ADVANCE PRAISE FOR *PRECIOUS LITTLE*

"You. Left. Me. Breathless....I honour and respect your willingness to be a light warrior and way shower in dark times."
– MARJORIE BEAUCAGE, Métis elder

"No novel I have read is as raw and fierce, nuanced and indelible as *Precious Little*....This book is vital, essential."
– LORRI NEILSEN GLENN, author of *Following the River: Traces of Red River Women*

"Carved from a true-to-the-bone honesty....Tremendous and touching to the core."
– LISA MOORE, award-winning author of *This is How We Love* and *February*

"This book is a must-read for the Innu...The dominant society also needs to read this book to understand what is happening to the Innu people and how we have struggled to enjoy life as it happens."
– MARY PIA BENUEN, Director for Primary Health Services, Sheshatshiu Innu First Nation

"An unforgettable journey....A deeply compassionate, insightful and unflinching story about grief, anger and hope."
– LESLIE VRYENHOEK, author of *We Will All Be Received*

"This character dreams my dreams. Anna takes me by the hand as she walks among my people. I could not let go of her hand until I had finished reading."
– CHRISTINE POKER, Director, Healing Lodge, Natuashish

"I couldn't put it down....A must read book."
– KATNEN BENUEN, Director, Health Commission, Mushuau Innu First Nation

for Esmée, Léo and the people of Natuashish

*

White people use different words, and it is hard to understand them. It is the same with the true Innu people. They speak hard Innu words, and some people don't understand them.

Kaniuekutat

Acts of appropriation are part of the process by which we make ourselves. Appropriating - taking something for one's own use - need not be synonymous with exploitation. This is especially true of cultural appropriation. The "use" one makes of what is appropriated is the crucial factor.

bell hooks

Try to feel, in your heart's core, the reality of others. This is the most painful thing in the world, probably, and the most necessary.

Margaret Laurence

PRECIOUS LITTLE

PRECIOUS LITTLE

CAMILLE FOUILLARD

Vagrant PRESS

Vagrant Press is an imprint of
Nimbus Publishing Limited
3660 Strawberry Hill St, Halifax, NS, B3K 5A9
(902) 455-4286 nimbus.ca

Printed and bound in Canada

Cover artwork: *Uashtuekapau (Northern Lights)* by Mary Ann Penashue
Editor: Carol Bruneau
Editor for the press: Whitney Moran
Interior Design: Rudi Tusek
Cover Design: Heather Bryan

NB1578

This is a work of fiction. While certain characters are inspired by real persons, and certain events by events which may have happened, the story is a work of the imagination not to be taken as a literal or documentary representation of its subject.

Library and Archives Canada Cataloguing in Publication

Title: Precious little : a novel / Camille Fouillard.
Names: Fouillard, Camille, author.
Identifiers: Canadiana (print) 20220259399 | Canadiana (ebook) 20220259437 | ISBN 9781774711088 (softcover) | ISBN 9781774711095 (EPUB)
Subjects: LCGFT: Novels.
Classification: LCC PS8611.O84 P74 2022 | DDC C813/.6—dc23

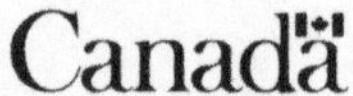

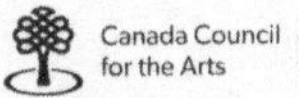

Nimbus Publishing acknowledges the financial support for its publishing activities from the Government of Canada, the Canada Council for the Arts, and from the Province of Nova Scotia. We are pleased to work in partnership with the Province of Nova Scotia to develop and promote our creative industries for the benefit of all Nova Scotians.

We acknowledge the support of ArtsNL, which last year invested $3.2 million to foster and promote the creation and enjoyment of the arts for the benefit of all Newfoundlanders and Labradorians.

A Note to the Reader

This novel is a work of fiction. I wrote this story always thinking of my experiences in Nitassinan with the Innu people. However, while some of the facts are true and geographic place names are real, the incidents and all the characters in this book, including the main character, are products of my imagination. I have known people like those I describe in the novel, and the main event is similar to one that occurred, but the details are fictional. As well, I take great liberties with geography and time, moving events forward and backward and from place to place to suit the narrative. Indigenous people are referred to as "Native," as that was the term used at the time the story occurs.

I know precious little, but I do know that I've been called to bear witness with the Innu to loss and grief, trauma, story, resistance and joy. Why tell, and how to tell? What is it like to tell? This is my story, flawed and incomplete, and only mine—an attempt to weave together some kind of whole from many separate and disparate bits and pieces, fragments of experiences, emotions, intuitions and knowledge, including the gaps and the unknowable of the Innu world.

I invite the reader to come along with me, to also witness and question everything, to believe my story or to suspend disbelief, to know in a different way, with no answers. I will not claim final authority of this story, nor say with any certainty what it all means.

Finally, for any mistakes I have made in my writing, interpretation, renderings, and thoughts, I am deeply sorry.

I.

We need your help. No "hello" or "how are you?" but I know who it is.

I highly doubt that, I respond, the calm of my morning coffee and bagel ruffled. I cradle the phone against my shoulder and wrap my cardigan tighter around my flannel pyjamas. I imagine Manish sitting at her own kitchen table at home, an abandoned white construction crew trailer.

We want to do a people's inquiry. And you can lead it, she says.

A 'people's inquiry.' Doesn't sound very Innu.

No response. A pregnant pause.

And, not a chance, I add.

It's about the house fire and the kids dying, she says, her voice diminished, constricted.

I stop chewing. A wave of sadness engulfs me. I resurface and lean into the phone.

Honestly, this sounds like a good idea, I say. But I'm not your person.

The sky outside my window looking over the St. John's Harbour is thick with clouds.

You *are* the person. We need you.

Need? I say, my brow knitting. How are your kids? Since the fire?

A faint, tinny echo of my voice scratches back to me over the phone line.

Not good.

I imagine breakfast with her three kids, huddled on the couch watching a video of *Sesame Street*, slurping their milk and Froot Loops.

Don't change the subject, she adds.

I've been thinking a lot about you. About everybody.

When I'd first heard the news about the fire on the radio just before dawn, I'd closed my eyes in a veil of tears and lain awake, rocking myself back and forth, something I'd been doing a lot since Dad died. Mark was away. The bed was vast and bereft. Eventually I'd gone down to the kitchen, boiled the kettle for a cup of coffee, stared at the stain at the bottom of my cup. I drank it slowly, watching the light of the rising sun dulled by the clouds meshing with the grey rock and grey buildings and fading snow, a hollowed womb ache from my miscarriage last year gnawing at me. I'd called Manish later that morning, but she couldn't talk.

She still can't talk about it, two weeks later.

So, you going to do this? Manish asks again.

Do I have to remind you what happened the last time I came up? The land claims meetings?

What?

Mostly nothing, remember? Did you even come?

It's not about you. Don't take it personally.

Well when Bay Street Bob showed up, abracadabra, people got real interested. Maybe I just need a law degree. Or a penis?

Manish's laugh explodes on the other end of the line.

We're interested this time. Honest, she says.

Really? The only interest I got last time was when I was heading home, walking to the airstrip. Suddenly there were three ATV's lining up: Tapit, Tanien and Sepastien, all offering me a ride to make damn sure I didn't miss my plane.

Manish laughs again, a girlish giggle this time.

Well, you can be a pain in the ass, she says.

Trying to butter me up?

We want you for this job.

I don't know.

Seriously, the feds turn us down. We have to do our own inquiry. This time you work with an Innu team.

Well even if *you* might think I'm the right person, what about the *guys*?

Your name is the only one come up. You say always we need to listen to the people, and how we should have a meeting to find out what people want. Now's your big chance.

A silence stretches out between us.

We never do anything like this before, she says. Just come. Support us. We need a supporter.

The guys are on good behaviour too, she adds. No booze charters, I promise.

As if she could even follow through on such a claim.

Nikaun, I hear a faraway child cry. Manish is being summoned.

I take you hunting, she says.

Let me think about it, I respond finally. I'll call you.

I hang up the phone, knowing I'm going to do this. How can I say no?

I'll work with you, I'll tell Manish when I call back, but I ain't leading nothing.

II.

Buckle your seat belt...if you have one, the co-pilot shouts from the cockpit of the red Twin Otter just before takeoff. I sit alert, immersed in the stink of fuel and cigarette smoke. It's been a week since the phone call, and I'm headed to Utshimassits, wearing my sealskin boots, shiny black and waterproof. An Inuit Elder from Nain had chewed the leather to soften it into gathers at the toes. At first I was a skeptic, and I'd jumped into puddles to test them.

Heat blasts at my toasty dry feet now, but a draft enters around the frosted window. I shiver, a chill persisting despite my snow pants, down jacket, long wool underwear, hat and mitts. All around me, passengers sit packed in parkas sporting hoods trimmed with fox or wolf tails. The plane's interior is grey-painted metal and cigarette butts litter the floor. The seats look like movie directors' chairs, vinyl fabric wrapped around metal frames. Cargo occupies some seats, strapped in and blocking windows.

People glance at me, look away quickly, mostly. A few say hello and smile. I smile back, enjoying the banter in Innu-aimun peppered with laughter and the odd cough. I'd like to know the scuttlebutt. A couple of women chat tête-à-tête in the front seat, bright-eyed toddlers propped on their knees, cuffing and pawing at each other like puppies. There's Maniaten who spent the year in St. John's getting her teacher's certificate. I'd taken her to a huge bingo in Pleasantville and she kept shushing me, leaning over onto my cards to stamp a number I'd missed. Just across the aisle from me is Toni, greasy hair falling into his eyes, and wearing a slick down jacket. I'm pretty sure he's making a little side money, spying for the military, or CSIS. They must be giving him cash for his efforts, unlike my Sheshatshiu friend Ben who used to get mickeys of rum for his tattling.

Shusi is sitting a couple of rows ahead of me, across the aisle. She'd stayed at my house when she was about to pop her last baby. She was in jail and they'd let her out early because she was so pregnant and couldn't fly home. I took her to the hospital when she went into labour in the middle of the night. The baby was huge and breech. Shushi had almost broken my hand, grasping so tightly as the doctor made the caesarean cut. Something had gone wrong on the other side of the screen blocking our view of the procedure.

You need to leave, the doctor had said. Right now.

The doctor said you have to go, the nurse echoed.

But Shusi had kept her grip on me, squeezing my hand so I could barely contain a scream, and I'd stayed, and the baby was dimpled and perfect with a full head of hair standing straight on end. Two days later the social worker came to fetch the baby and Shusi went home alone. For the whole seven months she was in there, she told me, no one in the penitentiary had talked to her about what she might do to be able to keep her baby.

Shusi smiles my way now; her hand flutters a wee wave. I smile back; my chest tightens at the memory.

That's the back of Emma, sitting just in front of Toni. She's a member of the health council, the first Innu nurse who, as a single mom, took her five kids and travelled to North Bay to study for her diploma. The Newfoundland government—Father Knows Best—won't recognize her credentials even if every other province does. Same thing happened with the tribal police who got their training in BC. The Band Council hired them all anyway.

It's a relief to be gone from St. John's, even with having to bow out of a contract—the task of mediating simmering politics among the Women's Centre staff, a sure case of post-pseudo-feminist-collective-syndrome. Saying goodbye to Mark wasn't hard. He was slipping into his usual late winter blues over the last month, a chronic "Am I the bad guy?" What does he want—for me to pat him on the back when he does dishes, folds laundry, as if he's doing me a favour? Can you just sort the damn clothes? And he's full of doom and gloom, a dark ominous cloud hanging overhead, my head, insisting that the government is going to call for a moratorium on the cod fishery. Like it was a personal affront. He claims it's gonna happen before the end of this year! I know he works for the fishermen's union but is that even possible?

Call me, he'd said as he held onto me outside airport security.

I didn't respond. He is perfectly cognizant that I hate phones, the chitty-chattiness of them.

Call me, he said again.

I'll try, I said, and reached up to give him a peck on the lips. He turned his head and it landed on his cheek.

Our mutual interests are not profound: camping, recycling, a couple of friends, elephants, music, a hate-on for Brian Mulroney, meticulous dishwashing, things like that. I've changed my mind about relationships; ours doesn't need to be complicated. We love each other. We're just not very good at it.

It was a relief to be leaving, a welcome break, even with a little Jiminy Cricket whispering on the edge of my consciousness: what are you doing? Are you sure about this?

I waved at Mark when I reached the top of the stairs, made it to the gate just as boarding started.

The plane is full, on this second lap of my journey. It starts to roll, snow-clouds erupting behind the propellers as it turns towards the runway, rambles over to one end, turns again, accelerates, and takes off into a brilliant blue sky. I reach for the *Downhomer*.

The first time I visited Davis Inlet was about ten years ago, when Manish invited me to lead a workshop on women's health. We'd met at a conference in Nain. I loved her face, the freckles across her nose and high cheekbones, her impish smile, even teeth between full lips. Her eyes were searching and intelligent, her hair thick and black, her laugh handy. I warmed to her ease with white people. *Kakeshau* is the word for white people, Manish had told me, eager to teach me her language.

And Utshimassits, she said, it means "Place of the Boss." It's the Innu name for Davis Inlet.

I wondered who the Boss was; I didn't ask, but assumed that person was *kakeshau*, like me.

I sat with her and Elders An-Pinamen and Mani-Pia at the conference, homing in on the three who were like sisters, heads hunched together. They were speaking Innu-aimun, a song whose rhythm and intonation I'd never heard, and laughing an infectious, deep belly laugh.

Come visit us, Manish had said, and so I did, being the eager community development worker that I was, at the ready to facilitate "social change." Eye roll. What I remember of the workshop was Manish struggling to translate for the group:

We don't have a word for 'health' in our language.

I wondered what else didn't translate, what else I didn't know, couldn't know, all the things I needed to unknow. Like what I'd heard the previous weekend at a dinner party in Goose Bay.

You're going to Davis Inlet? Tim had asked. By yourself?

Yeah, I've been invited to a women's meeting.

Be careful. Don't go out at night.

I think I'll be okay.

So you know those Davis Inlet Indians got free houses? Tim's girlfriend Liz had jumped in. Paid for with our taxes.

Your point is? I asked.

I heard when they first got houses they started dismantling them on the inside, she said. Two-by-four by two-by-four, wall by wall, for wood to burn in their stoves.

She pulled a strand of her blond hair behind her ear, eyebrows raised, looking my way.

I think that story is urban legend, I'd said. Without the urban.

It's true, she said, and went on about how those Indians were still getting houses, and still complaining; apparently houses weren't enough.

If I'd had my wits about me, I might have pointed out to Liz that if it was true that people weren't all that beholden, there was something about their impertinence and defiance I admired. So cheeky, stubborn, maybe desperate but also resourceful.

Even restrained as I was, it seemed like Liz was taking my going to Utshimassits as some kind of personal affront.

I'd looked over at Tim, holding his head down, chopping celery with fervour. He'd invited me over when we ran into each other at the Goose Bay airport. I knew him from an ethnomusicology class at the university, when we'd often studied and listened to world music together.

There's no pleasing those people, Liz continued.

She was baiting me. I'd stopped responding. She went on, an evangelist on a mission to convert. She applied the word 'baloney' to sexual abuse by priests. Canada stealing land? What nonsense!

Nuns and priests taught me respect and morals, she said. The Indians in this country were conquered. That's what humans have done forever. It's time they got over it.

Still Tim said nothing.

What a bunch of racist crap, I wanted to scream. But I was a guest and Good Little Catholic Girls are docile and quiet.

Were they really 'conquered?' I asked instead, my brow furrowed. What if a bunch of Innu set up their tent in your yard, made themselves at home, picked a few potatoes out of your garden, walked right into your house? Can we just get another bucket of water, use your toilet? You never invited them, but you don't mind, do you?

Manish had used this analogy at the Nain conference and it had stuck. She'd been talking to the Minister on the Status of Women, the Right Honourable Lush, who had opened the conference claiming he was a great supporter of women: he thought all men should have at least one. You can't even make this stuff up.

Lush and Liz would probably get along. I was avoiding her eyes at this point, just waiting for her to quote the CBC reporter who, when interviewed about Davis Inlet on the St. John's morning show, had described the Innu as "zombies" and "Walking Dead." A proud moment for our national broadcaster. He'd been there once, so he should know. Speaking of tax dollars.

Maybe we should change the subject, Tim said finally.

We? I said, trying to make a point.

A pitiful response. I wanted to find the right words. I can still feel the shame washing over me. Not that different from the feeling I had last year. Even after all these years, working on different projects, I can be mindless when it suits me. Manish had offered me a caribou heart. It was Valentine's Day, I was headed home from Utshimassits, and I had nothing for Mark who'd be waiting at the airport.

The perfect Valentine's Day gift! I told her as I thanked her.

No, she said with a grimace, but still I gave Mark the heart. I couldn't see the harm. It seemed so perfect. It's not too late to apologize about that.

I wish now I could've told Liz and Tim the story of that first visit to Utshimassits, when a group of women of all ages had made a place for me in their circle. We were in the church hall, a refuge from the stormy January night we had all trudged through to get there.

Let's tell stories, I'd suggested to the group, about what it's like to live here in Utshimassits. As women.

Silence. What kind of a workshop was this? they wondered. Finally Mani-Pia, one of the Elders who was at the Nain workshop, spoke up.

The women want to know about you, Manish translated. Your story, she says with a slight grin. Are you married? Where's your mom and dad?

I decided against disclosing my allergy to marriage, that I agree with feminists and Robert Louis Stevenson that marriage is a sort of friendship recognized by police.

I don't have a husband, I said. And my parents live in Manitoba, in the middle of Canada.

I pointed west, or at least where I thought west was. It was in that moment that I wondered for the very first time whose prairie lands the village of my childhood had been settled. It was years before I'd made the connection that my ancestors, who arrived on the shores of 'New France' in the 1600s, would surely have encountered the Innu, traded with them, shared food, clothing, tools, and weapons. The women around the circle that night may have wondered about that.

Do you have a baby? one of the younger women asked in English, her voice barely audible, curiosity trumping her shyness.

No baby.

The women discussed this for a while.

How come you have no babies? Manish translated, again with a smile, perhaps reading my discomfort about how my lifestyle might be interpreted, perhaps to let me know she was just the messenger?

I wasn't quite ready to tell them about my birth control practices or my abortion.

My mom had five babies by the time she was twenty-seven, I proffered, as compensation.

My status established, the women shared stories around the circle, bits about their lives since the government had settled them, only slightly more than a decade before. The talk was lively, like the women had just been waiting for the chance to tell their stories. Manish, who was sitting next to me, wrote scant notes so I could follow:

son-in-law beats her daughter, medevac to hospital in Goose Bay she say she can't talk to her grandson anymore he don't know the Innu words only in bush sometimes he listen he work so hard in bush he very proud

when priest come to live here he deliver babies her husband say not priest job we deliver own babies the women do in old days

she have baby when 16 years old, nurse ask her to sign paper she don't know paper say social worker take baby to NF give to family no one help to see her daughter again

I'd read the scribbled words on the foolscap, sat dumb and receptive, smiled at each woman, despite the incongruence of it. I nodded to show somehow that I was listening, that I understood what was being said. Finally I spoke, though I didn't know what to say.

This must be hard, I said, in a kind of a mutter.

Manishan translated my meagre words, and the women talked at length back and forth about what they might mean. Eventually Manish offered a morsel of translation.

The women say these are things that we have to live with, she said.

Mani-Pia spoke next, while women got up to pour themselves a cup of tea, still listening, heeding the story and nodding in agreement. A suffocating heat blasted from the radiator behind me. Something was gnawing at me, a texture, a weight, a lonely and opaque feeling, a fear I could lose my composure and tears or a confession might spill out. Manish was no longer taking notes, but finally she provided a summary in English.

Mani-Pia talked about how we were put on this island, Manish said. And we face so many problems, just like what happened to the boy Aieshess in the legend. His father left him on an island to die, but he survived, after he ride on the back of a Sea Caribou with antlers and conquer many obstacles. In the end he kill his father and rescue his mother. Then he turn her into a *pipitsheu*, the bird with a red breast.

I wondered about what the Sea Caribou stood for and who was the father, why the boy turned his mother into a robin, and whether it was time for me to try to facilitate. I had started this conversation, but my week-long training on workshop facilitation had not prepared me for this. There were so many threads to pursue, but with no segue the women carried on, darting occasional glances at me.

They want your help to form a women's group, Manish finally explained.

What kind of help? I asked, wondering what I could tell them about the purpose and ways of a women's group in Utshimassits. Precious little. I looked down at my clasped hands in my lap to catch my breath, think of something to say, get my bearings.

Before I could elicit an answer, the women all rose and scurried towards the door. On her way, Mani-Pia handed me a plastic bag.

A present, she said, surprising me with her English. She spoke again to Manish.

The women say you can help us get money from the government, Manish translated, as Mani-Pia headed out the door without a backward glance or goodbye.

Manish and I lingered to clean up, stack chairs and fold tables, take down the flip chart stand. The blank page glared back at me. I paused, rested my hands on the back of a chair.

How'd it go tonight? I'd asked, clearing my throat, bracing myself. What do you think? I added.

Next time we should bring cookies, she said. But it's good for the women to share stories—*tipatshimuna*. We all have a story, right?

True, I said.

Cookies? I thought. But what else?

What should we do now? I asked instead. We could write a proposal?

I never write one before.

Me neither, but I'm sure we can figure it out.

Inside the bag I found a pair of beaded moccasins trimmed with rabbit fur, just the right size.

Ten years later these moccasins are tucked away in my suitcase. I stare out the window at the whir of the propeller drawing the plane forward through the icy air. Manish never said who was funding this inquiry, only that it wasn't the government. "Inquiry"—that word is getting on my nerves.

Through the portholes on both sides of the plane, the black and white landscape stretches out below. Snowy barrens and endless mountains, bald rock, trees, rivers and valleys, marshlands, frozen ocean, deep blue sea on the far horizon. Not one solitary road. I spot an occasional snowmobile track, most visible along the shoreline or across a frozen lake or bay.

My eyes rest on the breadth of the man's shoulders in front of me. He's Innu and also staring intently out of the window, likely spotting animals invisible to me, outside of my consciousness. Like the time I drove across London, England, in a taxi with two Innu Elders. We were on a European tour to lobby against NATO jets practising to kill, flying low-level and dropping dummy bombs over Innu lands. I'd queried Shimun about what he thought of London's urban sprawl. He wanted to know about the small porcupine-like critter he'd spotted by a riverbank, a hedgehog, and when was duck season?

Atikuats! the man in front of me calls out, points a finger westward. A buzz spreads through the cabin. Below us an endless stream of caribou are running, thousands, like flowing beige ribbons in the wind, as far as we can see. The plane drops altitude and follows the procession, rows of them, now galloping faster as the plane descends. Occasionally they disperse, a break in the line, and then rally back in succession. How much of their lives do caribou spend on the run—running for food, from wolves, blackflies, bad weather, snowmobiles, hunters and planes, especially the military bombers flying at treetop level? Elder Mishta-Pinip had talked about caribou on the run at the land claims meeting, how it was hard on them. He talked about the moss they ate, how it was impregnated with *kakeshau* pollution.

They don't have any fat on their flesh anymore, he said. They don't taste the same.

Last spring I flew in a Beaver with five dead caribou. Manish's brother Tanien invited me along for the ride. She must have prodded him to invite me, knowing I'd be up for the adventure.

Hop on! he said, like he was asking me to jump into the back of a pickup truck.

He and a posse of hunters had shot the caribou in the Ashuapun area, near an abandoned runway and weather station at Border Beacon by the Quebec–Labrador border. An early spring thaw had made it impossible for them to haul the beasts back to the village by snowmobile, so the Band Council chartered a plane to fetch them.

We landed on the lake. Tanien got off the plane ahead of me and headed to the pile of caribou, threw each carcass one after another over his shoulder like large sacks of flour, piled them up in the back of the plane. He never asked for my help. The pilot had no snowshoes, so he was equally useless. The two of us climbed back aboard, inching our way around the new freight. I fastened my seat belt, feeling a little crowded. We took off and soon after, the unsecured mountain of carcasses shifted and jumped as the plane hit an air pocket. My heart fluttered as I imagined whirling around the cabin with the caribou in complete rigor mortis, the plane in a tailspin, but it regained its bearings and I regained my composure, eventually.

I turned to examine the large male caribou nearest me, his white penis sheath and his three-foot-wide antlers. A musky smell, slightly sweet and boreal, filled the cabin. I wanted to touch his small, well-furred ears, broad and blunt muzzle, and short tail. I reached over to inspect his hooves hollowed out like a scoop with crescent-shaped toes, and others higher up the leg. These were sharp-edged hooves useful for good purchase on rocks or ice, able to support the animal's bulk walking in deep snow and bog, paddling through water and digging through snow in search of food.

I sat back, looked over at Tanien, and nodded at the mass of caribou.

The Band Council hired you to go on this hunt? I asked, shouting over the drone of the engine. I was thinking how the bookkeeper must have cooked the books, balanced profit and loss with rectitude, or not—payments in and salaries paid out, at the whims and patronage of the chief. Did he have a column in his ledger for caribou hunting? *Shuniau.* Money doesn't work the same up here.

Yup, the band help us with the hunt, Tanien said. They pay for gas. Four Ski-Doos.

Where are these caribou going now?

I was calculating the expense of the hunt. A cost-benefit analysis: gas, ammunition, salaries, the charter—for how many pounds of meat?

We cut 'em up and make sure everybody get some. Elders first. And Tshinetshishepateu, the first Elder, because he tell us where to go. We have Innu rules about sharing. Innu laws, he'd said, grinning, his voice with a mocking edge. It's like our own Innu 'accountability.'

How did he know where to find the caribou?

He read the caribou bone, the shoulder bone.

The scapula, you mean?

Is that the word? In Innu is *utinikan.*

How does someone read a bone? I asked, at once fascinated and skeptical.

You put the bone over candle flame. The fire make marks when it burn the bone, like could be a black line or some spots. You look at the marks and you see a place, maybe a mountain or a river. I'm not sure. I never do it. But Tshinetshishepateu say he see a river and a lake, like where the Ashuapun-shipu run out of Ashuapun Lake. A place where caribou cross the river many times.

Wow, how do you learn to do that? I asked.

You have to be good hunter. And you dream it.

Dream it?

The best part of the hunt was my son, Tanien had said, ignoring my question. Mishen kill his first caribou. Twelve years old. I take him with me.

He shot a gun? He's got a gun license?

You should see the look on his face. His hands so cold he almost can't pull trigger. But he shoot it. He can't wait to go home tell his friends and mom.

Tanien's voice was buoyant above the thrum of the engine.

Then he had a story to tell, I'd said. The best part of the hunt?

True. He always remember that first caribou. Now Mishen take some meat to Tshinetshishepateu and we have a feast, a *makushan.* Mishen want to see how you crush the caribou bones and make *pimin* from the bone marrow. He say he want to ask Tshinetshishepateu to make a drum dance too.

I hope I can come.

Sure, but you dance like a chicken.

Haha. I'm not that bad.

My voice was getting hoarse from shouting over the engine. Tanien was in a talkative mood and I wanted to ask about *Katipenimitak,* the Caribou 'Master,' or was it Caribou 'God' or 'Spirit' or 'Man'? So many different translations for that word.

The large male caribou was staring at me.

Now, below me the endless stream of caribou continues to rush forward. Asking about *Katipenimitak* was likely trespassing. It's easy to be curious and transgress, but it's like a need, this desire to learn how to show respect to the animals and their spirits. Maybe *Katipenimitak* will drive these caribou all the way into Utshimassits? Is that thought also out of bounds?

The plane shakes and shudders and points its nose downward to start its descent. Last time I came, the plane landed with pontoons and the water had swished and splashed and roiled around the pilings of the wharf. The plane circles above the village, a smattering of tiny prefab houses scattered in rows parallel to the shore, jammed between the water and hills on three sides. Wisps of smoke escape from chimneys and random caribou carcasses are strewn on roofs. Snowmobiles skim their way north to the airstrip and then west around the bend along the coastline, past the garbage dump. The plane bounces with a sudden jerk as it lands on a snow-covered gravel runway. It turns and heads for the hangar.

The co-pilot pulls open the door and drops the ladder. I wait my turn, grab my knapsack, and step out into a snapping cold. The wind whips the smell of jet fuel all around me. The co-pilot begins to toss the luggage out helter-skelter. Everyone scrambles to retrieve theirs.

Manish is standing by the chain-link fence, a big grin on her face, a fleecy hat sitting lopsided on her head. She walks over and slaps me on the back.

Wanna ride? she asks.

You just want to dump me in a snowbank, I say.

I'd never do that, she says. She leads me to her snowmobile, throws my bag into the komatik, sits and settles, and signals for me to climb on behind her as if on horseback. I'm barely sitting when she guns it full throttle.

I got no brakes, she yells out.

Excellent! I shout back. The two of us bump and bounce through the air. The cold whips me in the face, slices through my parka. I crouch behind Manish to block the wind and hold fast to her nylon jacket covered in engine oil, like a mechanic's. We blast over to the government store and stop as abruptly as we took off. No brakes, she said.

You want to pick up some food before I take you to the Pasteens? Manish asks. I'll go drop off your gear and come back for you.

Sounds like a plan, I say. Manish kicks off and I walk into the store to fluorescent lights beaming down on me. Eyes all around seem to say 'what is she doing here?' Except Munik, an Elder I've often seen at meetings. She shuffles over in her moccasins to give me a peck on both cheeks. Like the French do.

Welcome back, Anna, she says, in English!

I grab a cart, look around at the paltry offerings on the shelves, and head for the produce cooler; it sports three bags of apples, a half-dozen cabbages, a small heap of oranges, two bunches of blackened bananas, small pickings of wizened turnips and potatoes, and yellow onions. I pick out an orange, a small cabbage—ignoring the $10 price tag—and one onion. Eyes still follow me around; a few catch mine. My smile goes unheeded.

The freezer also disappoints: French fries don't qualify as vegetables. Good thing I gave up being vegetarian. Labrador took care of that. Down another aisle, I pick up a jar of pasta sauce to study the ingredients. Apart from the high sodium content, the best before date has come and gone. My cart fills up with cans of kidney beans and tomatoes, chili powder, a bag of rice, a box of cereal, flour, baking powder, margarine, a box of UHT milk, some cheddar cheese, eggs, chocolate chip cookies, and a dozen candles.

The cashier tallies up my groceries. Next to the cash register sits a pile of last year's Advent calendars selling for $25. My attempts at small talk are met by the cashier's barely audible monosyllabics. I pay up, pack my groceries into two plastic bags, and exit to find Manish sitting on her snowmobile, exhaling perfect circles of smoke from her cigarette.

I'm staying at the Pasteens? I ask.

They said you can stay in the tent behind their house. No water and sewer, just like you asked for, Manish says. With a smirk.

I never said that.

I get no respect from this woman. My request was to stay with an Innu family. Last time I boarded at the nuns' house, and one night found myself staring at a poster of Our Sacred Heart of Jesus hung above the toilet with the words *Yes, Lord God, I believe!*, while kids sniffed gas from plastic bags outside the window, their laughter eerie and unholy. Like a cat in heat howling. It still baffles me how I went back to bed, tossed and turned, how Sister Helen and I both ignored them, even if we were heeding Manish's advice.

Leave them alone, she'd said. You don't know what they might do.

I don't like staying in the enclave of houses for white people in the village where they all have running water while the Innu have to haul buckets from a tap outside the band office.

Good thing I brought my sleeping bag, I say now. But will I need to get wood?

Don't worry, the Pasteens have three boys who can help. And if you want a shower, the mission sometimes lets people wash up there. Sister Alice has the key.

As long as I don't need to go to confession, I say.

Having my own space appeals to me: fetching water, cooking on a wood stove, keeping busy. The skeins of Newfoundland sheeps' wool in cheery colours that I brought to knit should help stave off melancholy, idle thoughts, panic.

Hop on, Manish orders, and I do, my two bags of groceries set between us. We drive past the Band Council building made of BC logs and the mission building with its makeshift bell tower and a side wall with a spraypainted graffiti image of a stick figure behind bars, a collar around his neck, and *jail the priest* scrawled underneath. We continue along the row of teachers' duplex residences, past a cavorting group of teenagers scantily dressed for the weather. The school, with its red iron siding and blue doors, flashes by on the right before we slide up over a big rock, a hub for gossip or ceremony, like a mass or wedding or drum dance. As Manish pulls back a little on the throttle, a couple of boys chase the Ski-Doo, trying to grab a free ride on the komatik's runners.

Nakate, nakate, Manish shouts in a shrill voice, as she turns the Ski-Doo right, steers around the back of a house, and stops just short of a tent doorway. The canvas sides of the tent are banked high with snow. I grab my groceries in one hand, swing the canvas door aside, and step in. A plywood floor has replaced the usual neatly interwoven fir boughs of a *nutshimits* tent. A fire crackles in a sheet metal stove to welcome me. A small table and two chairs sit in a far corner, next to a small shelf concocted out of scrap wood. In the left corner is a closet-like enclosure with a covered honey bucket and a curtain for a door, and on the back wall lies a thin foam mattress next to where Manish laid down my luggage.

I carry my grocery bags over to the shelf and begin to unload. This is where my quest to know ancient Innu secrets and the mysteries of Mother Earth has landed me. On a plywood floor in subzero March weather, with a honey bucket to dump cavalierly, like everyone else, not too close to anyone's doorway.

Should I worry about my camera and computer? I ask Manish, still standing in the doorway.

And sexy underwear. Don't leave them around if you're not here.

Gotcha.

A Ski-Doo roars up to the tent and stops abruptly. Sepastien pokes his head through the door.

Hey, Sepastien, how's it going? I say.

He enters with his long-legged gait.

Pushu, pushu. He reaches out to take both my hands in his and shakes them up and down with enthusiasm. He smells of woodsmoke and cigarettes and fuel and spruce trees.

Akat want to know if you need anything? he asks, casing the joint. What you got to sleep with?

This sleeping bag, it's Arctic down, and a camping mattress. I point to them, strapped onto my backpack.

That's no good.

It's supposed to be good for minus forty.

That little thing?

Sepastien turns and leaves, no goodbye. Manish and I follow him out of the tent as he climbs onto his snowmobile. We make our way over to the big rock. A couple of women, talking in hushed voices, look over at me.

Tan etin? I say. How's it going? The women giggle and ignore me, carry on with their conversation. The laughter and screams of children sliding down the hill behind us rise and fall as they run and whirl and tumble off their toboggan right next to us. Runny-nosed and rosy-cheeked, they grab the toboggan and head back up the hill.

Sepastien appears again on his snowmobile, a bundle on his lap. Manish and I follow him back into the tent as he rolls out two caribou skins.

One for under your sleeping bag and one over you, he says, with hand gestures to demonstrate.

Nice. My hands stroke the tan-and-oatmeal-coloured fur, like unbleached linen. They are just the right length to cover my whole body.

Will they bring good dreams? I ask.

I don't know, but they keep you warm.

Tshinashkumitin, I thank Sepastien. Two caribou have sacrificed themselves. Is Katipenimitak also owed my gratitude?

You can't sleep here alone, Sepastien says, still assessing my situation. I send kids over, Shuni or Shuash. Do you need something else?

A radio? I totally forgot mine. Do you know anyone who might have a spare one?

You can use ours. I send it with the kids.

He leaves again and Manish follows him out.

Meeting with the Elders tomorrow, she says. I can pick you up on my way.

That's okay, I can walk. What time?

Don't know. Innu time, she says with a smile. We should have tea and a snack to give them. I can make Innu donuts.

Let's make them here and you can show me how?

Okay I pick up the stuff to make them and come by first thing in the morning.

I follow Manish out of the tent. She roars away as I go to grab some wood for the night and early morning. A few junks lie scattered on the ground. Manish forgot to mention the details of my accommodation. I knock on the Pasteens' back door, which has, in place of a doorknob, a piece of nylon twine threaded through the hole to open and close it. No one answers. I can't just help myself to these few junks, can I?

Best I resurrect my inner lumberjack. I spot an axe plunged into a large log for storage, yank it free, and grab a piece of bucked wood from a small pile. Neither the chainsaw nor the axe had become my friend during the two years I lived in Sheshatshiu, but I know I can do this. I can. Tear wood asunder like at least some of my ancestors—all those coureurs de bois, homesteaders, refuted Métis—did for millennia and until only a few decades ago. My feet apart, shoulder width and square to my target, knees slightly bent, I swing the axe straight back over my head and surrender to its weight and power soaring through the air and smack into the far middle back of the round. Thunk! The two halves fall in opposite directions, the wood brittle from the cold. My heartbeat like a sledgehammer in my chest. Strike again down the centre of one of the halves. Bingo! There is no one around to see my triumph, cheer me on.

Manish would be proud. She'd asked me once why I was so useless with an axe. A grown woman.

When I was a kid and our house got cold, I turned a dial on a small box on the wall, I said. I'd shown her how, a gesture, a twist of the hand.

That explains everything, she'd said.

A couple armfuls of splits are piling up, and my shoulders ache from the concussive force of blow after blow. I place the wood into the curve of my arm and haul it into the tent. In the knick of time. There are just enough embers to coax into a hearty fire and I fill the stove to the brim.

I'd planned to whip up a chili, but can't be bothered. A fried egg will have to do, in this frying pan that looks barely wiped from its last use. My mother would be turning up her nose. I toast a slice of bread directly on the stovetop, boil a kettle for tea, and devour my egg and toast and peanut butter. Delicious. Vegetables can wait for tomorrow. The bucket holds barely enough water for dishes. I head for the Band Council building to fetch more, and maybe to find the radio that never showed up. My line to the outside world.

Mark would want to know I've made it, but that phone call requires more charm and coordination than I can muster right now.

III.

I walk right into Sepastien's kitchen without knocking, surprised to find no one home. No gaggle of kids, no heat. Cupboards ripped out of the wall, a stack of Gyproc and a table saw in the middle of the floor. Outside and around the back of the house, Tshinetshishepateu stands by a half-built canoe, its bare ribs jutting out of the snow. Last summer I'd watched him hammer and shape those ribs in perfect symmetry onto the frame, using the width of his hands, and the distance between his elbow and hand, to measure.

He acknowledges me with a slight nod. My mind whirls, searching for words. That familiar self-conscious whirl, always worse with an Elder. We both look away.

Tanite Sepastien mak Akat? I muster up in my halting Innu-aimun, failing as always to capture the cadence and inflection. The old man points to a tent perched on the hill behind the two houses to show me where I'll find Sepastien and Akat. His finger traces the length of an extension cord running out of Sepastien's house. He speaks Innu the whole time. His eyes are droopy, sad, guarded.

Tshinashkumitin, I say shyly, smiling in that way I have of over-smiling.

The cord leads me to another and what must be nine or ten more crawling through metre-deep snow up the hill before I reach the tent nestled in a grove of spruce trees—a *nutshimits* tent. I poke my head in the small opening above the door flap. The heat and stench of burning hair and bone assaults me, but I step in, my nose crinkled up in distaste. A caribou head, staked with a stick through the neck and nostril and thrust into the ground, grazes the side of the stove and stares up at me as it roasts. White bulging eyes with no pupils. Charred bone smoking and flesh sizzling where the fur has burnt away.

Come in, come in. Sepastien sits on an upside-down beef bucket, while Akat crouches at the back of the tent changing a baby's disposable diaper. I walk over and lean forward to give Akat a big awkward bear hug. With her small nicotine-stained hands, she grabs mine, squeezes and smiles. A smile that makes me feel like everything will be okay.

Nussim, she says, my granddaughter, as she stands with the babbling baby. She tucks her into a *ueuepishun*, a tiny hammock strung between two tent poles. She motions for me to sit on the floor of boughs. I love Akat, although the smattering of words we know in each other's languages turns most visits awkward in the time it takes to stoke the fire and throw another junk into the stove. I step around a box of dishes and random kitchen paraphernalia to sit down. To the left of the door on a trunk sits a thirty-two-inch television blasting out news from Bangor, Maine. Sepastien leans over, shifts the caribou head sideways, carves out a grilled cheek with a knife, and pops the flesh into his mouth.

Want some? he asks me. I shake my head.

We don't waste any of the caribou, he says. He must be calculating my thoughts. Tomorrow, Akat use the brain to tan the skin, he adds.

Speaking of skins, are you sure you can spare the ones you gave me today? I didn't realize you're also staying in a tent.

Just 'til the Band Council fix our house. You keep the skins. We have more.

But I don't see any amongst the mountain of bedding in the corner. Sepastien stands and flings the door flap open to freshen the air and I can see the last breaths of the sunset's reflection on the ice across the bay. The days are getting longer.

Nipishapun? asks Akat as she stands to pour me a cup of tea from a kettle on the stove. She offers me milk and sugar as well, *tshitshinapun*—the same word as 'breastmilk'—and *kashiuasht.* I scoop a spoonful of sugar and shake a few drops from the can of Carnation Milk into my cup to tame the tannins of the boiled tea.

Akat is speaking to Sepastien and I hear *utauna* more than once.

She's talking about my father? I ask.

Yeah, she say to tell you she sorry to hear he pass away, Sepastien says.

Thanks. I smile at Akat as tears well up.

He died so fast, I say, swallowing hard. The doctors said he had cancer and two weeks later, he was gone.

Were you there? Sepastien asks.

The whole family was, I say.

Sepastien translates, and Akat looks over at me and nods.

I got to say goodbye, I continue. But I wish our funerals were more like yours.

What you mean?

People seem closer here—the homemade coffin and the women dressing the body. The way everybody comes to the church and kisses the person, throws a handful of dirt on the coffin at the cemetery.

What happen with your father funeral?

The undertaker, you know, the man who works at the funeral home, he took the body away. I never had a chance to sit with my father one last time. I couldn't recognize him, lying in all that satin in the coffin. They wired his jaw shut. And the stuff they use to embalm—formaldehyde—stinky. It was weird.

As Sepastien translates for Akat, my mind wanders back to the church. I was the only one to kiss my father's cold forehead. The altar boy swung the thurible of burning incense, vases of flowers and pillar candles decorated the altar. We sang "The Lord is my Shepherd" and I got to read a pagan prayer by Starhawk, because the priest didn't know how to say no to my mother who does the books for the church. "I who am the beauty of the green earth and the white moon among the stars and the mysteries of the waters..." I began to cry halfway through the passage. I struggled to keep a sense of dignity, nose dripping; it took an eternity to get a hold of myself and be able to continue. We left the church to the choir singing "Ave Maria" and made our way to the graveyard where the coffin lay in a subzero hole, lined with a green rug and short brass fence-like enclosure, like he was being laid to rest in a living room. It was January. On the prairies.

The TV screen disrupts my reverie as it switches from Bangor news to a WWF wrestling match.

What happened? I ask. This is the first time I've seen a TV up this way playing something other than a video.

Somebody at the band office switch the channel, Sepastien says.

So *your* channel changed?

Yeah.

That sucks.

Not so bad. As long as it's not *All My Children*, Sepastien says.

What must Akat think of soap operas: all the beautiful people, shining chandeliers and chintzy florals, valances, gilded bathrooms. From no TV to satellite TV. Boom.

What does Akat think about having TV? I ask, wondering if it's replaced the community radio station as the soundtrack in every home. You might hear someone calling a truant to school or a drunk home, an Elder reciting a morning prayer or singing a hymn. Innu airwaves broadcast bingo, jokes and stories, warnings about places to avoid going through the ice, Innu songs, country and western songs, political rants, items for sale, a Friday night dance, an announcement about the doctor's visit.

She likes Mr. Bean, Sepastien responds as Akat looks up and smiles. I nod to concur. Her large square glasses are oversized for her face and have snuck down her nose. Her face seems disfigured and asymmetrical, reconfigured from damaged tendons and fractured bones. Sepastien has hinted at their troubles, and I've never pressed for details. *Minushkuess*: her fine and delicate features still hint at her

Innu nickname, Pretty Girl. A patrician face with an aquiline nose, and lips that must have been small and full at the same time. In Sheshatshiu, my neighbour Nishapet occasionally came knocking on my door with a bloodied and black-eyed face, looking for shelter for the night. I'd let her in and she'd head to the couch while I fetched her a blanket. Sometimes I'd give her a cup of tea to help settle her down.

How did you two meet? I ask now, trying to imagine the two as teens, needing to imagine a more innocent time.

We were at a gathering in Sheshatshiu, before many houses built, Sepastien says. In old days gatherings were when kids get match up and married. I see Akat. She is a hard worker. I really want to marry her, but I can't just go up to her. I gotta ask her parents.

So what happened? I ask.

I can see that Akat is listening keenly.

I am scared so I send my uncle to talk to them, Sepastien says. He have to go two times. I think she don't want me.

And did she?

Akat is smiling now, looking coy. She jumps in with her own version.

She say no one bother to talk to her, Sepastien translates. She say she don't even know her parents give her away to be married.

What did she think of that?

I'm looking at Akat as she responds, no need for translation.

She say she don't want to come near me.

Sepastien does not crack a smile while Akat chuckles, both hands on her mouth.

Did you have another boyfriend, *tshitimush*? I ask.

My question inspires more laughter from Akat, gales of it, as she slaps her hands on her thighs.

Tapue, tapue, she nods her head. Other man, *napeu*, and scared are the two things she manages in English. She laughs with an even deeper hilarity, and continues, her face animated.

Sepastien translates, like the words taste bad as they roll off his tongue. Funny he's still translating and hasn't shut the story down.

She say she too shy to marry me. She think I pretty good looking, but I dress bad.

"Hair like Johnny Cash," Akat says as she smooths her hair back with a swirl, and she bursts into laughter again, a contagious cackle. She mumbles something else under her breath, and Sepastien cracks a smile, surrenders, the two now in a counterpoint of he-he-he-he. I always miss the best lines.

Nice story, I say. I'd love to see a picture of your wedding.

I borrow a suit and she borrow the white dress, Sepastien says. And even we borrow the rings. But the priest won't take a picture. He say I'm too drunk.

His voice wanders and trails off.

Who cares, he says, barely audible.

So why you come back here this time? he asks, changing the subject.

Manish called me to ask if I'd help organize a people's inquiry, I say. About the kids dying in the fire.

Tshekuan 'inquiry'? Sepastien asks with a quizzical look.

I'm not sure what an inquiry is or does, to be honest, I say. I've never been part of one. We'll have to talk and figure it out.

I hope it don't have anything to do with the police going around asking questions.

Are they going to lay charges? I ask.

I'd been thinking about running into the parents whose children died, what it would be like to look into their eyes, the sting of it.

Lay charges? Sepastien shoots a glare at me.

Against the parents. For leaving the kids out alone so late at night?

Well, they have to go to hospital to charge Manishan. She say she just want to die. People watching Tshani too, a suicide watch. The others cry all the time, they never go out of their house.

You don't think the parents should be held responsible?

By going to jail?

I don't know?

You think they should go stand in front of one of your so-called judges, they say guilty or not guilty? Then they live in a cage and sleep in a bed next to a toilet. Teach them a lesson?

So, what do you think should happen?

Those parents are never free from memories, thinking about their kids all the time. All the time. They never forget. You want to punish them more?

I don't know.

You don't know? But you *kakeshauts* always know everything.

Akat looks sullen as she gently swings the baby in her *ueuepishun*. Sepastien must be translating the conversation for her, his voice shaking, thick and hoarse. I sit stunned and blink back tears. The wind outside howls, sucks the heat out of the wood stove and straight up into the sky.

They make a mistake, Sepastien adds, as he turns to open the cooler next to him. A very big mistake. They pay for it, every day. Go ahead, put us all in jail.

He takes out a bundle from a grocery bag and heaves it at me.

Here, from my net this morning, he says. Your breakfast tomorrow. Go home now.

Akat does not look at me. I take his gift, open the bag to find a small char, spotted grey, steely turquoise and white, the fins on its belly coral, hinting at the colour of its flesh.

Thanks. I shift to stand. Iame, iame apishish. Little goodbye, I say, as I get up, my voice like it's on hands and knees. I grab my water bucket and exit smack into the icy chill. I slip and slide and sink out of control down the hill through the snow and faint shadows of the half moon. No street lamps to illuminate my way home.

Teach them a lesson? Sepastien wasn't asking a question.

I stare up at the Milky Way, its billions of stars spilled across the night sky.

You white people always know everything, he said.

I have no damn business being here.

I reach a snowmobile track at the bottom of the hill, slow down, and trudge along gloomily. The wind has its hackles up now, yanking at my hat and parka, slinging snow in great cosmic swirls around me. A chill shivers through me. There's no solution to some things. No peace, no absolution, no restitution. A price to be paid for everything.

Put us all in jail!

I step around a tree lying close to the ground, a stoic and brave tree. Unlike me. Hands in my pocket, head down and thrust forward, eyes glazed with determination to forget the whole thing. The fire in my stove will be out when I get home.

At the village tap I fill my bucket with icy water and continue on my way. Footsteps crunch behind me, someone running to catch up on the packed snow. I turn to see Shuni, tall and lanky, a purple wool beret barely covering her ears, wisps of hair and a long braid, her gait agile, restless like a pony. I want to reach over and zip up her jacket. She's coiled a sleeping bag around her neck like a scarf and carries a pillow under one arm.

Hey, Shuni.

You thinking real hard, she says.

How can you tell?

I call you many times and you never answer.

Sorry. I can't hear very well with my hood on. So where are you off to?

My dad say I come and stay with you. And he say to give you this.

She hands over a small transistor radio and leans over to grab the handle of the water bucket and ease my load.

IV.

I wake in a pool of grief this morning. I thought I'd never see my father again, but there he was in my dream last night. I don't usually remember dreams, but this one is so vivid. I was watching a play at the LSPU theatre hall in St. John's, a spectator, but strangely I was also an actor in a small room backstage getting ready to play an Innu woman. Feeling squeamish about it. I placed a traditional Innu hat over my sassy short hair. It was made of black and red wool felt and decorated with beads and a brocade ribbon. Attached to it were two small coils of hair wrapped in black cloth that hung over my ears. I wore a simple long shift of supple beige caribou skin, embellished with a crosshatch of red, yellow, and blue designs painted along the hem: parallel lines, triangles flanked by paired curves with end spirals, a zigzag of circular medallions. Designs infused with the magic of the sun and moon, river, mountain and hunting trail, sexual potency, the heart and soul of *Katipenimetak*, the Caribou Master, all to be revealed during the play.

It was time to apply my makeup, make myself look Innu, but there was only white makeup. I'd misunderstood. I was meant to play a mime. I smeared it on. I started to panic at my brash white face in the mirror, whitey-white *kakeshau*, my heart pounding, tha-thump, tha-thump, like it was about to burst out of my chest. This was not going to work. This was not what I'd signed up for.

I heard a knock on the door and opened it to find my father, drunk and a little scary. But he said calm down, I looked just fine the way I was. In the mirror I saw my mother standing in the corner of the room. She was staring at me, wearing an apron, arms folded, looking grim and unhappy. How did she get in?

Mom, you need to take off your apron. We're in a theatre.

She looked at me with a blank stare.

My father seemed oblivious to my mother, grabbed my hands, and started to dance a silly dance. My father who never danced. His hands were big and heavy, needling. And why was there no one to play the drum? I worried he would follow me on stage, drunk, and then everyone would know. I broke into a sweat, and heard the curtain call.

Break a leg, my father whispered as he let go of my hand and pushed me gently out of the dressing room. My mother still said nothing. The stage was my bedroom in St. John's, flowery wallpaper, cozy in a warm golden light. I stepped into the hallway which was not a hallway at all, but a doorless narrow passage, miles and miles long. I no longer knew where I was. I didn't know anything.

I've got to pull myself together. I've got to find a way. I walked and walked around several corners, and finally came to a flight of stairs that crumbled as I descended. I started falling, falling, into a white expanse of nothingness. Finally, I might be in Labrador. What a relief! The set was supposed to be in *nutshimits*, but there were no hills, no bay, no tents, no trees, no barrens. Nothing. I looked around, a scream rising in my throat.

The curtain came down and the audience stood to applause.

The dream has left me immobilized, my body still snared in a deep sleep. Slow, deep breath in. And again. Like an archaeologist, I ferret out each bone until my skeleton feels all there, intact, a precise and beautiful instrument. Calm down.

I fell asleep last night thinking about grief, how it's almost a relief to be here. This job might be a distraction and surely a haven.

In some strange way. Innu people don't generally give advice. What should I do? I've often asked, and *muk^u tshin* is their usual response. 'It's up to you.'

No one here will try to tell me to write in my journal, or go to a grief support group, or give me books about grieving, suggest I take an art course or get a dog. It's time to pull up my bootstraps. Grief can turn you into a foreigner, an undesirable. I won't have to worry about how sad I look, or watch people sway to a safer topic or cross the street to avoid me altogether. People will keep you at bay, where there is less danger of contagion. No one here will advise me about the clinical stages of grief: denial, anger, bargaining and depression. As if there isn't a million ways to grieve.

I don't have to pretend or wear a mask or makeup, contrary to my dream.

Shuni hasn't stirred yet. She got up in the middle of the night to light the fire. Does a stove fire stir up memories of the house fire? She knew those kids. I might ask her about it when the time seems right, if that ever happens. Manish told me once that for days after the person has passed, Elders will tell children not to go outside, especially not at night, for fear the spirits will take them along with them on their journey. Maybe this is what I felt the night my father died. I ended up sleeping in the bed with my mother—every other bed in our family home occupied. I felt him there, the charge that was his soul not yet evaporated, like there were three of us in the bed. It was crowded.

At least the Innu here all seem to believe in an afterlife, often recounting dreams of loved ones who've passed, visiting them, almost always in *nutshimits.* So happy, so peaceful out there, they say. I mainly believe dead is dead. Life doesn't go on; it goes nowhere. Death goes on. My father might appear in a dream, but I'll never really see him again, never again chat with him as we drive around the farm to check on the crops, or fry up partridge and add brown sugar to cantaloupe, pick baby dandelion greens in the spring to sauté in butter and flambé with vinegar, argue about the NDP and the

Liberals, or pour him a glass of Scotch against my better judgment. I'll never again laugh at his quirky wit, or answer his questions with explanations he'll never understand. Why won't you shave your legs? Why are you working up there? Why don't you buy yourself a car? Why don't you marry Mark?

Did he really want to know?

I rise, shake off the caribou skin and sleeping bag along with my dream, slip into my moccasins and parka, and step out the door as stealthily as possible.

The sun is slowly peering over the horizon, its light filtering through a crystal fog that has drifted in from the night. Heavy and laden, this cold white and amber ghost of the frozen Labrador Sea is crawling westward through the village and beyond to blanket the hills and trees. A few stars linger. I catch a whiff of smoke puffing out of nearby chimneys and lamplight glowing from the Pasteens' kitchen window. I want to see inside, but my view is masked by dirt, frost, and condensation. We still haven't talked about rent and wood. I want a fixed and fair amount; they'll want their share of what's available, and I never seem to know what that means. In my culture, money is measured; a loan is a desperate act, somewhat shameful. I hoard my money. I am responsible for myself, I have to look after myself, that's how I was raised.

I walk over to the big rock, and as far as I can see and hear, there is no one else stirring out of doors.

Back at the tent, Shuni has disappeared and I'm relieved, not being much of a morning person. I lift the lid off the water bucket to find a sheet of ice has formed, enough that I need to fetch the axe outside to crack it. I pour a little water into the washbasin and scoop some up with my hands to splash over my face. The icy water shocks, steals my breath. I pour some into the kettle and open the stove door to light the fire, a task I love. I stack a handful of twigs around a crinkled sheet of *The Labradorian,* teepee style, to let the air circulate, and strike a match. I add two small junks and at once the flame is snapping with confidence, a large one.

The caribou skin dress from my dream is still with me, in the corner of my eye. I wish I could touch it. At least the whole costume seemed like real Innu, and not braids, random beads, and a feather headdress.

V.

I'm sipping the last of my morning coffee when Manish arrives with the fixings for making donuts: flour, brown sugar, baking powder, raisins, corn oil, and her own frying pan.

She throws the ingredients into a bowl, adds water, and stirs the whole into a batter. She spoons out a small ball of dough, stretches it out to make a hole in the middle, and drops it into a hot sizzling pan of oil on the stove. I've made sure to keep the fire blasting and now pull the door flap open for relief.

Where are we meeting? I ask as she flips the dough over with the spatula. My morning consternation seems to have dissipated.

Innu Nation office, should be okay, Manish says.

What about the Band Council rec hall?

Steps too steep for some *tshishennuats.*

And the mission hall? It might be more comfortable?

I don't want the priest walking in.

Manish is already establishing some terms of reference.

I'd organized an education conference for the Native Friendship Centre a few years back, attended by Sepastien and Kistin, who worked as a teacher's aide. They'd talked of problems with the school: the furnace was often broken, sometimes there was no water, some teachers were hitting kids, and the kids were only learning *kakeshau* culture—why couldn't kids get credits for learning about the beaver and hunting and *nutshimits*? For these highly inflammatory statements, the priest saw fit to call them both out during the Sunday service. The way I heard it, even Sister Alice walked out.

We can make the Innu Nation office comfortable, I say. Turn up the heat, place the chairs in a circle.

Manish nods absently, her thoughts elsewhere.

Will it be a real Elders' meeting, I wonder. The last one I'd been at was the one about land claims with lawyers and government negotiators. Sepastien was meant to translate, but it seemed to me he barely did his job. Of course it was hard to know. Too many impossible words probably, or not enough time. People had a plane to catch. Through the presentations by lawyers and Tapit, the Innu Nation's chief negotiator, and during the discussion that ensued, almost all in English, the Elders just sat shuffling in their seats, sometimes dozing off. The talk was about non-renewable resources and surface and subsurface rights, land classifications, royalties, compensation, FEARO, co-management, expropriation, impact benefit agreements, the short list, interim measures. The time had come to get a framework agreement together.

Finally, to my great relief, Tapit turned to ask the Elder Mishta-Pinip to speak. Earlier that day in the office, Tapit had been in deep conversation with the old man. Maybe he was prepping Mishta-Pinip, coaching him about the meeting and what he should say. Tapit's uneasy straddling of worlds might sometimes be a little like mine.

Mishta-Pinip had stood up to speak as those around him sat at attention. He spoke fast, forcefully, like he knew all that had just been said. He seemed fed up. I longed for the unedited, unabbreviated version of his words. Sitting next to Manish, my eyes pleaded with her, and she leaned over to whisper the gist of the old man's oration. He said as a kid he'd pulled a toboggan when his family travelled from Uashat to Uashkaikan, from Sept-Îles maybe to Fort Chimo? And he'd watched his father hunt caribou with a spear many times.

I never went to school, he said. His school was *nutshimits*, his teachers were the land and the animals. He talked about how the mission showed cowboy and Indian movies in the church hall, how rocks could move on their own, how bears wore ties and suits and could speak *kakeshau*, how an evil creature spirit—*Manitu-utshu*—lived in the mountain by Muskrat Falls and was not to be disturbed. *Manitu-utshu* was known to exact revenge. He decried how he'd lost a canoe and cache with the flooding of Meshikamau, and his grandfather's grave was also flooded. The military could go fly their jets somewhere else. One jet flew so low over his camp he could see the pilot's face, and it near gave him a heart attack, sent the baby screaming. He added that his father was a *kamiteut* who used his powers for good, not like that other *kamiteut* whose name shall remain unspoken. Whatever had become of his grandchildren, he wanted to know. He could no longer understand them. Finally he sat down and Sebastien translated for the group, a calculated offering. He left out the part about the rocks and the bears, how his father was a *kamiteut*.

Tapit must have been shaking his head on the inside. Minutes after Mishta-Pinip sat down, the meeting was adjourned and the *kakeshauts* managed to catch their plane.

Manish spoons a donut out of the frying pan and adds it to the mounting stack of them on the table.

I'll get the coffee urn at the band office, she says. Can you pick up tea bags, sugar, and Carnation Milk at the store? Meet you at the office after lunch. I'll make sure Elders have a ride. Tapit and Shuash can help with that. You can set up.

Sure thing, *Utshimashkueu*.

I like it when she's Boss Woman.

And don't you forget it, she says.

No worries there.

I am setting up the flip chart stand when Tshinetshishepateu and Manikanet, the oldest couple of the village, hobble in, soon followed by Shushana, who is tiny and hunchbacked. Their legs are bent like archer's bows, shaped by decades of walking in bearpaw snowshoes and sitting on boughs. Or maybe it's from rickets. Tshenish and An-Pinamen arrive, then Shinipest, Tuma, Etuet, Mani-Pia, Akat's parents, Mishta-Pinip and Manteshkueu, and finally the Katshinaks, Tshakapeshes and Mistenapeos. I'm glad to see that both the drinking and non-drinking factions are here. I'm longing to take pictures, but that would be so *kakeshau*-on-safari. Better to be less conspicuous, although people here mostly seem to love to get their picture taken, especially when I send them copies, which turns into multiple requests and having to make more copies, endless copies over the years. The price I pay for the privilege. Still my camera's going to stay in my backpack.

The women wear long plaid or flowery cotton skirts over dark pants, their hair tucked under a tuque or a woolen red, green, or blue Ukrainian scarf. On their feet are rainbow-striped socks and tanned caribou-skin moccasins with colourful beadwork. A few of them wear chain necklaces with crosses almost as big as my hand.

My grandmother used to wear a rosary as a necklace. As a child I figured she wore it in case she might need to break into prayer, recite a decade of Hail Marys at a moment's notice. Some of the men are wearing green-and-black-checkered hunting jackets. A couple sport aviator bifocal glasses, and Tuma has wrapped a faded and grimy yellow cloth around his head. He reminds me of Innu people in Father Whitehead's old photographs from the 1920s, taken when people looked unabashed into a camera—whether smiling or serious—guileless, unself-conscious. Maybe life was simpler back then.

Manish asks Manteshkueu to say a prayer. I like prayers in Innu, when I can't understand a word they're saying. This meeting warrants a prayer of gratitude, a chance to hear from Elders before any plans get made. A number of leaders are here, including Tapit, Kanikuen, Sepastien, and Shushep, but Manish is the one leading the meeting. She is speaking again.

We've asked you to this meeting to talk about the fire, I imagine her saying. She stops after a couple of sentences. Her face tightens, tears well up. She looks over at me, and signals to the flip chart. My own tears are handy and I want to put my arms around her. What is she saying? Does she want me to continue? I can't do that. Instead, I nod at her with a half-smile.

I marvel at her standing up front, presiding. There was a time when people insisted I facilitate meetings. Are meetings even "chaired" in the Innu world? And the last time I'd been here and gone door-to-door or stopped women on the road to invite them to the land claims meeting, some told me their husbands wouldn't allow it.

We need to talk about this. It's one of the saddest things that ever happened to us, Manish says in English now, then switches back to Innu, having regained her bearings.

There's no need for translation. She's reminding them about the Rich family who drowned not so long ago, and all the young people they've lost over the last few years. How something needs to be done. For the children.

Tshinetshishepateu, as the oldest in the community, is the first to respond. He takes the pipe out of his mouth and tucks it into his breast pocket. He leans forward in his chair, elbows on his knees, his head hunched over and cradled in his hands. He speaks a long time. I catch the occasional bits, what sound like words I know—*auassats, tshishennuats, utshimauts, ishkuteu, mitshuap*—children, Elders, leaders, fire, house—but not enough to know what he's saying. Finally, he leans back.

Shash, he says, enough. No one translates for me.

Each Elder speaks in turn, telling their inscrutable stories. The muted and deep music of each voice on its journey lulls me into a daze. Their speech is, like the prayers of my childhood, interminable, the droning incantation of a rosary recited, a soundtrack to my thoughts. It wouldn't make sense to translate everything for me. This is a conversation they need to have amongst themselves. Translation can kill most meetings, stretching the conversation to numb everyone's mind, double the time and sometimes more. Vital threads lost with the starting and stopping, fragmented bits and elusive equivocations, deliberate or unavoidable.

My mind meanders.

The office is a concoction of two trailers merged. Everything and everyone working here look a little worn and tired. The walls are painted a steely blue that sucks up the light. Two windows on the back end of the room are boarded up. The fluorescent bulbs buzz a low-level white noise and reflect a jaundiced light on everyone. They are discharging mercury vapour. I'd tried to sweep the floor earlier, but my efforts barely touched the years of accumulated dirt and grime. There's no water or toilet in the building.

Several large topographical maps taped together hang on the wall by the entrance. This morning I'd traced my hands over the mountain ranges and along river valleys. I'd looked more closely at the names, so many names for such a large, "uninhabited" territory—as DND describes it when they're trying to promote, or excuse, their low-level military flight training. Innu place names are scrawled everywhere, and English names are scratched out and replaced with Innu ones. What looks like dozens of corrections, maybe hundreds, have been added. Mushuau-shipu for George River, Mishta-shantesh for Daniel's Rattle, Mishta-shipu for Churchill River, Uashat for Sept-Îles, Akami-uapishk^{u} for the Mealy Mountains. A red marker has traced a number of trails, covering impressive swaths of the territory, including inside the military training zones. How many meetings have I been at where maps are the focus? People point to places with certainty and precision, break out into a story, seeing in their mind's eye the actual place.

This is the world I keep wanting to enter—the one with Innu names. I'm not much interested in reading anthropological accounts "about" the Innu. They mostly feel suspect. First of all, where are the women? Well, except for Eleanor Leacock. And did the researchers understand enough Innu-aimun to get it right? Did they know about all that is not translatable? Did they have the right to share the information? How were their words filtered; what was left out?

I don't like to leave those books lying around for the Innu to see when they visit, don't want to feel like I'm in on some secret about them that they don't know.

There is a whole world to experience, apart from maps, books, and old photographs. The smell of tobacco from the old man's pipe and the incantation of his song, the stretch of a beaver skin on a frame, the knobby hands of a woman plucking a goose, the giggles of a child teaching me Innu-aimun and fussing over my pronunciation. Sitting around the circle in a teepee covered in caribou skins or birchbark, under distant stars. Stars for celestial navigation. Dead reckoning. The dreamer *ishkueu* mixes her dyes and paints the lines of her dream onto the caribou hide, in exaltation to the Animal Spirits—maybe she would teach me?

Here I go again, trespassing. And then again, it's likely my ancestors consorted with Innu generations ago. My family tree is sketchy, but I do know my mom's lineage includes a fille du roi, Madeleine Dubois, one of eight hundred or more girls rounded up by King Louis XIV and sent to the New World to make babies, establish roots, strengthen the colony. Ships filled with filles, an exceptionally rare and valuable cargo, landed on Nitassinan's shores and straight into an infernal winter. Forget the romantic image of history books. A man could choose a fille to be his wife like a butcher chooses a lamb amidst the flock. Charming. Was she poor, unwanted, an orphan, maybe a fille de joie? She wasn't likely a sweet and dainty coquette, more like tough and rugged as a manly man, and then some. Hopefully not too obedient. She looked the Innu in the eyes. Would Manish and Madeleine have been friends if they'd met? Imagine the movie, a different story from the white man's history book, starring Manish and me—an unlikely friendship but she saves my butt that first year. She shows me how to snare a rabbit and fish, clean a skin, sew moccasins, dry meat. I teach her how to garden. She wears a dress made of caribou hide like in my dream, and me with my farthingale and padded bum roll.

This chair is hard, my butt stiff. Tshinetshishepateu is speaking again. Is the conversation still about the fire or inquiry, or has it taken a circuitous route? I'm daydreaming about costumes at a meeting about children dying. I abandon my perch by the flip chart, grab a notepad and pen from the table along the wall, and slip into the chair by Sepastien. He takes the pen and paper from me, responding to my pleading eyes, and begins to write.

He say his grandson who die last year he knock on his door night before fire tell him something bad will happen

Tshinetshishepateu pauses as if to listen, but no one speaks. And then he goes on and Sepastien keeps writing.

He say reason children die is we not look after caribou bones make Katipenimitak angry we throw bones for dogs bones everywhere we should take care caribou bones

This gets everybody going again as the conversation makes its way around the circle one more time. I point to the paper on Sepastien's lap, but he only shrugs. I'm on my own.

There are ghosts and caribou bones, and spiritual practices and meaning and social order that make no sense to me, and I'm not meant to know. I was raised to believe in a virgin mother, and receiving God in a small bland host placed on my tongue by a priest in long robes. We eat and drink the body and blood of our saviour. Like cannibals.

Finally, Manish looks over at me.

They think it's a good idea we talk about the fire, she says. They say we need to talk to everybody. To hear everybody's story.

Everybody? I ask. That would be hundreds, wouldn't it?

We can't leave anybody out.

Okay, I say, without explaining my reservations.

What about the *kakeshauts*? Teachers, Sister Alice and Sister Marie, the priest, nurse, social worker?

Mauats, Manish says before she has even translated for the Elders. They are nodding in agreement.

That was clear.

Did they say exactly what we should ask people to talk about? I ask.

Manish translates my question and the conversation starts up again, still animated. No slouching, squirming in chairs, or escape artists. Time to serve tea and donuts. I'm pouring a cup for Tuma when Manish finally summarizes their discussion.

They want us to ask people what happen to us after the white man came into our lives, she says. How the church change our lives? How Social Services change us? And the school, police, doctors, nurses, the store, government. All of them.

Good questions, I say as I offer milk and sugar to Kananin.

They've not come up with any direct questions about the fire.

You might also want to ask people what needs to be done to stop these things from happening? I suggest.

Manish translates this and again the Elders are nodding before she's finished.

Who will do this work? I ask. You need a team who can talk to everybody. Men and women, different clans, drinkers and non-drinkers, all ages.

This spurs more talk as the plate of donuts makes its way around the circle. By the time everyone has swallowed their last bite, Manish walks over to the flip chart and writes down three names.

Sepastien is really good writer, and he talk to everybody. That man's not shy. Shustin work with Social Services. Her English is good. Hard worker. She work at school before and kids like her too. Kananin is an Elder, so people know this is a serious thing we're doing. She work in school too in the past, she write Innu-aimun good, and everybody her family, related to her, like granddaughter, cousin, brother, auntie, son-in-law. Big family.

Sounds good.

We should talk about money. I don't like to, and I won't look after it, but I want to know about salaries.

It would be good if we all get paid the same, I say, those of us working on this.

Manish translates and the Elders nod. Mishta-Pinip makes a comment that cracks everybody up. I look around curious, my eyebrows raised, but no one translates the joke.

I have one more question, I say. "People's inquiry," it doesn't sound very friendly, in English anyway. It's a word for government and lawyers. How will you explain it in Innu-aimun? What should we call it?

Another lively chat and Manish turns again to write on the flip chart: *Mamunitau Tshitaianimuanu.*

It means Gathering Voices, she says.

Way more inviting. I say. Is there anything else we need to decide on now?

Mishta-Pinip speaks up and I can hear *Mr. Bean.*

His favourite show, Manish mouths to me from across the room, pointing at her watch. Mr. Bean apparently has taken the village by storm. Manish thanks everyone, and the Elders get up. Tshinetshishepateu and Manikanet are heading my way.

Miam miam, tshinashkumitin, Tshinetshishepateu says as he shakes my hand, and Manikanet follows suit. I'm not sure what I've done to deserve their gratitude, but my heart does a little dance. I haven't done any writing at all on the flip chart, but I do feel rather like capital letters and exclamation marks inside.

Good stuff, I say to Tapit as we leave the building.

I don't know. People fighting too much all the time in this town, he says. I just can't see it, how it can work.

You know better than me. But it does feel like something. A good start, anyway.

Maybe. He climbs onto his snowmobile and takes off, stirring up a cloud of snow.

Manish has followed us out. She looks despondent.

Why so glum? I thought that meeting went great, I say, which is funny seeing as I wasn't privy to most of the discussion. We're both headed home towards the big rock.

So embarrassed, Manish says. Crying like that.

You're not the last person who'll be crying about this.

She doesn't respond and we walk on, our footsteps a syncopated beat, crunching on the hard path.

Maybe the Elders are right, Manish says finally.

About what?

If we tell the story of what happen to us, if we do that, maybe things can be better.

Yes, we can hope.

Will people be able to stand it—opening all this up again? Manish asks, shaking her head.

What else can you do?

Snowflakes fall gently and define the whispers of the wind. We reach her trailer.

You coming in? she asks. We step straight into her living room, dark with wood panelling and a beat-up rug that's never seen a vacuum. Long strips of what must be caribou meat are drying above the wood stove in the corner. Manish sees me looking at the *passauaia.*

Wanna try some?

Sure.

I take a tentative bite of the dried meat. It still has a slight coppery taste of blood, like sucking on a paper cut. Chewy.

Hi, Pien, I say.

Manish's husband sits on the couch, scowling at me. He barely grunts a response, and gets up to go into the bedroom. Shuts the door. His usual response. Moccasins and socks, hats and scarves are draped on a string above the wood stove, four rifles sit on a wall rack, and in the corner of the cluttered kitchen stands a half-filled snowshoe with a ball of sinew hanging from it.

You're spending lots of time on the land, I say to Manish.

I won't when I'm chief.

What do you mean, when you're chief?

The guys have decided I should be chief. They are all worried about this inquiry. No one wants to be left holding the bag.

I'll gladly hold that bag with you, I say, smiling. And it's great, you being chief.

They're pretty sure I can win. The election is set for next week.

That's fast, I say. When was this decided?

We had a meeting yesterday. We talk about it at the meeting today. So it's going to happen.

What'll I do in the meantime? I wonder. And are all the election rules and regulations being followed?

So now you've got a campaign to run? I ask instead.

My only campaign is no booze, Manish says. I won't buy votes.

A woman and no booze, I say. That should be interesting.

Manish smiles conspiratorially.

You don't mind being chief?

I'm a bit worried about my kids. Will I be able to take them on the land? And all those meetings with government...She grimaces.

You'll be good for them.

The two of us sit quiet, sip our tea.

At least now, one of our commissioners, Sepastien, is not bootlegging anymore, Manish says. It wouldn't look good for the inquiry.

Shagger, I say. I talked to him about that last summer, told him I'd tell his sister Penash, and sic her on him if he didn't quit.

You think that did it, why he quit?

Who knows? I say, shrugging. I best get home. I think I'm out of water.

Wanna ride?

Mauats. I'm working on my muscles, I say as I raise my forearm, flex it, and head for the door.

By the way, you're moving in with Shustin and her family. Safer during the election.

Okay with me, I say as I exit. Nice to know someone's looking after me.

I decide against yelling out to Pien that he can come out now.

VI.

Over the next week, I catch a few candidates' posters hung in the store and in offices around the village. They're homemade, photocopied pictures with marker-scrawled names. *Vote for John Jacobish*, all in English. One morning I recognize Manish's voice on the radio and I'm pretty sure I hear *mamunitau tshitaianimuanu.* I think she may be talking up the inquiry. So she *is* campaigning.

Maybe we should have a flyer about Gathering Voices to hand out door-to-door.

Sure, Manish says when I ask her about it.

I've made the move to Shustin's. She claims I haven't displaced anyone. They haul mattresses into the living room every night, and the lot of them sleep together as a family, just like in a tent. I have my own room.

We always do that, she said to me. So we don't get lonely.

Loneliness, I've learned, can be a perilous thing around here, related to feeling excluded and longing for people.

Loneliness, Manish told me once, can lead to the living wanting to die to be with loved ones, or the dead longing to be with loved ones still alive and coming to take them with them to their nether world.

Aren't you lonely? she asked me. I was living on my own then.

I know loneliness, aching, sorrowful, but having my own room is a relief, not a lonely thing.

I ask the kids if they like to draw, how I need a picture to put on the flyer. Napess volunteers and spends the better part of the night crouched over his sheet of paper at the kitchen table, sketching with a sure hand. He draws an Innu drum filled with a *nutshimits* scene—Canada geese and ducks flying over a rising sun and hills, two Innu paddling in a canoe, a caribou and bear and fox on the lakeshore. He adds pastel hues with coloured pencils. I could just hug him, but had best spare him the embarassment.

Wow, awesome job, I tell him. Maybe the Band Council can pay you for it?

His face beams.

The drawing will also make a wicked report cover.

The flyer needs to be bilingual. Shustin is not sure how to write in Innu-aimun, but between the two of us we manage to sound out the words phonetically, how most people write anyway. People keep telling me no *kakeshau* is going to tell them how to write their own language, linguist or not, and not many people seem to have cottoned on to the beauty of standardized spellings for word recognition.

Tipatshimu, we spell out; share your story. Take out the "n" at the end of the word, and the noun for "story" has come alive, a request. And Gathering Voices is about sharing stories. People here call almost any kind of sharing a story. We, all our thoughts and experiences, are stories. It has me thinking about my own story, how it stops with me, how little I know about even my parents' lives, never mind generations back.

I head out to the Innu Nation office to photocopy the flyer. I shrink Napess's drawing with the photocopier at the band office, cut and paste the image onto a clean sheet, and type the text in a simple and bold font, which looks like twigs lined up together in the shape of letters. The creaking photocopier manages to spit out a hundred copies, but with a lamentable streak running through every one of them, a desecration of Napess's artwork. It'll have to do.

No one bites at my hint about having to drop off the flyer door-to-door. That leaves me, and hopefully my doing this won't scare people away. It's hard to know. My first stop is a tiny, ramshackle monopoly house, multiplied many times over across the village.

My mittened hand taps a muffled knock on the door. The only people around here who knock are the nurse, the social worker, the priest or nun, but I can't bring myself to just walk in. A ragamuffin girl, round-faced and rosy-cheeked, opens the door.

Hi, I say, and she looks at me wide-eyed, runs back into the house. A large beef bucket is perched in the middle of the porch. It might be a honey bucket. I walk by it. A man sits next to the stove smoking a pipe, and a girl is washing dishes in a plastic basin on the kitchen counter. Mani-Pia, who was at the Elders' meeting, sits at the table beading the tongue of a moccasin. A couple of kids are jumping on the bed in a bedroom that is no larger than two snowmobiles sitting side by side and can just barely accommodate a double bed. Next to it is one of those infamous bathrooms with a toilet and tub, but no water. The room is now used for storage and strewn with *nutshimiu* stuff and other sundry gear.

A whole village was constructed from scratch with no running water. Did the engineers forget to survey the area? Did they figure these people are used to living in tents so they don't need much water, nothing too big? We'll give them dollhouses, with pictures on the wall, tiny windows, for Mommy and Daddy and Dick and Jane—no *nukum* or *nimushum*, adopted kids, or slew of grandchildren built into the design.

Everyone is staring at the intruder. The usual bare light bulb frowns down at me from the middle of the ceiling. All the walls intact, closing in on me. I don't want to be a voyeur.

Hi, I say again, with a smile. *Pushu.*

The man looks over to Mani-Pia.

Auei e? he asks, wondering if she knows who I am.

I just want to give you this, I say, and I hand a flyer to Mani-Pia. About the *mamunitau tshitaianimuanu,* I stumble through these endless syllables: mah-moo-nee-tah-oo chee-tah-yah-nee-mwa-noo. I've been practicing.

Eukuan miam, Mani-Pia says. Good.

She carries on in Innu to the man, must be her husband. He wasn't at the Elders' meeting with her. Hopefully she's filling him in. The TV is on and a CNN reporter is talking about the aftermath of the collapse of the Soviet Union and the Cold War. The World Bank and the IMF are coming to the rescue, humanitarians that they are. That should be good news but they should also do something about George Bush and his military industrial complex. Will this affect the NATO base at Goose Bay and low-flying jets assaulting Innu camps?

A teenage girl with a baby in her arms opens the door from a second bedroom no larger than the first. The baby takes one look at me and starts shrieking at the top of his lungs, a piercing scream. Everyone cracks up.

Next thing I know there's a cup of tea for me on the table. I still have ninety-nine flyers, but it can't hurt to have a little sit-down.

Good meeting with the *tshishennuats*, I say, looking over at Mani-Pia. She nods. What is she thinking about all this business? Even at the meeting, people have only talked about the fire in passing, with eyes squinted, as if they can't stand to have their eyes wide open, to see all of anything at once. I'm not much for asking questions to make conversation, which is what most *kakeshauts* do, and are expected to do. I don't want to be the interviewer. I don't want to interrogate, pump people for information, turn into a journalist, an anthropologist, a nosy pest. I want to be infused with knowledge or somehow experience it, breathe it in.

The TV is a distraction. Charles and Diana are splitting and Madonna has signed a $60 million deal.

The conversation continues around me with its lilting cadence, back and forth. Sometimes they glance over at me. The heat from the stove envelops me as I fix my eyes on Mani-Pia's hands sewing and weaving her beads into a flower pattern on the caribou skin. Arthritic joints swollen on rounded fingers. Hands to dress and undress a baby, set a snare, knead bread, hands that are awkward with a pencil, writing slowly and judiciously. Does she know how to write? The ends of her fingernails are black the whole way around the edge. Bulging veins criss-cross the top of each hand.

I made moccasins once, I say. Small ones. Akat showed me.

Mani-Pia nods, unimpressed.

More breaking news on TV. There must be no one in the band office to change the channel, but everyone's eyes have turned to the television set as a well-coiffed man announces that the police who beat Rodney King in Los Angeles have been acquitted. The video that captured their guilt is playing. The news shifts to South Africa where people have voted to end apartheid and then Vandana Shiva, my all-time favourite environmentalist, is on mainstream news. She's talking about thirty thousand children dying in Sri Lanka every year from bad water. Six kids were lost here; multiply that by five thousand. News has a way of neutering a message, not driving it home. Or maybe it's me. I can't take it in.

No one is talking. A mute hospitality for the *kakeshau iskhueu.*

The baby looks at me intently, cooing now. I even manage to elicit a smile from him before he buries his face in his mother's shoulder. I'd best get going. I wave my goodbyes. The sun has gone down and I'm never going to get these flyers delivered.

I walk to the next house and knock on the door.

I keep knocking, one house and then the next, surprising people, never sure what I'll find on the other side of the door. It's a quiet night. Most houses are overflowing with people; some are clean and tidy, others not so much; some friendly, others not so much. People walk or drive by me on snowmobiles. One of them stops.

Auei tshin? The handsome young driver wants to know who I am and why am I here.

Ninu Anna. I try to explain. I'm working here, with the Elders and Innu Nation, about the fire.

That should totally confuse him. I hand him a flyer.

We're going to gather voices, I say, ask people to talk about the fire and why these things are happening.

He takes off again as I watch the flyer I gave him twirl into the air in his wake. I pick it up and carry on. Another man stops to talk to me.

I thought you were breaking into my house, he says, pointing to the door I just left.

That's funny.

We exchange goodbyes, and I continue on my way.

The flyer is likely a waste of time and paper. Can people read? It'll come in handy as fire starter. A *kakeshau ishkueu* knocking on doors about gathering voices? But it's something concrete, this walking around and talking to people. Beats speculating and overthinking while I wait for something to happen.

At the end of the harbourside row of houses by the frozen shore, is a gap. A house missing. My eyes struggle to make out a few details. The moon and stars are hiding. There is a silhouette of a metal kitchen chair with no seat, a wood stove minus the stovepipe, a metal bedframe and other scattered debris under a blanket of snow. Darkness.

The house.

I don't want to look—it's all too private, too awful. The dark night is a blessing. Manish had told me the story that morning. She'd come into the office while I was photocopying the flyer. She handed me a photo: six small coffins, three white, two grey and a blue one, lined up in a row below the altar at the front of the church. On each coffin was rested a sheet of paper with the child's snapshot and his or her name printed in marker underneath, along with a plastic red rose and a cloth with a small yellow embroidered cross. My heart sank deep at the image. I held back tears.

What happened, Manish? I asked. I've only heard what was reported on the radio and in the papers.

For once, they pretty well get it right, she said. It was Valentine's Day, freezing outside, really cold. A charter come in with booze that day and there's a dance at the school, a couple parties in the night. The kids are out alone, from three different families; the oldest was eleven and the youngest was nine. They are brothers and sisters, cousins. Roaming around. People say they were sniffing. The house is empty so they must have gone in out of the cold. No one sure how the fire start, but by the time people see smoke, flames are breaking through the roof. I can still see it, the smoke, the flames, a lot of flames. Probably they have bags of gas. At first we don't know the kids are trapped inside. There's nothing we can do. No water. No truck, no pump. We got no water.

She'd paused and looked up, gazing into space.

My father try to go in the house, but he can't see nothing. When the sun come up, we saw the bones, she said.

Our eyes locked and we said nothing for a long time. The image had pulled us in, together. We looked away as our eyes welled up.

What were their names? I finally asked. The children?

Mani-Akat, Shinipest, Kanikuen, Simeon, Shunian and the youngest Kiti.

I couldn't fully grasp what she'd just told me. Who ran door to door, panicked, pumped with adrenaline and cortisol, maybe alcohol, screaming, Are your children home? How did the purveyor of bad news break the news to the parents? Was there someone to hold them close, or maybe walk home with them and sit up all night? Was it morning before they knew for sure, while in the chilled air the sun rose red and blazing, oblivious, the whole village staggering from the blow?

Those are all the parents, sitting in the front row, Manish said, pointing at the picture.

I stared at their faces, as if they might hold answers. They looked so young, huddled and hunched, muffled in their winter jackets, tuques, scarves and beaver hats, as if the multiple layers of attire might stave off the sorrow as well as the cold. How many times does guilt amplify grief? Hundreds of people were packed in behind the parents. An ocean of sad and sombre faces. Some eyes cursed the camera; others looked down to avoid it. There had to be uncontrolled sobs, small children squirming and screeching everyone's desolation.

Outside, maybe the day was grim and stormy in pitiable sympathy. Had the priest managed to offer words of comfort or did he preach fire and brimstone? Did he mention this is what happens when you leave your children alone at night? Hard to imagine what words he might have used. Easier to imagine what followed; how everyone, including the little children, might have queued down the middle of the church to make their way to the caskets to say a little prayer by each coffin, how they might have wanted to lean over and plant a kiss on the cheeks of all the children to say a final goodbye. But no. After the fire, the coffins remained closed.

I wanted to find it in myself to be kind, compassionate. There was no other response. But in my heart was anger, and right next to the anger, helplessness. Look after your children. Can we just look after the children?

This picture should go in the report, I'd said to Manish as I handed the photo back, my words slow and controlled. Lest we forget.

It was a hard thing to say. I was thinking about the work at hand. I was changing the subject, shutting down, trying to move on.

Now, as I turn away from the remains of the house and head back to Shustin's, the darkness distorts. Images shape-shift through my tears, impossible to reassemble into some sensible pattern, familiar, mundane. There is none, not even a moon. The wind lashes my face. We are told there is a God. All my encounters tonight swirl around in my head. Grief is all around me, hitting, over and over again. No one has been spared.

VII.

I'm climbing the hill when I run into Tumi. Last time I'd seen him was in Goose Bay when he'd snuck me past the airline agent, with her list of passengers, onto a chartered plane headed for Utshimassits. The charter was already at capacity with the volleyball team, so three kids packed into a double seat to make room for me. Tumi was slick that way.

You coming to the party? he asks now.

What party?

I don't tell him I'm not much in the mood, the remains of the house still under my skin, its ghosts clinging on to me.

At my house. Come on in. Take a load off, Tumi says, smiling a goofy grin, the ear flaps of his beaver hat flapping.

What's the occasion? I ask.

There was no party an hour ago when I was dropping off the flyer. Tumi's smile is pretty inviting; he'd have a few things to say about all of this, the fire, the work. I want to go and I shouldn't, but it might be useful. It might be good for me, or not. Probably not. I'd be better off getting my sleep. I need my beauty sleep.

Election party, Tumi says. Napaen wants to be chief.

I didn't know Napaen was running...I don't know. I was just heading home.

Each word measured. I've vowed to myself I'd avoid this kind of revelry, but here I am being all kinds of indecisive. Just say no, do it. Heed the warnings.

Just one beer. Come on, Tumi insists.

We're all lonely for something, wanting to demolish old things in our path—ugggh, just say no—but I follow Tumi as he leads the way into his house and a cloud of cigarette smoke. Mark should be here; he always jumps at a party invitation. He's more the party animal, everyone's and no one's friend, a drown your sorrows type, and always trying to get me to go out more, especially on those sluggish days when I'm wallowing and drawing the curtains. He's good for me that way.

The room is blocked and maybe it's a chance to talk up the inquiry. Or not. Two towering stacks of two-fours stand against the back wall by the couch.

That's a lot of beer, I say.

Imported them myself from Hopedale by komatik, Tumi says.

A number of people are sitting on the linoleum floor. A few familiar faces smile back at me. Matshiu from the "job readiness training" program I taught when I lived in Sheshatshiu—training people for jobs that didn't exist—gets a nod from me. Matshiu's a wicked cartoonist. My favourite was of a funeral procession of animals: caribou, bears, wolves, foxes, geese, rabbits, moles, partridge, as far as the eye could see, all standing upright like humans, following a lumber truck on a road gouged through the forest.

Shakanin sits at the kitchen table. She sat next to me at a court hearing in Goose Bay over an 'illegal' caribou hunt. Three Innu men had been charged and lost six caribou and all their hunting gear: snowmobiles, komatiks, guns, ammo.

What does that mean, she kept saying under her breath, and I'd done my best to translate. Why hunting caribou, getting food for their families, being Innu, was a crime.

She slides over to one side of her chair now and points to the other half for me to share with her. On the couch sits Manish's Pien huddled between Napaen, the candidate, on one side and another large man on the other. All three are still wearing their parkas. Tumi slumps into a padded chair next to me. Must be his wife who just gave up her seat for him and now sits on one of the armrests. He doesn't introduce me.

The chair has multiple cigarette burns, and the stuffing protrudes in a couple of places. Handsome Boy, who was on the snowmobile earlier, strums a guitar, singing a country and western Innu song, something about the land and *Nimushum*, his grandfather. Live entertainment.

When did you get here? Shakanin asks.

Last Thursday.

Why did you come?

I'm working with the Band and Innu Nation to get people talking about the fire and what needs to be done.

Another *kakeshau* here to save the Innu, Pien pipes up from across the room, his voice oily and manly. Scowling, same as he was a few days ago at his house.

Here to make a few bucks off the Innu, eh? he asks.

What's it to you, Pien?

My beer is warm and bitter.

That would be *Peter* to you *Ms.* Anna.

I smile, a slight curl of my lip, a lying kind of serving-the-public smile. My mask in tact. People here call each other by their Innu name. Is there a problem if I do too? Not that I've ever actually discussed this with anybody, like so many other things. I've just tried it on for size. The rules are unclear, but it seems like people have different names for different contexts. Most people have a Christian name, an English and an Innu version—a throwback from the Oblates. This is the first time anyone has complained.

Whatever you want, *Peter*, I say, my voice a snigger. Sometimes my derision is ambivalent: I can be both repelled by and attracted to the fight.

Tshinetshishepateu once shared how people used to be given their names by *Katipenimitak* through dreams or singing. I knew this practice was pretty much gone—children now severed so soon after birth from their culture. But some Innu names persist as "nicknames." There is *Petapan* and *Ashini* and *Atikuss*, Dawn and Rock and Baby Caribou. Sometimes it's hard to get a translation for someone's nickname, people refuse, so I avoid using these. And there's Pishum who dropped

Bernadette, Penatet in Innu. She prefers *Pishum*—Sunshine—to a saint's name, and signs her name with it too.

Some people seem to like it when I use their Innu name, most seem indifferent. And when I write reports, most people are happy to have their Innu name attached to one of their quotes, but not their English one.

Pien is probably just being crooked.

You haven't answered my question, he insists.

I just said, we're working on an inquiry, Gathering Voices.

I know what he's doing. He's smart; I haven't given him enough credit. I do that with men sometimes.

Inquiry. What the hell is that? he says.

I wish I could tell him, what it is, what it will be. And I want to tell him I was invited, by his wife in fact. I could just say that I'm here as a guest. I'll try to do a good job.

Leave her alone, Shakanin says. I shoot her a grateful look.

My brother, she says, pointing her chin up towards him. Pien snarls my way again and resumes his banter with Napaen.

How are your parents doing? I ask Shakanin.

Worried. About their grandchildren. Since the fire. Worried about me. My drinking.

She raises her bottle of beer to punctuate her words.

I should go on home out of it, she adds.

Yeah, me too.

A toddler toddles in the midst of it all. His big sister, who must be around seven, is keeping an eye on him. The boy is playful, looks around the room with intelligent eyes, like he was born whole and awake. He wears only a diaper. He runs and stops and jumps and twirls, stretching the limits of his body; his sister follows almost in step, like a synchronized dance.

Hey *kakeshau ishkueu*, I'm still waiting to find out why you're here, Pien says, tossing his loathing across the room at me again, right on target, bullseye.

People are always talking about me as *kakeshau ishkueu* in my presence, but they use my name when they're talking to me directly. Except for towering Tanien; he calls me Shorty sometimes, short for Shortcake. Affectionately, I think.

I'm a government spy, collecting classified information, I say, to gales of laughter.

Apparently I can be hilarious and entertaining. Mark would be proud of me. I can do this. I can do this party.

Tshekuan? A woman from across the room has missed the joke. I'm impressed with the number of people keen to translate that statement. Pien is clearly not impressed but has no comeback.

A book lies at my feet, half sticking out from under Tumi's chair, and I lean over to pick it up. Books are often my refuge and solace. They're rare around here, except for the odd Newfoundland joke book, *Old Farmer's Almanac*, or Georg Henriksen's *Hunters of the Barrens*. I wasn't expecting to find Franz Fanon's *The Wretched of the Earth*.

I have yet to get around to reading this book. The title always makes me pause. It's about colonization, which I've gleaned Fanon describes as a form of violence, and how it's not only the land that gets colonized, but also people's minds, hearts, and souls. The book brings me back to Germany, during the anti-NATO European tour. The two Elders, their son, and his family and I were hosted by the Green Party and its leader, Petra Kelly, had an executive assistant who was an exiled Black Panther. He'd told me *The Wretched of the Earth* was the Panthers' bible.

The Panthers are more about Fanon than Martin Luther King and civil disobedience, he'd said.

I hadn't totally grasped what he meant, did not want to seem the innocent that I was and never asked.

The book's cover has an image of a black man with a cage around his head, like a prison. The cage is white and the man holds a key in his hand. I should seriously read this book, and what better place to do that? I leaf through the pages; Fanon has included a poem, some kind of musical work, and case studies. Not the usual dry academic fare. I didn't know he was a psychiatrist, and from Martinique.

I look up and the toddler has picked up a roll of duct tape. I watch as he rolls it across the floor towards me. He runs after it, but I grab and hand it back. Just as he reaches to catch it, I pull it away behind my back, and magically it reappears in my other hand. He squeals with delight, so unguarded and sweet. He reaches again and I hand it over. He snatches it and decides to sit at my feet to discover what else it can do. A bracelet, an anklet, a hat. Crash-landing. Oops. He laughs a belly laugh.

I want to wrap my arms around the child, quietly sign off from the party, head home, take him with me over the hill, to another place, somewhere safer, away from his earthly assignment, just this minute. I'll give him back. A great white saviour, for a second. His older sister still has her eye on him and I feel safer with this child at my feet. Somehow.

I leaf through the book, pause on a random page to grasp the odd sentence. The language is dense, *the colonizers' language*, Fanon might call it—big words: imperialism, pacification, pathology and liberation, bourgeoisie, and genocide. How about *epidermalization*? A simmering anger burns off each page.

Colonial domination has disrupted in a *spectacular fashion the cultural life of a conquered people.* True enough around here.

Another page reads how the West has corrupted leaders of the colonized state, making them put their own interests above the interests of the people. And *every effort is made to bring the colonized person to admit the inferiority...* and *to recognize the unreality of his "nation," and, in the last extreme, the confused and imperfect character of his own biological structure.* There is talk around here about Innu nationhood, like with *Innu kananatuapatshet*, an attempt by Tapit and others to organize and unite the Quebec and Labrador Innu. They've used nationhood as their argument in court—this is their land, they've never signed a treaty, and Canada's law is a foreign law. One judge believed them, even if his ruling got overturned two seconds later.

Clearly the ravages of colonization are all around me. Right here at this party.

Shakanin stands and walks over to the fridge. She must be looking for another cold one. I want to say, Go on home out of it, but I'm one to talk. She closes the fridge door, a beer in hand. Someone has stuck a poster onto it with masking tape. The poster is red, blue, and yellow with tiny little pictures of food: bread, eggs, lettuce, bananas, a carton of fresh milk, a bottle of ketchup, an ear of corn, with *What kind of food should you keep in the bottom of the refrigerator?* and *What kind of food should you keep in the top shelf of the refrigerator?* A burning issue up here. When was the last time they saw fresh corn?

A couple dozen beer bottles are now strewn over the table around the largest ashtray ever, and a woman across the room butts her cigarette out on the floor with her boot. The decibel level in the room has risen. And I'm still here.

Fanon is an ideal escape, a kind of vindication? I might like to argue with him about some of this, except no doubt he'd make mincemeat out of me. At the level of individuals, violence is a cleansing force. It frees the Native from his inferiority complex and from his despair and inaction; it makes him fearless and restores his self-respect. I might want to counter that decolonization does not always involve violence, but Tapit would be a way better debater. He's often quoting Ghandi, in defense of Innu civil disobedience, and talks about how non-violent protests have made the Innu proud and strong. Fanon would then point out how Canada has sent armed police and soldiers more than once to keep the Innu and others in check. The two would agree about ways the violence gets turned inward.

This your book? I ask Tumi.

Ralph gave me that. Bedtime reading, he told me.

You mean the guy from Denmark.

Yeah, he photocopy it too and pass it around to some other guys.

One of the chosen ones, are you? I tease. Not an easy read, is it?

I knew Ralph, an anthropology student, from the Native Peoples' Support Group in St. John's. He liked to accuse me of being more Innu than the Innu, of romanticizing the culture as lost in history.

I try to read some of it, Tumi says. Ralph tell me what it's about, something like the Black man need to be free from wanting to be white. I don't want to be white. I'm Innu.

You might agree with some of his other ideas though, I say.

Maybe. I don't read books much.

But Tapit's been reading it for sure, I say. That must be where he's getting all that language, those words he likes to use at meetings with *kakeshauts*.

Yeah, all those words is why Innu people walk out sometimes, Tumi says.

A lot of white people don't like that language either, I say. People get called communists for talking like that.

What's a communist anyway? Tumi asks.

I shift in my chair, run my hand through my hair. I'm not sure how to answer that, even if John Crosbie, our federal minister of justice looking after Newfoundland's interests, has called me a commie on CBC radio more than once. A communist: Little Old Me.

It's what people who are trespassing and destroying your land will call you if you tell them you don't like it, I say to Tumi.

I take a long sip of my beer. Tumi is pondering my words. I can see the wheels turning. Redbaiting. Red's my favourite colour. I lean my elbow on the table and rest my chin on my hand. It doesn't take much to be called a communist. Organize a few anti-NATO protests, speak at a couple, get quoted in the media. Make the odd call to an open-line radio program that likes to propagate lies about the Innu. Convince unions and churches to send out press releases with messages of support. The most egregious: live with and work for the Innu. To hang out with the Innu apparently is suspect. Red Indian lover. You must be an outsider. You must be a deviant, or disturbed, a radical, probably a missionary with the delusions of a saviour. Or you're running away from something. Maybe you're a New Ager itching to appropriate, to heal and get saved. Or you might be an alcoholic, a codependent, a reject. Definitely a lost soul. Next thing you know you'll be claiming a long-lost Sioux relative. You must be a bleeding heart, a needy bleeding heart. I might be a little of all of those things.

My grandfather talk about this stuff sometime, like what this guy is writing, Tumi says, interrupting my rumination.

I rather listen to *Nimushum*'s stories, he continues. He say the same thing. How white people keep stealing our land. And our kids' minds too, with their school.

Sounds like your grandfather and this Fanon guy are on the same page on that point, I say.

Tumi won't get his political education from me. I prefer reading novels to Marx. Last year I was written up in a feature article about NATO in Labrador in our so-called "national" Global Times. The centrefold article said little about the Innu, but I was profiled as an anthropologist of "Marxist obedience," "overtly anti-militaristic," spreading misinformation and manipulating the natives. Who knew I was an academic with such fervour and power? You'd think the journalist might have bothered to talk to me. I imagine myself more of a hippie wearing a flowery dress than an ideology-mad politico, an agent working against the state. More of a Volkswagen van–driving kind of woman living with copatriots in a nutshimits commune close to the land, in the woods, lovely, dark, and deep, hunting, foraging, and growing our own food, living off the grid, trading bread recipes and braiding garlic ropes, a clown troupe organizing the next sit-in. I'm more the kind of woman who howls at the moon and dreams of throwing pies in the faces of politicians. Yes, I could be a pie-throwing terrorist. Or a small tart–throwing terrorist—easier to sneak in, or snack on, should my plan fall through. Let them put that in my CSIS file. Not the violence Fanon had in mind. Oh dear, I don't mean to make light of Fanon.

Handsome Boy has sidled over and sits across the table from me. He looks like he's had one too many—no, maybe three or four. I hadn't noticed when he was playing his guitar. A pall of cigarette smoke, acrid and thick, hovers above us. Someone opens the window and -25°C air blows through the room, crawls up my sleeve. I shiver.

That's enough politics, Handsome Boy says.

He's been eavesdropping.

Auei tshin? I ask him.

Samish, he says. Hey, my band wrote a song. About the kids in the fire. Wanna hear it?

I nod, keen, my eyes wide and inviting. He brushes the strings of his guitar with a pick, a slow strum with a chord progression reminiscent of Kashtin's melancholic *Akua Tuta*, a warm and lush sound. He hums a couple bars before he begins to sing a plaintive lament. He can really play, even with a few too many. For a moment the room goes quiet.

Beautiful...and sad, I say when he's done, even if I can't understand the words.

Sad thing that happen here, he says.

Really sad, I say as I watch his fingers move along the fretboard, silently picking out chords.

Hey, do you think you could write down the words to your song, for a report? I ask. I'm working with people here to talk about what happened. Can we put your song in the report?

Sure thing, he says.

Behind him hangs a picture of the Virgin Mary, crowned with a fan of birdtails, beige and brown feathers, perhaps a hawk's—*shakutamuatsh.* A small ceramic angel hangs next to it, looking lonely. The opposite wall has a Dan George poster with a large rosary draped around it. *The only thing necessary for tranquility in the world is that every child grows up happy,* pronounces the poster. Next to it hang an Innu drum, a dream catcher with a fringe of eagle feathers, a crucifix, and a tree branch decorated with Christmas ornaments.

I been sobering eight months before tonight, Samish says.

That's good, I said.

You can quit again, you know, I want to say, but don't.

Tired of going to jail, me, he says, as he strokes the stubble on his chin.

People often confide in me, all manner of confessions. They might knock on my door, walk right into my tent, or stop me on the road, and the next thing I know they're telling me about their lives, their indiscretions, and not just minor misdeeds. It happens to me on planes too. Mostly I don't mind. If I listen close enough, things maybe can make sense, anything at all.

Why were you in jail? I've learned to ask direct questions.

Last time because I hit the policeman. But now I have daughter, she born in August. I quit because of my girl.

What about tonight?

I quit again. Tomorrow I go to *nutshimits*. Best place to quit. I don't even think about it there.

I do that too, go in the woods or by the ocean, when I need to feel better.

I don't sniff now, never. I have my friends and my family, my girl. I play my music too.

Good for you.

You want the words to our song. I can do that.

There is only a slight slur to his talk. The chatter in the room has ramped up.

So, where's your husband? Samish asks as he takes a swig of his beer.

My boyfriend's in St. John's, I say.

Definitely time to hit the road; it's obvious where this could go. But before I can move, Samish stands, teetering as he places his guitar against the wall. He walks right over to me, sways and staggers. He leans in close, very close, to whisper into my ear—as if the whole room isn't looking now, doesn't know what he's about to say. His eyes are puffy and bloodshot.

Let's go to your tent, he says, his breath laced with tobacco smoke. Alcohol emanates from his pores, mixed with an acrid underarm smell. He's right on top of me now.

Get off me, I say, in a kind of shouted whisper.

People are watching and he will pay for this. He might not remember, but he'll be reminded and he won't like it. I'm trying to shove him off me, my heartbeat has picked up. I should have left when the going was good. Teeth clenched, I force him back, my hand on his chest, my head tilted forward to shield him off. I push again and he leans back in, and I push again in a back and forth dance. I can hear laughter and beer bottles clinking, and then a crescendo of cheering. He won't easily live this one down. There may be a reckoning for me too. Hopefully his girlfriend won't hear about it.

Get. Off. Me, I say again, still under my breath, my voice hoarse and snarly, panic rising in my chest.

The outside door opens and bangs against the wall. A very tall and loud woman wearing an oversized camouflage hunting jacket barges in. Heads turn and watch as she marches straight over to the action in our corner. She says something indecipherable. She must have been at another party. Her eyes look wild and mismatched.

She teeters around the children, grabs Samish with two hands, hauls him right off me.

Thanks, I say, exhaling finally, shaking off my panic. She is grabbing at Samish's T-shirt.

Pets mini, she says. She wants his T-shirt with its Innu Nation flag—green, white,and blue bands emblazoned horizontally across the front, superimposed with caribou antlers bracketing a snowshoe in the middle. She's hauling it over his head. Goose bumps spread across his now bare and hairless chest, his tiny nipples stand erect.

My chance to leave. I stand, step around Samish and the missus and the kids.

Hey *kakeshau ishkueu*, you done researching the "psychology" of the drunk Innu? Pien is shouting through the crowd now, out of sight.

He should read Fanon, I'm thinking, as I beeline my way to the door, struggling to keep my balance, shaking, unsteady.

And where's your man? Pien asks.

He's on a roll now.

Or you too good for men? Are you a fucking lesbian? Go on, get out, go right back to where you belong. You just here to stir up trouble with our women.

Thanks for the beer, I say, with a nod towards Tumi.

A feeble *kakeshau* attempt to divert the conversation. I could've at least told Pien to lay off. Or asked him what was wrong with lesbians. Instead, I am still smiling, frigging *smiling*. Napaen is in the porch, hauling in a large beef bucket.

My secret recipe, he says.

Probably a homebrew concoction: sugar, molasses, and yeast stirred into boiling water and left overnight to ferment.

Samish has followed me. Shirtless, he squeezes into me against the side of the doorway, trapping me again. I tilt my head down to escape his breath, the smell of alcohol still metabolizing, a hint of the sweet and sour fermentation of stomach acids distilling, like fruit cocktail gone bad. A smell from my childhood. My heart is beating out of my chest. The paint on the doorway is peeling.

Get off me. Let me go, I say. Go put a shirt on.

You lonely? I make you not lonely. I wan...

You want to let me go.

Napaen, just inside the door, says something our way, loud enough for everyone to hear. The room cracks up. There is an edge in their laughter and Samish winces.

He thinks he's *kakeshau*, I imagine Napaen saying. This goading would be an insult up there with the worst, as bad as *atim^u^ mitike*—dog's penis. *Kakeshau* meaning: you're being so white, betraying your culture, trying to be better than everybody else, too competitive, selfish, you think you can tell people what to do, you're a know-it-all and arrogant...

I slip under Samish's arm and make my getaway, pick up my gait and don't look back.

I can get drawn to all the wrong things, walk about with a kind of vertigo, settle into nothingness, and accept this.

Fight or flight. There is a loneliness in both, and all I want is to be left alone.

I pull my parka tight around my neck and scurry up the hill to Shustin's. I don't look over my shoulder. This is why the women wouldn't let me stay in the tent. We have to look out for each other.

People will surely be talking. Last time something like this happened, I was the one broadcasting it. I'd told Shustin and Manish about it. I'd told everybody any chance I got; it was my attempt at vigilante justice. I'd been staying at a teachers' house, they were away, I'd forgotten to lock the door, and Tshani had staggered in piss drunk.

I want sex, he'd said with a slur.

Would you like a cup of tea, I said.

I also served him eggs and toast, to distract him. We'd connect, he'd forget what he came for and leave. But he'd backed me onto the couch, his knee on my shoulder. There were spaces between his teeth, yellowed from cigarettes and plaque. He kept saying, I want sex, and I just kept talking, telling him about my grandmother and how she used to make me and my cousins race on our bums across the kitchen floor for quarters. I told him how she hobbled with one leg shorter than the other, but she still had ten kids even if she was crippled. And she had no running water. I didn't tell him how much she didn't like Indians.

A knock on the door had saved me. Tshani let me go so I could answer it, and he'd left, scurried around me and the kids at the door, without saying goodbye.

Wolves howl from a distance as I pass by Manish's house. Her lights are out. She's not waiting up for Pien. Shustin's door is locked. I knock hard and again. They think it's a drunk knocking and they're not opening.

It was a close call that time with Tshani and I was tempted to tell the police, but I couldn't. I didn't like the power of it. If it was somewhere else I might have, although the police weren't likely to pay attention. And if they did, they'd make it all my fault, like they did with my friend Simone at her rape trial when that creep with the Corvette got away with it. Here, the police might well take note. Tshani was Innu, and this was different: a vulnerable white woman crying danger. And I wasn't hurt really, was I? That's what I told myself. He was on probation, and he could lose his freedom, and there was his family who needed him to hunt and fish. There was the shame of it, and fear, but I couldn't quite muster up anger. My sense of guilt—at being someone deemed worthy of protection, but only in this instance, in ways that protection could endanger others—had stayed my anger. It was like I wasn't entitled to anger.

The truth is that my entitlement was not to feel that anger, but its absence. My lack of anger was a luxury. Like now. I can afford to bypass anger, to dance around it even if it hovers, electric, a button I can turn off.

I bang on the door again.

Shustin, it's me, Anna, I call out, feeling bad about waking the whole house. Finally I hear the click of the deadbolt slipping back into the door.

Sorry, I was just at Tumi's, at a party.

Go to bed, she says, a weary contempt in her voice.

In the bathroom, I scoop out cold water from the bucket and pour it into the washbasin. I look into the small mirror on the wall, avoiding my eyes. At least I didn't drink too much. I know *drunk*. Halfway through your second drink, you feel warm and cozy, one giant vibrating being, then everyone in the room is your best friend, even complete strangers. Something happens. You almost weep with gratitude they're so sympathetic. You keep chasing this euphoria all wretched night. You forget all your problems, then head for the bathroom and forget your new friends. You stand up and lose your balance but that doesn't stop you from hitting the dance floor. You stumble into people, or spill your drink all over them—that's how I met Mark—the entire freaking world is so beautiful, you're on top of it and ready to go to another party. Then your hearing dulls and everything gets slow-mo, and your skin is super-sensitive, the alcohol is visiting your brain, it's settled in, the world begins to swirl, you're starved, and then you throw up and hopefully you're not alone and you make it home to your own bed without blacking out or waking up next to a stranger. And the next morning, it's pheww, that was close.

I quit doing that.

I close my eyes, bend forward to splash water over my face, and see the charred remains of the wood stove, the skeletons of the chair and bedframe. I dry off and head to bed, burrow under the blankets. My weary body is begging for sleep. The cold of my sadness creeps in and settles into bed with me.

VIII.

It's Monday. The election has come and gone, uneventful, no calamity or major collective hangover to keep us from getting down to work. There must be at least some undercurrent of bitter aftermath but instead, Napaen, the defeated candidate, has been given a job with the inquiry.

He'll talk to the drinkers, Manish says. Her first decision as new chief. Were the Elders in on it?

The news does not thrill me. Hopefully he'll work out, at least stay out of our way and not badmouth us too much. I'm not holding my breath.

It's time to get down to business. Two and a half weeks here and what have I got to show for my time? As luck would have it, a March blizzard has moseyed into town and shut down the school, store, Band and Innu Nation offices. I trudge through blinding winds, head-butting against drifting snow to let Shustin, Sepastien, Kananin and Napaen know we need to get started.

Nine A.M. tomorrow, I say, like the predictable *kakeshau* I am.

I fetch the Innu Nation office key from Kananin's daughter Pishum, who works there. Our team is about to invade her space. I reorganize tables in the main room, haul a large rectangular one to the centre, pull up a bunch of chairs, and drag the other tables along the windowed wall. I pick up garbage, throw coffee mugs into my knapsack to bring them to Shushtin's to wash. I haven't moved back to my tent yet. Shustin says there's no need for me to go back, which is nice of her, but I don't want to overstay my welcome. I may want my own space again.

Random sheets of paper are scattered on all surfaces—documents from lawyers, the Assembly of First Nations, the Department of Indian and Northern Affairs, and an audited statement by Barnes and Associates. Many are scrawled and doodled, people's names written over and over like they were practising cursive writing. *CONFIDENTIAL* is stamped on some. I stack them all into a tidy pile on a corner table.

Also strewn about are copies of *Windspeaker*, the national Native newspaper. March 16, 1992, a recent issue. Elijah Harper has scuttled the Meech Lake Accord. "Harper has sunk Canada's latest attempt to pencil out constitutional rights for its First Peoples," reads the lead. His "no" at the back of the Manitoba Legislative Assembly was soft-spoken. He holds an eagle feather in the accompanying photo, looking dignified, his hair pulled back in a ponytail. Back home the papers reported that Clyde Wells was the guy who quashed it.

A headline reads *Healing Wounds from Bitter Memories in Kanesatake.* Two years after the seventy-eight-day standoff, women are calling for services to help people heal from the trauma and divisions in the community. In this paper the Mohawks are Kanien'kehà:ka of the Haudenosaunee. "The nation has been ripped off multiple times over the last three centuries, first by the religious Order of the St. Sulpice, then government and finally the town of Oka," the paper reads. There's no reference to an "Oka crisis," but a quote by a sixteen-year-old girl, stabbed by a soldier's bayonet when the army stormed the blockade, is highlighted in large text and giant quotation marks: "I was with my 4-year-old sister. I still have nightmares."

I'd followed that story closely and this was the first mention I'd heard of a stabbing.

The already iconic picture of a baby-faced warrior staring down a baby-faced soldier surrounded by tall pines in dappled sunlight illustrates the story. Next to it someone has underlined a line of text over and over with a red pen.

For the Mohawks, it was one land grab too many.

Always it's about the land. The notion of "land claims" is mocked here. *Who* exactly is claiming the land? Mishta-Pinip ranted about this at last year's meetings, pointing fingers at government officials, including the Right Honourable Minister. I was taking careful notes from Tapit's translation.

It is for *Tshishe-utshimau*—the government—to show us how he has walked and lived on this land, Mishta-Pinip said. Does the government know the different lakes and rivers and mountains, has he even seen them? The trees and plants and the medicines? The government need to show us how he knows the animals and how to show *ishpitenitamun*—respect—to them. I know every bit of this land, from Uashkaikan to Uashat.

There was nothing of the braggart in Mishta-Pinip's voice. There was anger and there was love, also conveyed in the translation by Tapit, his voice rising, intense. Did love for one's homeland carry any weight in the land claims process? What of their gods and spirits? Oral testimony? Mishta-Pinip could cite references too. His grandfather had bequeathed his stories to him.

Did your grandfather tell you stories about this land? Mishta-Pinip had asked the Indian Affairs Minister directly. He wasn't wasting his time with a deputy minister or some other underling. He was addressing the government *utshimau*, the chief.

Did your people give a name to every stream on this land? Mishta-Pinip asked him. What do you know about our *ashkui*?

Mishta-Pinip had proclaimed his people were prepared to fight for their land, and asked whether the government had plans to send in the troops, like they did at Kanasetake?

I was staying with Tapit and his family that time. His oldest son, Pashen, was still living at home, with his girlfriend and their new baby. Everyone else was out the first night after the meetings and Pashen was alone in the house. He brought it up.

What you think of Oka? he asked me, sitting on the couch bouncing his baby on his lap.

I went to a powwow there last year, in Kanesatake. Those Pines are amazing, I said. I'm a tree hugger, I'd fight for them.

And they wanted to bulldoze the cemetery.

Yeah, to build a golf course, I said. It's crazy.

What you think of the warriors? Pashen had looked over at me, his eyes piercing, trying to read my reaction, as he planted a kiss on the top of the baby's head.

I'll be honest. They scare me.

There's guys all over the country joining the military, they train to be soldiers. Then they go home warriors to their rez. To defend their lands.

He was dropping kisses when he'd said this. Little feather kisses all over the top of the baby's head, as he continued to look me in the eye. I didn't know anyone from here who'd been in the military.

But they'll be up against the Canadian military, I said. There were at least a thousand soldiers deployed with tanks at Kanesetake. What chance do they stand?

I was imagining my nose in the baby's fine hair, inhaling her sweet smell too.

At least they go down fighting, Pashen said, looking away. I'd started playing peekaboo with the baby, eliciting a two-toothed grin, then a cackle of laughter.

I don't trust guns, I said. Even if I do like the idea of the Warriors taking directions from the clan mothers.

Pashen smiled.

This chain of command was unclear to me, but what did I know?

The baby had started to fuss. At first her whine was a squeak, then it grew insistent, building with each protest as she tried to squirm out of his arms.

There must be a better way, I continued.

But I didn't know what that was. I'd been at a national solidarity meeting when a Native leader had talked about how he dismantles cities on his land—in his mind. I had thought he was speaking metaphorically. But what was he to do? What about the Innu and their paperless culture being required to document their land use for a government process? Someone else's game with someone else's rules. Stacked. And in the meantime, anyone at all who wants to stake a claim for mining anywhere in Nitassinan only has to fill out a few forms. There are 250,000 claims registered already. Easy peasy. No lawyer needed.

What about the protests? I asked Pashen. They're working pretty good.

Are they? he said.

The protests had been peaceful so far, amazingly so. I'd stood outside the chain-link fence of the Goose Bay airport a couple of years ago to take photos while women carrying babies, Elders singing hymns, along with men, children and youth, broke through to walk onto the runways and face off against NATO F-16s about to take off, killing machines designed to fly below radar to reach their targets. But to hear the Commanding Officer go on about clinical strikes, collateral damage, and soft targets—that would be human bodies—you'd swear they were talking etiquette, a military Amy Vanderbilt guide on polite and proper warfare.

Mamu, mamu. Stay together. Hold hands, Nush had said to the children as they crawled through the hole in the fence. Be good. On the runway she waved an Innu flag above the crowd of protestors sitting on the ground refusing to budge. The planes were stopped in their tracks. They turned around and headed back to the hangar. My heart pumping madly, I'd laughed and cheered through my fear. Clicking away with my camera, I captured all the camaraderie and giggling while soldiers dragged bodies from the ground and onto a bus. No one was hurt, but a few were arrested. There was honour in being a ringleader, even behind bars. Back at the camp, Tapit and Penute quoted Ghandi to the CBC reporter, speaking human rights and civil disobedience and reclaiming their homeland.

Where peace groups failed, Innu actions brought attention to the lunacy of the Cold War. That sounds a bit shrill, I'm told, when

I rant, seething over this patriarchal paranoïa, gazillions of dollars spent on killer planes, toxic fuel, top guns, bombs, nuclear missiles. Smart and virile young men sacrificed: grandsons, sons, husbands, fathers, friends, lovers. The waste of resources, wealth, genius. No one takes me seriously, even the people in our peace group. They like to quote Gwynne Dyer.

Hysteria is grossly underrated.

You're being naïve, I'm told. You need to be realistic.

Let's be realistic and bomb the world over multiple times.

Pashen was right. The Innu may be proud of their courage and brazen actions, protests have united people, but are they closer to reclaiming their land?

Maybe protests made this inquiry possible.

The Innu can do this. Yes they can.

I fold the newspaper in half. A dull headache has edged in behind my eyes. Time for some fresh air. I gather up all the other copies and stack them next to the pile of random paper and files.

Outside the frosty window, two kids, small kids, walk by carrying a bucket of water, splishing and splashing with each step.

I reach for a roll of flip chart paper and remove the elastic. I tear off multiple sheets, tape them together and plaster a whole wall. There is possibility in large blank sheets of paper.

In Innu there's only one word for paper—*mashinanikan*—whether it's a book or report, flyer, court order, ticket, invoice, government form, poster, report card, newspaper, receipt, scribbler, journal, what have you.

Now all we need is an agenda. I should go home and map one out, in my *mashinanikana.* And tomorrow we will meet in the *mashinaikanitshuap* or "building for paper."

IX.

My agenda can wait. I'm off tobogganing with Shustin's daughter Epa this afternoon in a world of fat, swirling snowflakes. It's easy to get sidetracked with this family, enjoying the ease and warmth and laughter of its cocoon. It's also called procrastination. Shustin looked rather preoccupied preparing a caribou stew and *pakueshikai* for her parents, while the two boys tormented their little sister. Might as well make myself useful, and it could clear up my headache. Only Epa bit at the chance to go sliding when I suggested it to the three kids.

Epa is now bundled up in a black snowsuit, must be her brother's hand-me-down. A fox fur someone added to the hood frames her face, while a lime green scarf is wrapped around her neck. I tuck in the ends of the scarf just to be safe. She plops herself down on the toboggan first and I squat and manoeuvre myself behind, my legs stretched out on either side of her. We burrow a track as we slide. With each run we hurtle down at increasing speeds. Epa's squeals are bloodcurdling.

You like Medusa? Epa shouts out to me at the top of her lungs as we rip down the hill yet again, hanging on tight, snowflakes smacking us in the face.

You mean the woman with the snakes for hair on her head? I ask.

We've landed at the bottom of the hill, Epa sprawled across me, her boot dangerously close to my nose.

Yeah.

No. She's creepy.

Epa slides her whole body over my head to get up.

She scary, she says.

How do you know about Medusa?

I see picture in a book. What about people have black skin?

You mean, do I like them?

Yeah.

We head back up the hill.

Sure, why not? I say.

Me too. Epa pauses for a moment. She seems deep in thought.

Did those kids do something bad? she asks.

I don't register.

What kids? I ask.

The kids who die in fire?

Oh, of course you mean those kids. No, sweetie, it wasn't their fault, no, no, not their fault at all...Come here, I say, as I draw her to me, let her head rest on my shoulder. She doesn't resist.

The small girl inside of me is triggered, the one always on the verge of crying these days, the one who needs me to do a lot of crying for her.

Maybe it was the *atshen* come get them, Epa says,as she pulls away from me.

What are *atshen*?

You know, they eat people, Epa explains. Or maybe somebody light the fire to save the people?

A fire to save the people?

Nimushum tell me the story. The Grandfather Eagle was hungry, but his claws was no good.

Epa has curled her fingers into claws of her own and is scratching at me as she continues her story.

The man make the Grandfather Eagle claws sharp for him so then he can hunt again.

Her right hand starts filing away at an invisible claw, a quick back and forth motion.

Now Grandfather Eagle claws so sharp he catch five caribou with one claw and five caribou with other claw.

Epa has thrown off her mitts and is showing me two fistfuls, each clutching five whole caribou.

Holee, I say.

Epa's eyes are wide open, as if she's only just heard this story for the first time herself. We stand close, caressed by the falling snow. I'm marvelling at Epa's English, how quickly she's picked it up with only a couple years of schooling. Maybe she's watching a lot of TV. And she remembers this story so well!

Grandfather Eagle give the man all the caribou, she continues, because he save his life.

He was a good eagle, I say.

Yes, but his wife, Grandmother Eagle, she is bad, very bad. She eat the people. She try to kill the man. She throw him on a big rock. But he not dead so she take him back to the nest.

What happened?

Grandfather Eagle say he help the man, but he can't. Grandmother Eagle his wife fly faster than him. The man say he make fire in the nest. He tell Grandfather Eagle to stay away, but Grandfather Eagle say he stay and burn to help the man, because the man help him. That's what happen. Grandfather Eagle die in the fire.

What happened to the man?

He run away from the fire and when the fire is finish, the man take the back of Grandfather Eagle, his back is not burned, and the man put grass and rocks in it. He make his back full, like he fill a bag. Then he take a knife and cut the back of the old Grandfather Eagle in many pieces and throw the pieces all around.

Epa is swinging her hand around, throwing the pieces of the old Grandfather Eagle's back.

The pieces turn into small animals, like *uapush* and *nitshik*^{u}, she says.

And then?

The man go home and tell his wife now he have to save the people because Grandfather Eagle save him. The end, she says, looking pleased with herself.

Wow, you tell a mean story, Epa.

I'm not sure what the story has to do with the fire, and the children, and saving the people. Snowflakes have subsided and the sky is clearing. The moon appears behind a cloud against the blue sky. It holds itself in the sky, beaming down on us.

Is it time for hot chocolate? I ask.

Ehe. Beat you to the house.

And she does.

I've been here for sixteen days. This is what I get paid to do.

X.

I'm still awake and it's the wee hours. It's been a couple nights of tossing and turning like this, mulling over what we should do as a team to pull off this inquiry. The red-digit number on the alarm clock by the bed shifts relentlessly, one minute after the other, and still no sleep. The wind is banging against the window as the moon slowly crawls across the sky. I still need to exorcise "inquiry" from my mind, expel thoughts of judges, a panel of experts, lawyers' arguments and witness testimonies. There will be no cross-examination. So then what?

It was pointless to go to the library before heading up here. I knew there'd be no handbook, no how-to manual on public inquiries in Mushuau Innu land. Still, I should have come more prepared. Was it confidence, courage, or common sense that landed me here without a clue? Keep the slate blank, I'd thought. It seemed like a better idea back in St. John's.

It's like this. Reading volumes of books and journal articles full of theory and lingo and lofty ideas does not help. I've parachuted into this village more than once filled with purpose and a spectacular plan, with this crazy assumption, deep-seated, that I should know better, that I can "help." My spaceship has touched down. Now what? What was I thinking? And my language, all the jargon. How can I make this work? It can't.

Most times I find myself waiting around for people to tell me what to do, while they wait for me to tell them what to do.

Silence is a good plan, and listening. I will execute it rigorously. I'm all ears.

Remember the Elders' meeting? We do already have a half-hatched plan. Don't we?

Gathering voices.

What are the chances this can work? Too many things get started here and before you know it, they've fallen apart.

This is why they've brought me here, so the whole thing can rest on my shoulders.

The night sky outside my window is black, moonless, smothered with stars. Someone is up and making their way to the bathroom. A door squeaks; there's a little quiet and then the sound of the lid on the honey bucket being replaced. The door squeaks again. Footsteps in the hallway. Shustin and her husband are whispering, easy volleys of words, back and forth.

Like when I'd whispered at my father's bedside the night before he died. It was my turn to spend the night at the hospital. I'd arrived early evening and as always rushed over to hug him, and I'd hung on for a wordless moment to keep the tears at bay. I took hold of one of his hands, turned in on itself, like in the distorted pose of a modern dance. His limbs had shrunk to bone. His skin was mottled and no longer fit his body. His knees, his toes, his hands had turned blue. He smelled of soured scallion, the odour of a body no longer able to eat, whose tissues were shutting down, kidneys failing; the smell of infection he could no longer cough up. The day before, I'd left the hospital with a pain in my side absorbed from him, a fist clenched around multiple organs. I wanted morphine too.

He could barely speak, only monosyllables. There was no more TV, no pills to administer, no waiting for the tablets to labour down his throat to make sure he didn't choke. Only an IV and a bedpan. Mostly he slept, his breathing raspy and gurgly, irregular, sometimes with pauses of thirty or forty seconds, then a feeble gasp. The nurse showed me how to swab glycerine in his mouth to keep it from drying out. She coddled us, the whole family, made us all feel useful, sensing each of our failings and letting us know it was okay, we were good, we were showing up.

Hearing is the last sense to go, she'd said.

Was it to comfort us, give us something to do, a chance to speak to all our unfinished business. Was it true?

That night I'd leaned in close and whispered all the things I'd never talked to him about: why I split up with his favourite of my boyfriends, why I went through that phase where I shaved my head and not my legs, about my canoe trip down the Zambezi River and the family of elephants cavorting and showering each other with their trunks, how I wanted kids but I might never get it together, how this country was going to hell in a handbasket, especially with Mulroney's free trade agreement, how I couldn't refuse invitations from the Innu to work with them, how I forgave him for that licking when I was sixteen, how I figured he was an agnostic like me, how death was mainly about the absence of those you love, why did he have to die now, we'd only just started to talk?

But before sitting back into the chair again and laying my head down on the bed rail in search of sleep, I'd planted a kiss on his forehead and whispered one last thing.

You can go now. It's okay.

He died the following morning, shortly after I'd gone home. I'd figured my way through that hardest moment of my life, so surely I can do this now. Breathe deeply. Get some sleep. Try savasana, the corpse pose in yoga, total relaxation. Still the mind, inhale. Breathe in slowly and exhale, follow my breath out. Pause. Keep returning to the breath.

The body is more willing than the (flailing) mind.

I can do it, walk into the great unknown, trust myself.

Maybe I should write to Mom. I can't sleep anyway, could use some respite from this tossing and turning. I've been wanting to since I got here, and she hates phones even more than me.

I get up to find paper and a pen in my backpack, head back to bed, draw the covers up to my waist.

I made it, the letter starts off. I've been here a couple of weeks, settled in now. I've been thinking a lot about you, how you're doing.

Words elude me. What to tell her? Each day our respective grief has been reaching out across half a continent. What must it be like to care for someone for years, morning, noon, and night, and then have the person gone? The unending absence. The week I stayed behind after Dad's funeral, the two of us had kept our sorrow in check. Sometimes we have to build a wall around our hearts, to keep it hermetic and sturdy, then once we've tended to the heartbreak, polished up the scarring, made it look nice and presentable, we can start taking the wall down, plank by plank. We all do that; don't we all protect ourselves, in the face of our broken world? And if we don't, is there any way to keep from breaking? My mother had shooed me away when I offered to stay behind, help ease her into her new life.

Go on, she said. Don't worry about me.

Your days must be long now that you don't have Dad to look after, I write. *I hope the house isn't too empty. I'm being well looked after up here. Our work is finally coming together, we've had meetings and I'm working with a great team. I've been knitting up a storm, making a hat for Mark. Thanks for showing me that seed stitch! We'll soon start actually talking to people, "gathering voices" they call it here. We'll probably do some workshops. I'm staying with the nuns, so you'll be glad to know I have running water, china cups and saucers, a doily on the coffee table. You can smell the lemon oil, haha, brings back memories of being a little girl. Remember when I was in grade one and I wanted to be a nun when I grew up? Mother Superior, I liked the sound of that, and wearing a veil and a flowing gown every day. But couldn't it be red instead of black and white?*

I'm surrounded with sad people here, as you can imagine. Everybody is so sad, we're all grieving together. I fit right in.

I gotta go. Big training day today. Thanks, Mom, for everything, looking after Dad and us, those last days. Love ya.

A wave of loneliness rushes over me as I think of her reading that.

A weird letter, but something; written with my fountain pen, emerald ink, my best handwriting. It's almost like we are close. I fold the paper, set it next to my shoes. I can grab an Innu Nation envelope tomorrow and walk it over to Mata's house, a.k.a. the post office.

I must have dropped off to sleep quickly after I turned off the light. Eyes open now and I'm still a refugee in a foreign land. Birds are making a racket outside the bedroom window. I'm not sure what kind of birds, but they are restless, erupting, mocking the hill behind the house.

Creeping Self-Doubt. I'm the champion of second-guessing myself. It's a kind of anticipation of bad karma, a foreboding of the 'shouldawouldacouldas' that are about to exact revenge. It's too late. I'm doomed. Come on, you did your best under the circumstances. This stringent standard of perfection. Having prescience is not within the human realm of possibility. I may have done my best, but still, deep inside, I'm never good enough.

Come work with the Innu. Required skill: know how to feel inadequate.

Must I get up?

I seem to have misplaced my audacity.

Like when I'd worked in "job readiness training" with Sheshatshiu adults a few years back, that interminable fall. It was a program that allowed governments to swap people between programs—unemployment insurance benefits, training allowances and welfare. The irony of me teaching people here any kind of 'life skills' was not lost on me or my students. I was meant to help them with things like "problem-solving, communication skills, personal qualities and work ethic, interpersonal and teamwork skills." I had them journalling and role playing, prided myself on being a "popular educator." They were also meant to learn how to put together resumes and how to do interviews. All this to get them ready to apply for jobs that did not exist from here to kingdom come. A patronage appointment by a relative or friend in power was their best bet to get a job, like the way our Senate works, although I wanted to believe there was a kind of Innu protocol at play, one not dissimilar to the way they shared the kill from a hunt, with its own sense of equity or righteousness. Either way, jobs were scarce.

I gave all my students A's. They should have been grading me. I was the one being trained.

For one assignment, my student Matshiu, the cartoonist, handed me a sketch he'd drawn of two Innu guys in a canoe out at sea headed for an oil rig in the distance. In a speech bubble, one guy was saying to the other: *All that role-playing and drawing pictures really help me get a job on this rig.* He thought I'd be pissed off, but I just laughed.

You should get a job with *The Labradorian.* They need a cartoonist, I told him.

Mostly, be kind: my job was to ensure I did not let kindness slide through the cracks. But I wasn't trying to be kind when I'd said that to him. I meant it. I should have helped him with his letter, but he didn't ask, I didn't want to be too pushy. I should have been pushy.

Maybe it's time to take a chance here, now?

I look at the clock, it's only 6:30. I can call Mark. Get up and get to the office early and use the phone. The house is cold, and I didn't sleep enough, but I need to talk to *somebody.*

I roll onto my side, struggle out from under my warm blankets, trip over a boot and twist my ankle. Limp over to the bathroom and honey bucket corner, turn my nose up at the smell. Really time to discard its contents. I throw my clothes on, grab a piece of *pakueshikai* and skip firing up the wood stove, my job as the first one up.

This call is probably a bad idea, but I pick up the phone and dial home. The phone brrrings, brrrings again, and finally Mark picks up. I woke him.

Hello? he says, his voice gravelly.

It's me.

What's up? Mark says. Tell me. I want to know everything.

Of course he would, so eager even in his groggy state. He is a continent and a strait and an island away, not to mention mountains and river valleys, a whole world. This is a mistake. A burning smell of accumulated dust from the heater I just turned on fills the room.

We haven't really started yet, I say.

Really? You don't have much time. I don't need to tell you that.

Well, you just did.

Long pause. He's a man and he wants to hear about the plan.

We don't really have a plan yet, I say.

So, what's happening?

Words fail me again. How can I tell him about the picture, the remains of the house, Epa's story, never mind the party scene? No matter what words come out of my mouth, they'll somehow be disemboweled, taken out of context, left starving for air. An anecdote can be blasphemous or at least a betrayal. Do I have a right to tell?

Why exactly did I want to make this call?

I'm visiting a lot, going for walks, a few meetings, I say. We did get a little advice from the Elders, well actually quite a bit. So maybe that's our plan. What about you? Is the union still sending you to be an observer in the South African elections?

No decision on who's going yet. Everything's same 'ole around here. Work and meetings, playing hockey, jamming with the boys, a few beers. I think I'll take a cooking class. I miss your cooking.

I bet you do.

But getting back to you. You looking after yourself?

Sure, somebody's got to. I'm staying with Shustin and her family, they like my cooking too.

I figure he'll scold me if I tell him I'm thinking of going back to the tent. You don't need to do that to yourself, he'll say. He'll get all legalistic about the elections and red-blooded about Samish, although emotions are not really his thing. I commented on his lack of emotion once and soon after he feigned rage, stomping up and down the hallway, shouting, even after I apologized. I should have been scared but I wasn't convinced by his performance.

I can't bear any advice from him about this job. And I'm really not about to tell him my period might be a little late. My breasts feel a little tender, but it's just a week, maybe two, not too late at all even if I am rather punctual.

Did I ever tell you the story about the frogs infesting our back yard when I was a kid? I ask him instead.

You wanna tell me a story about frogs?

Humour me.

Fire away, Mark says.

There were hundreds, maybe thousands. Every time you took a step in the back yard, five or six, ten frogs would jump in every direction. Another step and ten more leaped out. Like little frog explosions.

Were you scared of them?

I got used to them even if they always made me gasp a little, my heart aflutter, but one day, my mom sent us out—me and my brothers and cousins—to get rid of them.

Sounds like a team sport.

That's what the boys thought. It was a big competition to see who could get the most. My cousin Martin kept count.

How'd you catch 'em?

With our hands. You had to hold them tight, get 'em in a cardboard box before they escaped. We filled a huge box.

That sounds kind of gross.

That's the least of it. My brother, you know Alex, poured gasoline over the box and struck a match to it, lit the whole thing on fire.

So, is this a confession?

I never told anybody that story before.

I was a frog murderer. In the world of the Innu, there is *Anikapeu*, the Frogman. As the story goes, he trapped a young girl in quicksand near Meshikamau Lake. He wouldn't give her back, claiming she'd always be happy and never grow old. I don't think *Anikapeu* would be impressed with my story. There would be restitution, a reckoning for our slaughter.

Well you did get the job done, Mark says. Sounds like they were taking over.

I guess.

You hardly ever talk about your childhood.

Really? There's more where that came from. Storytelling as atonement.

You must be Catholic.

Don't hold it against me.

You're forgiven.

I miss you.

Call again. Don't wait so long.

I hang up the phone, wondering why I'd thought about those frogs, and whether Mark and I would make it. Damn, what if I'm pregnant?

The burning frogs had sizzled and crackled, the smell of charred flesh had clung to our nostrils. I didn't tell Mark about the two burrowing owls that had swooped down right over the smoky remains of the box that day. They'd flown so close to me, claws extended, one of them glaring, holding me captive with his unblinking yellow eyes.

A snowmobile snarls by so close it might drive right through the door into the office. A restlessness hangs low and persistent across the village.

Am I meant to push a little when we meet this morning? I'm pretty sure being pushy is not an Innu thing. I have this vision of doing some "theatre of the oppressed," or how we could videotape interviews and play them on the community channel. The Elders never asked for theatre or cameras. What I mostly need to do is surrender. Move over, misguided ego.

They've got this. My job is to convince them of that. And assume nothing, especially that my English is making sense.

Just before coming up here this time, a friend did a runes reading for me. It's an old Norse tradition. She'd scattered a bunch of lapis lazuli stones engraved with markings that looked like a foreign alphabet.

Pick a stone, she said. Glide your hand over the stones, and one will call out to you.

I picked one randomly.

Know that you do not know what to do, was the message. No kidding. Pre-patriarchal wisdom.

The importance of doing nothing, of not jumping the gun. Very shortly I'll facilitate something—start to do a kind of training? Minutes away now. Who's gonna do what? Or rather, who can do what? That might be the most important thing. Start there. Figure it out. Together. Find the right words for the questions, especially in Innu-aimun. Clear, precise.

The great unknown might just be very straightforward. I'll do what I usually do. The trick will be to endure my own ignorance. When I say stupid things, I'll blush with misery and embarrassment, rebound, stay good-humoured, and keep trying.

My stomach churns at the thought. I put my arms around myself. This is not a performance.

I'll just need to trust that I don't know what to do. Let this not be a failure. Let my white ass not do further harm.

People think some kind of deep compulsion propels me into this work. I have to have a good reason. It's not like I intended to have this life. Sometimes I look in the mirror, I mean really look, and I see that my face has adjusted to it.

Hopefully people will show up. I look at my watch.

XI.

I'm thinking it would be good to spend some time ourselves talking about what's happened to the Mushuau Innu over the last twenty years or so, I say. We'll have our own little inquiry or Gathering Voices. Amongst ourselves, over the next few days. This'll warm us up so we can help other people tell their stories.

My voice sounds so clear and certain.

The team sits staring at me after I managed to cajole them all into joining me at my table so we could start. Sepastien and Napaen had walked in a half hour late and Shustin and Kananin sat in a corner as far away from me as possible deep in conversation.

Let's all sit in this circle, I said, so we can all see each other.

We've covered the preamble, a recap of the Elders' meeting, why we're here and what our mandate is. I should have asked Manish or one of the Elders to launch us, brief us on our mission. I also should have prepared a rallying speech to start off, but we might as well just dig right in. We've touched on what our roles are, what mine might be. They know what the nurse does, what the priest or teacher does, and the social worker, but I'm a different kind of creature.

I'm here to listen and learn, to try to understand, like you, and to help the group, help all of us figure out how to do this job, I tell them.

Sepastien's chin is pointed up, a slight grimace on his face, the same expression he's had since he pulled up his chair. It's not a nod or a no, not a smirk or a shrug, but clearly he's not convinced. He's wearing a Montreal Canadiens hockey jersey; sometimes you can find a treasure in the mission clothes bin. Napaen is still wearing his trapper hat, the flaps tied up. He looks downright snarly. They might start heckling any minute.

Sound good? I ask, ignoring the body language.

Shustin translates for Kananin, and she's nodding. Both sit with their arms folded.

I'll try to write what you say on this paper, or draw it, I say. If I forget something, let me know, or you can come up and fill in the blanks. Sound okay?

No response.

What should we start with? I ask.

The school, Sepastien says.

That was quick. Okay, let's do this.

I write SCHOOL in the middle of a sheet and circle it, then add a simple line drawing of a sprawling building, with double doors and a bunch of windows.

What's the Innu word for it?

Kashkutamatsheutshuap. Sepastien repeats the word, sounding it out syllable by syllable as I write it in the circle.

By the way, maybe you want to take notes too, I say. It'll be good practice for when you go out and talk to people.

Shustin grabs the pads of paper and pens from the middle of the table and passes them around.

So, let's talk about what's happened since the school came into your lives, I say.

School is English and the kids don't learn Innu culture, Sepastien pitches in.

He could monopolize this process, but I say nothing. A lesson learned that time Tapit told me off at a public meeting when I suggested someone else might want a chance to speak.

You *kakeshauts* always think you can tell us what to do, Tapit had shouted at me. At least it felt like shouting.

Many people had walked out of the meeting during his bluster, but then they'd slowly trickled back in once he sat down again. Afterwards, some had made a point of letting me know it was good to try to include others in the conversation. Maybe Tapit was just happy to monopolize. I'd made a suggestion, but I must have imposed, not hedged enough? Everyone listens to the hunter as he gives an account of his exploits. No one interrupts. The storyteller is a guide, like an *utshimau*. You listen, surrender your right to argue, debate, object, or demand evidence. Being admonished by a *kakeshau* woman made it worse. I'll let Sepastien riff as he likes.

I write *no Innu culture* on the flip chart and draw a line to connect it to *SCHOOL*.

Can you explain that? I ask, feeling teacher-ish. And what happened then?

There are no Innu teachers and only Innu assistants, no Innu books, history, geography, or legends and games, almost no Innu-aimun instruction. The group is warming up. Shustin talks about how *kakeshau* teachers have no experience, and how they hit kids with a ruler, how they explain things over and over but no one understands because kids don't speak English, especially in the younger grades.

I want to ask about Epa and her English, say how good it is. What does it mean that a small Innu girl can now speak English so well? But I don't.

I draw a little stick girl and boy with question marks over their heads, and a stick kid with a bubble over her head dreaming about caribou, while the stick teacher is talking about giraffes, also in a bubble. Then a small stick kid is punching another one in the eye, his fist a small circle. Another kid is running away from the school because she's quit.

Drawings are less likely to get lost in translation.

Kananin has been mostly quiet to this point, whispering an occasional comment in Shustin's ear, followed by a discussion between the two, and eventually she says, *enkuan miam.* Good—she sees, so she must be caught up. Still, she seems in a bit of a trance, doodling with red, yellow, and blue markers, drawing Innu graphics like the ones on the dress I wore in my dream about performing at the LSPU hall. Sometimes she writes a few words, traces over them again and again, and every so often she looks up when someone's speaking, and laughs and nods at the right moments.

The bit of translation allows me to catch up with the recording.

Napaen, arms crossed, stares at the wall, rocking back and forth on the back legs of his chair. Makes me nervous that he'll fall back. He removes his hat and runs his hand through his hair. Not a word from him yet.

The school have leaks and no running water, Shustin translates for Kananin. If this was *kakeshau* school, they shut it down. She also say kids can't learn because they don't have a breakfast. And the kids can't go to *nutshimits* with their parents if they go to school.

Innu kids like foreigners in their own school, Sepastien says.

What do you think, Napaen? I finally ask. His thick hair is standing on end, assertive.

This is our school, not the *kakeshau* teacher school, he says.

He's still rocking his chair back and forth. As a child, my mother might have smacked me for doing that. The impossibility of his words, the truth of them, hangs in the air. I wait to see if he has anything else to add.

What about sexual abuse by teachers and brothers? he says after a long pause. Girls and boys. Write that down on your paper.

My stomach recoils at his words, pulls into itself. Napaen's mouth is still moving, but his words aren't getting in. My attention blurs, thoughts rattled and disorganized. My body is thinking for me now. It has kept score.

Have I missed anything? I ask finally, my back turned on the group. My mind scrambles to refocus.

Did you want to say more about that? I ask, as I write *sexual abuse* on the wall. No stick people image for this one.

There's only cover-ups, every time, Napaen says. People talk to the principal and write letters to school board, but they do nothing. And letters to the Bishop about the brothers. He just move them away.

Napaen's chair has come to a standstill.

First the *kakeshauts* take our land, then our language, then our kids, he goes on. They take our kids and do whatever they want. That's how the school change us.

I don't know how to respond. My mind is still rushing around. I want to say I'm sorry.

I'm sorry, I say, my voice lowered. I inhale, but it's as if the air can't get in.

Everyone is looking straight ahead and we sit for a moment. Sepastien is leaning forward holding his head in his hands, his elbows propped on the table.

Does anyone else have something to add to what Napaen has shared? I ask finally, feeling a numbness settle amidst the discomfort and the cruelty. Too much dissonance to hold inside of me.

It's true what he say. Sepastien looks up, shifting on his chair.

Mishimenitakuan, I say. It is sad.

I wish I knew the word for horrible.

Tshishue matshen, I add. It is bad, which doesn't quite cut it either.

Did people go to the police? I ask.

Napaen mutters and Sepastien grumbles a reply. What are they saying? Shustin rubs her forehead as if to erase her thoughts. Other stories are hovering maybe. Unspeakable.

Time for a break, Napaen says as he pulls a pack of cigarettes from his coat pocket.

I'll plug in the kettle, I say. Can we all come back in fifteen?

Too bad you don't know how to draw, Sepastien says as he sidles up to me, grabs a cup and teabag, and plugs in the kettle before I get a chance.

We reconvene and Kananin is sitting at attention. She's got something to say.

We were talking about abuse of the children, I say. The worst kind of abuse. Shall we continue from where we left off? My voice is so composed.

The fluorescent lights blink and resume their raspy buzz. Napaen pulls a pack of cigarettes and a lighter from his coat pocket and don't tell me he's going to smoke here, he just had a smoke break, but he does light up and blows smoke rings in my direction.

Kananin begins her story. She seems to have ignored my question, and her words spill out like they were practised, indisputable, as if she's been sitting on the brink and finally the dam has opened. There are Innu who speak, voice an opinion, tell a story, and although I can't understand, I know their words are poetry. She is one of them.

This could take a while and my measly trove of Innu-aimun is irritating. Colossally. How is it that I still can't speak this language? It's not from lack of trying, carrying a notebook around, writing down new words, constantly querying children who don't mind repeating a word or phrase over and over until I got it right and they no longer mocked me. I took a course when I lived in Sheshatshiu.

Apparently, my capacity to remember an endless configuration of the same syllables is limited. There are only twelve letters in the Innu alphabet—four vowels with maybe twice that many sounds and about twenty consonant and cluster sounds—compared to English, where we have over two hundred. Like *Kameshkeshkatinau-nipi* is the name of the lake in *nutshimits* where the Ashinis hosted me for the month a few years back. Disappointment Lake. It took the better part of a snowshoe trek with Muiss to memorize that one, hearing and repeating it over and over as we searched for partridge. It still doesn't roll off my tongue.

Pronunciations can be so subtle. Take *namesh*, or *nimish*. The two sound exactly the same to me, but one is a "fish" and the other is "my older sister." And I'm liable to say I plan to cook my older sister for supper tonight.

Tan eshinikashuin? I once asked a boy in Utshimassits his name.

You Sheshatshiu Innu? he responded.

You got it, I jested as he looked at me, surprised.

It turns out Sheshatshiu and Utshimassiu Innu have a hard time understanding each other, and I'm meant to tackle not one but two dialects. I can hear the difference even as words remain indecipherable. The Utshimassiu dialect is a melody more nasal than the rhythmic song of the Sheshatshiu dialect with its percussive accents to wake a baby in a mother's belly.

Kananin is all revved up now, her eyes fierce, glinting, and knowing behind large square glasses that have slid down her nose. Curly wisps of long black hair have escaped from her navy beret and frame her face. She is speaking the language of black spruce and brilliant water, craggy mountains, barrens, blue sky, and galloping caribou. In this world, a helicopter is a dragonfly and a train is a fire-sled, a star can be human, June is the Moon of the Flower, and September the Moon when caribou have regrown a full set of antlers.

If Kananin used more anglicisms, I might understand a bit. To be honest my initial zeal to learn has waned. *Utshimau*, I just heard *utshimau*, one of those words that resists translation. Could she be talking about a principal or is she on some nomadic meandering that has nothing to do with the school? If she's talking about the old days, *utshimau* was the leader of the hunt: skilled, knowledgeable, experienced, and humble, someone who dreamed the hunt and played the drum and had good relations with the Animal Spirits. *Utshimau* nowadays is also an elected leader with the Band Council or Innu Nation. *Tshishe-utshimau* is the Big Boss, or government. And *utshimau* can be a goalie, store clerk, or king. *Mitshim-utshimau*, Boss of the Food, is a social worker. One thing that's pretty certain is that a traditional *utshimau* is more wise and generous than bossy.

A couple years ago Mishta-Pinip called me *utshimashkueutshenitakushu*, or something like that, when I interviewed him about the health benefits of the outpost program.

You say you feel stronger in *nutshimits*. Can you explain that? I'd asked him.

Manish was translating.

Mishta-Pinip looked me in the eye like he could see right through me, then turned to his wife. I thought I heard him say something about a "Boss Woman."

What did he just say? I asked Manish.

Something like, She seems to be strong woman.

I asked her to spell it out so I could look it up in the dictionary. I found it, or a spelling that was close enough, and the definition was, She seems to have a proud and honourable character/temperament. Innu people don't talk like that.

What he meant to say was *utshimashkueutshenimu*, Manish had said with a smile.

Meaning? I asked.

She thinks herself a great lady.

That's mean, I said.

I'm hardly hoity-toity.

Kananin has stopped talking. She still seems so agitated, on the edge of tears maybe, angry, her cheeks flushed. She trounces me with her look. What? She starts again and I try to catch another word.

The grammar is what defeats me. There was a time when flesh-eating *atshen* rioting at my door would not have pulled me away from my studying Innu grammar. *The Language of the Montagnais and Naskapi in Labrador* consumed many of my nights, but I had a hard time making sense of it.

If only it were as easy as translating a word for a word. Often, I'm given a whole sentence instead of an equivalent word. English has ready-made words—you can look them up in the dictionary. But with Innu-aimun so many English words only exist in action. Ask a kid what a 'glass' is in Innu-aimun, and he'll say "it's for drinking." A *kamakunuesht* is a policeman, or more precisely "the man who locks people up."

Or a request for the translation of a whole sentence is met with a single Innu word, a complicated combination of a root verb, with a selection from hundreds of affixes—syllables stuck in front or at the back of the root, each encoded with little bits of meaning, things that we usually have whole words for, like feelings, adverbs, adjectives, possessive pronouns.

It's like a game, and people create words as they speak. The possibilities are endless and where is the logic of it?

Take gender. *En français* the whole world is divided up into male or female, but in Innu-aimun "she" and "he" are the same. Innu gender is about being animate or inanimate. Everything—person, animal, or thing—is spoken about as alive or not. It should be obvious—like animals, humans, plants, and gods are alive, therefore animate—but it isn't. Stones and stars, the moon and the sun are animate. At least some stones are. The body is alive, but not its parts. A spruce tree is, but not a juniper or berry. A snowshoe and an oar are alive, but not a canoe. Bread is, but not candy or beets. Snow is alive, but not river or fire. Fire is inanimate? And things deemed animate are not just spoken of as alive, but as if they were human. Animals are spoken of as "who," and a man might take a caribou or a beaver for a wife. A bear can wear a suit and chat with humans in their language.

It's like I have to try to listen, to hear with another part of my brain. Like listening to Kananin now, as she twirls a strand of hair around her finger, her head slightly cocked, gathering her thoughts. There is meaning in gestures, a tone of voice, a pause. She's staring hard at the corner of the table as her words flow again. I can hear that her *tipatshimun* is an old one, but her outrage is fresh. She sits up, taps her hand on the table like she's playing a drum, then points an index finger in the air three times, articulates each syllable with gritted teeth.

She's obviously not confused about gender or exasperated with verb conjugations—they're the real trouble with this language, and at least three-quarters of Innu words are verbs. Give me English, where verbs have three possible endings—walks, walked, walking. But in Innu, there are four possible forms. It depends if the verb is transitive or intransitive and if the subject is animate or inanimate. If a person can figure these out, there's all those affixes to choose from to indicate who did what to whom and how and when, and even the mood they were in. Add the prefix *tshishu* to the verb root for walk—*shkateu*, and you're talking about how Manish pissed Sepastien off by walking too far ahead of him. Only a linguist could understand after a lifetime of work. It's like my brain needs a new circuitry, and not even then.

When are you going to learn our language? Manish keeps asking. And I feel terrible. It seems so pressing and relevant when I'm here, and then I go home and there's no one to practise with.

Some words have stuck marvellously, like *mitike*, the word for penis in the Sheshatshiu dialect. It sounds a lot like mitigation, a word used frequently by bureaucrats and businesspeople when they're discussing how they want to take or destroy Innu land. Mention of the word "mitigation" cracks up a roomful of Innu every time. This word is not that useful.

There's also a whole thing about truth. In Innu it's important to indicate whether something really happened, or in a dream, if it's second-hand information, whether it's certain or possible, inferred or real. Does it happen all the time or only occasionally? I'm only just catching on to this. These preoccupations don't seem that important in English so I've often edited them out, and I shouldn't have.

Maybe someday I'll speak as well as a two-year-old, and in the meantime I'm left with the oppressor's language, as Adrienne Rich would say. My ancestors' sins are right there in my university-educated words, and atonement demands more than a scattered Innu word thrown in.

Finally, Kananin stops and stands to fetch herself a cup of tea. Surprisingly the noun for "word" is inanimate, but "voice" is animate. *Akuatshitakushu*—Kananin has a voice and has just made herself heard loud and clear. That may be Sheshatshiu Innu-aimun, probably a completely different word here. But never mind, voices are alive and we're gathering them.

Sepastien responds to my hangdog eyes.

Her story is long, he says. I try to remember everything she say.

He sits up and gazes out the window.

At first she talk about when she start work at school, the principal bring her to the classroom and give her some books. After school she have to wash the floor like a janitor. Her pay is very low. She never have training. She ask for courses, but nobody listen. She have to quit.

She say in the old days there's no such thing as a school. Innu people used to teach the children. Everything they need to survive. The white people say we don't have an education but our Elders, she say they know more than a professor at university.

I draw a stick person with a walking stick, words flowing out of her mouth turning into lines swirling all around, capturing words and drawings in their orbit: a tent, a caribou, a sun and a moon.

I can so draw.

Sepastien looks over to Kananin for a cue. What has he missed? She reminds him with a few sentences.

She say when she's a small girl, the priest sometimes show the children little bit how to read and write. She don't know what grade one is when she is small. Then in old Davis Inlet a teacher come. That teacher is very dangerous, he beat up kids a lot. He laugh and make fun of clothes kids wear. And then the nun try to teach kids Innu language. But most what we learn is to read the Bible.

My stick person has a veil and holds a book with a cross on the cover. Kananin is watching me intently.

She talk about her late father, he tell her stories and legends, *tipatshimuna* and *atanukuna*, that is how she learn about the bush. She say she can see the picture in her mind, *nutshimits* and the animals. Then the school is build, and it's like the people stuck in the community, like a jail.

That's easy to draw: a house with bars over the windows. Sepastien has paused and Napaen butts in.

Families can't go to *nutshimits* without the children, he says. The government say he take the children away if they don't go to school. The social worker take away some of our kids anyway. Kananin say is better and more easy to learn from our parents. Now what happen is kids don't want to go to *nutshimits.* Kids afraid to fail if they go to *nutshimits* for two months, and they afraid too that the social worker take them away, in school they failing all the time.

You go, Napaen says as he nods at Sepastien, who looks over to Kananin again for another cue. She prompts him with "Sister Alice."

Oh yes, she talk about when Sister Alice ask her to work in school. And she go back. She is the one to teach Innu-aimun, and the kids listen and learning good. When people camp in the bays, the teachers visit the camps every Saturday. They understand more about Innu culture. One time the principal send a teacher to a camp in Sango Bay. She stay there and teach all the children in the camp. She just stay at the camp the whole time. The teachers back then always visit us, even at night in the village.

Now she say it seems white teachers want the children to live like white people. And white people too proud to help the Innu. They too proud to care about Innu people. That's it. That's what Kananin say.

Kananin is nodding. She knows more English than she lets on.

Have we missed anything? I ask. And how are these things connected?

Everyone pitches in, Napaen has stopped rocking his chair, and more words and drawings fill the sheets of paper. Lines are drawn to connect topics and issues and stories and stick people, and pretty soon we have a tangly, chaotic, amazing, horrible web of a mess.

All of it. That's what happen, Sepastien said.

Everyone is staring at the wall.

We did good, Shustin says.

With that, they all get up and head for the door.

Great start, I call after them. See you back here for 1:00. This afternoon we'll do police and church.

Over the next couple of days, we contemplate the impact on the Innu of each of the various institutions. By the end of it we could fill a book to rival Fanon's *The Wretched of the Earth.*

Now what? I say. The next thing is to figure out how we're actually going to do this work, this gathering of voices. Any suggestions?

A long pause.

We will go to the houses, talk to the people, have a kitchen meeting, Sepastien says finally, the first to speak, as usual. We drink some tea with them. Or we can go to the people's tents in *nutshimits.*

Kananin and I go together, says Shustin. We both write the notes. We talk about it and we want to show some old pictures first. They have a slide show with the old pictures at the mission. Then the people can see how we live in the old days. I see Sister Alice at church and I already ask to borrow it. The Elders really love the old pictures.

That sounds perfect, I say.

We can make a paper with all the questions and we give one to every house and leave some copies at the Band office, and Innu Nation and the store, Sepastien says.

At the clinic too, and social services, Shustin adds.

Suggestions add up on the flip chart.

We have to talk to the kids in school, and the ones that don't go to school. And the workers at the Band and Innu Nation. The construction women trainees.

The youth council too, and women working with family violence project.

Tepi, my daughter, is in a play at school, Shustin says. They get ready for the festival in Kuspe. They show the play in the school gym here next month. The play is call *Kaiatshits,* The Boneman. Tepi say it's history play about Utshimassits. They talk about the same thing, what happen to us.

I could take pictures of the play, I suggest. We need pictures for the report, old ones and new ones. They can be part of the story. Maybe some of you have pictures too, that we can put in the report?

I have big box of pictures, good ones, Shushtin says. I check them out.

Miam, I say. Now we need to figure out who's going to talk to who?

Sepastien grabs a sheet of flip chart paper and a marker and starts to draw a map of the village, methodically, until every house has been logged. Kananin has plugged in the kettle. This could take a while. Sepastien writes down the family name on each tiny house, and the four of them begin to volunteer, discuss, and bicker about who'll go to which house.

What else do we need to do? I ask.

The Alcohol Program, they do a research. They have some numbers, Shustin says. They talk about them at inter-agency meeting. About all the number of people who die because of alcohol. And how many people have drinking problem. They count the people in each house.

Mixed methods, it's called, I can't help but say.

I don't explain qualitative and quantitative methodologies, but it turns out gathering voices is a kind of research.

I'll make a sheet, I say, and you can fill it out for each person, so we can track people, their names, ages, number of children, education, work, whether they're married, stuff like that.

Now the questions. What are we going to ask? The Elders said we need to ask how the school, church, social services, the store, the clinic, the police, and government have changed people since you were settled in Utshimassits.

We can ask them if they think school destroy our culture. Yes or no, Sepastien suggests.

Asking people about how the school has changed people is a good question. But we want to stay away from yes or no questions.

Whatever you say, Boss, Sepastien says.

I am not *utshimashkueu*, I say. But it's better to have open questions, like, has the school changed us? Or how has the school changed us? Then people can talk about the good and the bad, and they can tell their stories. Does that make sense?

Ehe, okay, let's do it.

Napaen's lost his snarl. I can't really read his face but he may be on board, at least for the moment.

What else do we need to ask people?

Kananin speaks up, and her words rattle the room. Sepastien's foot is jiggling under the table, and Napaen has started rocking again. Shustin translates.

Kananin says we have to ask why the fire happened, but not just the fire, other tragedies, so many people dying. And we have to ask what do we do to stop this from happening.

Kananin wipes a tear from the corner of her eye with the knuckle of her index finger.

We decide on seven questions, including how people were settled in Utshimassits, what is happening with the children nowadays, what people need to do to regain control of their lives, and how to not bring the problems of Utshimassits when the community is moved to a new location.

I haven't heard about a relocation, I say, eyebrows raised. Sepastien just made it sound like a done deal.

We have no water, Shustin says.

And we can't hunt on this island, for months, says Sepastien. Because of ice at Mishta-shantesh in spring and fall—you know Daniel's Rattle—we can't get to the mainland. That's where we hunt all the time.

There's an air in his voice that says do we really have to explain this to you?

Moving a whole village is a big thing, I say.

We having a big move, you'll see.

Okay, I say, unconvinced, but this is not my inquiry. Who's going to pay? almost slips out of my mouth.

We spend the rest of the morning translating the questions. They need to be clear and everyone has to be comfortable with the wording. "How has the school changed us?" does not seem that complicated to me, but a lot of debate ensues, arguments over the untranslatability of worlds and nuances I can't imagine. Sebastien is at the flip chart writing, crossing words out, adding new ones, and crossing them out as well.

Superfluous to this exercise, I'm still listening as I write a few notes about what we've been doing and how the planning evolved for the report. I draw up a calendar on a sheet of flip chart paper, and tape it to the wall, to record events and the names of people interviewed. Sepastien is rewriting the questions in Innu, along with the participant information sheet I've put together, to produce a bilingual questionnaire for people who might prefer writing to talking.

We'll need consent forms, I say.

We don't need one of your papers for this, Napaen says. Nobody will do an interview if they have to sign a paper.

But the group agrees to ask participants on the information sheet if we can use their Innu names in the report, in case we want to quote them.

In the afternoon the team practices interviewing each other. They start off with a script they've come up with on their own, how to explain what we're doing. They are self-conscious and shy at first, serious, and then they start taking on characters and they're hamming it up, laughing, coming up with every ridiculous and real kind of resistance they might run into.

Go away; don't bug me, Napaen says in his role play when asked if he'll do an interview.

Doors slam and there is cursing. Giggling. When Sepastien plays Mishta-Pinip, he goes on and off topic and no one can get a word in edgewise to steer him back. The whole time, they are taking notes.

Are we good? I ask at the end of the day.

No response.

Just have a chat, I say. The questions are only a guide. Listen to their stories. Listen carefully. Ask them to explain. Give them time. Ask them to slow down so you can catch up with your note-taking. It'll work out. You'll see. Easy.

But I know it is anything but.

XII.

Every day this week the team has arrived with their interview notes. They pop in at different times with their scant jottings, barely two pages of foolscap from an interview when they've been gone all morning or afternoon. I long to sit in on the interviews, to know the full story, to grasp every nuance. We need to do justice to the voices.

Are you writing down their exact words, just like they said them? I ask. If they say, "I did this," you should write those exact words down, not "she said she did this."

It's silly advice. While they're taking notes, listening, and asking questions, they're simultaneously translating what they're hearing into English. Except for Kananin's Innu-aimun in beautiful penmanship, just like the nuns taught her.

You can tell them to slow down, I say.

We should have used recorders, but machines can be intimidating, and transcribing takes forever. Not to mention, we don't have any and the store doesn't carry them.

I worry about their notes, what they've managed to capture. I was oblivious to the challenges of translating for the longest time, took translations at face value. I had no idea how loaded each of the translator's choices were, how vexing and disappointing—every word and sentence approximating, omitting, compensating, permutating. Translators sometimes just make something up.

Wanting things to be perfect is one of the most annoying afflictions of being white.

Six weeks left and we're meant to talk to everybody, and somehow report on it all.

Overlap in Shustin and Kananin's notes is comforting, and also the fact that there are no contradictions. Sometimes their notes are different when one has captured what the other missed.

I'm not sure what you mean here, I ask sometimes. Can you clarify? And I might get responses of things that never made it on the page. I jot them down.

Shanut and Shinipest love the old pictures, Shustin says. They talk about how everybody is so skinny, healthy. No diabetes.

The photos are amazing: a small boy who would be in primary school today saws wood with a hand saw next to a respectable pile of wood; a whole family and all their gear in a canoe coming ashore; a woman cleaning a caribou skin with her *mitshikuai* next to a boy playing a string game. My favourite one is of Shustin, around ten years old, looking straight into the camera with such swagger, two partridges tied on a string draped over one shoulder, a shotgun over the other. Everyone capable, having a purpose.

Shanut tell us the story of her grandfather, Shustin continues. He is the first chief. The priest pick him. He is the chief but he can't play the drum no more. The priest walk into a *makushan* and just grab the drum from him. She's just a little girl when she see that. She feel sorry for her grandfather.

Shustin and Sepastien take turns translating Kananin's notes into English.

Notes keep adding up. Papers, the team calls them. I call them data.

Sepastien's scrawls on the whole are more substantial and detailed. He writes so eloquently, with barely a couple years of schooling. He may also be editorializing.

A military ship come to old Davis Inlet about thirty years ago. It has many different flags. A priest and other people are all dressed up. A government person is on the ship and he want to meet with Innu people. He is the representative of the Queen. I don't know who he was. The priest is the translator. Maybe he speak Innu good enough for that job. After the Queen's man finish his speech, we are told what he say, whoever he is. He say that before he come he think the Innu people has everything—houses, water and sewage. Now he see it's not true. When he go back, he say, he tell the Queen what he see, that Innu people still living in tents.

What happen is the government way of thinking take a hold of us, now people depend on services we have here. Even if services not working for the people, they still buy that idea. The dependency is there, and it will be there for long long time. Services suppose to help us, but they destroy our spirit of going to nutshimits by thinking we need these goods and services.

Stories to do with the rocky road to settlement and its impacts come to life with Sepastien's notes. He's used to writing reports from working with the Alcohol Program. Not that he prides himself on the writing aspect of his job and being good at it. He told me the best work he did there was when he took the men hunting.

Hunting is my counselling session, he said. The man come back with a caribou and he is happy. I write that in my report.

It's odd to think of Sepastien in an office with a filing cabinet of documents instead of revving up his chainsaw or skinning and butchering a caribou.

Napaen is also a good writer, but his notes are inconsistent. Sometimes they seem a little too pat and predictable or frighteningly similar from one interview to the next, and other times he's only noted one comment for the whole interview. But his notes can also be excellent—diligent and specific.

> *Hunting laws a fucking joke. The Innu can only hunt in fall. Then no food for so many months. Government try to starve us, or they poison us with store food. My brother lose his skidoo and all his caribou last winter when Wildlife officer catch him, take all his gear.*
>
> *My grandmother die with a big cross around her neck all the time. The priest give it to her. None of her beliefs are visible except for the big cross. It seem like her beliefs are buried by this cross.*
>
> *The government give us a lot of money, but we spend the money on bills and food and building material. We give all the money back to the government store. Is like recycling. And then we pay the government taxes for working.*

Questions about people's education and employment on the participant information sheet seem to be putting people on the spot. One woman responded *Country of Higher Learning* for her education level. I make new copies of the sheet. I've added *nutshimits* as an education option, and *kanatuiut*, or hunter, for employment.

The pile of transcripts grows. By the second week, notes are handed over with such confidence I wonder, who I am to doubt any of this? As stories and details and facts and opinions accumulate, the promise of a bigger picture emerges. Lots of earnest and candid words, but still begging for elaboration, raising more questions than they answer. When the man beats up the woman, what kind of help does she need? What kind of help does the man need? What needs to happen to stop the violence? What needs to happen to bring back the old spiritual ways?

That priest was our teacher. He is very hard on us, make us very scared. He hurt us a lot. One time he kick my father when I was a little girl. I couldn't believe the priest beat people up. He tell the people the shaking tent is evil, that people are talking to the devil in the shaking tent. The priest get rid of the shaman and the shaking tent. Maybe people think if they don't listen to the priest, we all die. But the shaman is a gift from God. He cure people, help hunters find the animals. He help families know what other people doing in the other hunting grounds, if they're okay.

The picture will get bigger, but it'll still be a snapshot. There is so much not being said, unspeakable words, all the stories in people's body language that remain undocumented. Still, even if the stories are not being fully excavated or probed, truth can be gleaned from their incompleteness, in what is not being said, the silences, between the telling of what happened and explaining it. Sometimes these are the things that cry out to be heard, more than some of the recollections actually shared.

Memory can be a tricky thing, I say to Manish when she asks me how things are going.

What do you mean? she says.

No two people tell a story the same way, even if they're talking about the same thing.

That's true. Depends on how they feel about it, I guess.

Yeah, sometimes I can read the feelings in their words, like anger, sorrow, mercy. Sometimes I can tell people are confused by the question. Or maybe they don't want to share.

I guess people forget things too, Manish says, And there's shame and they want to protect somebody, maybe himself.

It's hard to talk about the hard things. We want to forget the really horrible things. Like my friend, her uncle raped her. One day last summer, she woke up on top of Signal Hill and had no idea how she got there, but she remembered. She said it was like her body was all bruised up again. Makes you wonder what's true or real.

Your friend know it happen though, right? Manish says, even if now her story is not like when it really happen.

We stash these memories away, out of reach, don't we? Like you said, to protect ourselves, survive even. Maybe.

Manish is right. The past was lived and then it becomes the story we make up and tell. Memories can be revised fictions based on all manner of conjecture and fancy, suspicions and "supposings." No one can ever know or see again who they were in a memory. There might be the temptation to lie, consciously or unconsciously, to sculpt a story into one's own image or impression of it. Or it can be rationalized away, like my own story, true and real enough, burrowing away out of reach. Almost. Remembering it feels like a finger on a wood stove. I pull away quickly and bury the knowledge, deeply, again. The past can feel like the only thing we have any control over: we can do with it what we will.

But it'll be okay. Even if some stories get revamped, or even shut out, the truth will find its way to the top. Contradictions might show up yet, and some facts may be disputed, but mostly people are recounting the same epic saga. People know what's happened, what's going on. They share their story and deserve our trust. They are giving away their story. And maybe its burden is also shared. Our job is to somehow weave the stories together into a tapestry.

I'm not sure if it's allowed, or who's making up the rules, but I'm dying to show Manish some of the notes. She might be able to tell who said what.

Wanna see what people are saying? I ask, as I shuffle through my papers searching for a few gems.

Look what some people said about the store, I tell her as she reaches for a couple of sheets. Such perfect answers.

People are afraid to go to nutshimits because the store is all they care about. In the past we don't care about the store. We always on the move. We don't care if the store have a lot of food or no food. The children today depend on can food or junk food. They eat too much candy. Now people addicted to white man's food, and some people getting sick from it.

Does government not know his school teach us to read and now we know how to read best before dates on the food in store?

Yes, all true, Manish says. What else you got?

Some people can really break your heart, I say as I hand her more.

We have to travel to Goose Bay hospital to have our babies. I wait for a month there and I am really homesick. I don't know anybody I miss my little girl and my husband. When I come back home, my little girl don't want to come to me. She don't know me anymore. She still little. It is really hard for the women to be far from their families so long. We have midwives in the community. They can help the women have their babies. I was born in a tent in nutshimits. They take that away from us.

We are seeing the children upset, sad, lonely. There is a lot of neglect all the time. The children see all that is happening. They need love, cared for and happy. Some are left alone at night. Some stay all over the place at night, staying at other homes when their parents party. They sleep from house to house. They afraid to go home to see drinking and fighting. In the old days, children are not allowed to stay out late at night. Now they are angry, breaking windows, stealing, driving skidoos to hurt themselves. Our children learn from us. They are crying within their hearts and losing their pride. Our children need us and we need them.

Manish winces as she's reading. I can feel her heart sinking, my own in tandem. She looks right through me, her gaze somewhere else. She says nothing.

There's the saucy people too, I say, wanting to bring her back. She absently takes the sheet out of my hand.

When the people move to another place, and there is running water, it's going to be easier and faster to make home brew.

Manish cracks up. She's back. Haha. Her laugh surprises me. The irony in that comment was all pathos and anger to me.

You haven't said much, I say.

She looks at me, still says nothing.

Wait, has anybody interviewed you yet? I ask.

No.

I should interview you. How about it? I can do some of the interviews, can't I?

Catch me if you can, she says with a coy smile. She escapes out the door, shuffling by Napaen who must be dropping off more notes.

He reeks of anger as he slams his papers on my desk. He looks everywhere but at me. I'm taking him in calmly, having taken a shine to him over the last couple of weeks. He has no idea, and we hardly talk, but he is teaching me about anger, how anger can be compassion, how it can reveal what we wish to protect, how it is a response to our inner powerlessness, fear, incoherence in our day-to-day. Not to mention that he gets the best responses about the justice system. When he's good, he's really good.

What's happening, I ask, not expecting him to open up or anything.

I gotta go, he says, and heads for the door.

Hey, Napaen, I call out, just as the door is about to slam. *Tshinashkumetin.* Good work.

I leaf through his notes and pause on a longer entry.

I been to jail myself. When the police tell me I break the law, I don't know what he say. If a person do not speak English they just say yes to the police. The police scare the person. The police write a paper, read it to you and then you just make signature with an X. With no person there translating the kakeshau words. The police sometimes do a lot of damage to Innu. A drunk person is arrested, charge and send to jail. Once he get out, he learn nothing and he afraid to go back to jail. In jail, he just eat, work, play. No Innu people visit him. No counseling at all for his problem.

Wow, he's done it again.

It's time for another newsletter, so I write up a two-pager outlining what we've been up to, maybe inspire people to participate. *GET IN TOUCH AND TALK TO US* in capital letters headlines the second page. Quotes plucked from the transcripts are highlighted in a bold font and scattered throughout. They reflect a range of voices on a range of issues. Straight from the horse's mouth. Or kind of, since it's been translated into English and I've cleaned up the grammar a tiny bit. Hopefully the quotes are close enough to what people said.

The social worker and doctor are the only ones to help battered women, for the sake of the women's lives.

We listen to government too much. We depend on them too much. The government should not control our lives. We should sue government for their actions in the past. Use the money for relocation.

Some young people very good hunters but they are like kakeshauts. They don't respect the animals. In my day, every part of the animal is important. The skull have to be hung on the tree. The elder should be teacher in school.

The nurse was mad at me and say that I don't wash my kids. She send me home and tell me to wash my baby at home. There is water at the clinic. I am really tired to carry the water all the time. The nurse should know we don't have running water.

We have to blame ourselves. We been drinking a lot and our children follow our ways. When a person drink, they leave the children alone in the house, while they look for some homebrew. The village is filled with alcohol. If the white people leave us alone our lives would be better. We start to drink and neglect the children. Anyway, we can't blame anyone. God is responsible for every one of us and for everything. We don't know what he thinks.

Tears had welled up when I first typed this last bit. These words, from Mani-Pia, so damning and devastating, are the most honest and candid I've heard anyone say about the fire up to now. Was she crying when she spoke them? I can't imagine her crying. I wanted to have a good wail of a cry with her. Was she angry? I'd read her words again and they'd stayed with me, snuck under my skin and settled in.

This newsletter needs to get done.

I need your help with the newsletter, I say to the team at our Wednesday morning meeting. Shustin and Sepastien agree to read it through. It's a formality. White people have this thing about wanting everyone to think like them, but people here pretty much never comment on anything I write, and I'm quite sure it's not because it's all so perfect.

They tell me it's fine, as predicted. Napaen has left, apparently not inclined to help out. Sepastien translates the text into Innu-aimun, which means the quotes go through a second translation. Will people recognize their words? Shustin and Kananin help me go through copies of *Windspeaker* and government propaganda to scoop out images and graphic art. Copyright seems from another world up here. I play with the images, cut out the background of a couple, accentuate contours with a marker, and drop them on the page to break up the text, invite the reader.

The newsletter requires blasted hours at the photocopier, refilling the paper tray, pressing the start button, unjamming paper, kicking and pounding the machine into submission. Why exactly is this my job? I'm always worrying about doing too much and I know that sometimes the best thing to do is nothing. Stay out of the way. A new habit for me is to end the day tracking every little thing I might have done that someone here could be doing. If someone here can do a job, then my handling it is exactly the opposite of what I should be doing. Stop that, I make a mental note, and vow to do better the next day. And then sometimes it can mean doing the less fun jobs, like fighting with this damn photocopier.

Shustin and Kananin help me compile and staple the pages together. They seem relieved to take a break from interviewing. It takes some moxie to try to do something new and different in your own village, to approach neighbours, poke your head in a tent doorway, and ask people to talk about the thing they most want to forget right now. In the meantime, Sepastien has agreed to take the newsletter to the radio airwaves.

Everybody else goes home early. All round, Napaen excluded, the newsletter was a great team effort.

Time for me to go home early too. The trail that runs up the hill at the end of the village beckons. I follow a snowmobile track. The wind sweeps the snow in long swaths, dusting over rabbit tracks along my way. Ducks and geese will soon be heading north. The days are getting longer. In the old days of this world, there would have been just light and dark, the position of the sun and the moon and the stars, daylight shrinking and lengthening to signal the changing of the seasons. Time must have been measured by what could be done in the daylight available, what chores could be completed, the distance that could be travelled. More work is becoming possible now, at least for those communing with the Land. Metres of snow still cover the ground, but the meltdown has started. Plants shiver below and the Earth aches for a glimpse of the sun's rays, while the village continues to say a long goodbye to those they've lost. And we are listening.

XIII.

On the weekend Shustin invites me ice-fishing with her mother, Mishta-Pinamen. Maybe she was missing me, since I'd moved back into the Pasteens' tent after the election partying ended. I was grateful to still be part of the family. My hook was the only one to snag a trout, the length of a newborn baby, my biggest ever. It rebelled against its capture, flopping wildly on the ice, but finally its life petered out enough to grab and gift it to Mishta-Pinamen. She seemed grateful and surprised. I was only following Innu protocol. She looked at me as if she was seeing me for the very first time.

Week six. I have no idea what's happened, but everyone has disappeared. No one has shown up for morning check-ins and it's Wednesday. We were meant to have our weekly meeting this morning. The transcripts are now typed onto my laptop and I've started analyzing them, identifying recurring themes, points of agreement, opposing opinions, stories that illustrate and bring to life the issues they relate. It's early to be doing that, but I need to be busy at something.

Names of people interviewed populate our list, and we need to add the women construction trainees and Innu classroom assistants who participated in a group interview yesterday. The list is starting to look impressive, but still a ways from including the "everybody" the Elders want.

A few tentative attempts at writing have left me mostly fretting about it, how the words might exploit or betray, and the price people may have to pay for them, how there'll be no way of knowing any of this. Is that just paranoia? Will we get the information people need, the answers? Only a pittance of what's being shared is recorded. So much will never be reported. Will people even recognize their words? Writing at this point is jumping the gun.

In the meantime, where are the notes from yesterday's focus group? And no other "papers" have been submitted this week. They need to be typed up. We have a little over a month left. The clock ticks as surely as spring advances with its longer days and the slow melt of snow. My patience and apprehension have turned into annoyance, a slight anger. A hole is being whittled away in the belly of my self-defense. What is wrong with me? That familiar fiend of incompetency creeps into my cells and consciousness. Exposed. It's about me now. I'm always the spectator, the bystander, a little ridiculous and paranoid, outside the conversation and the action. What is my role again? I'm achy and hormonal too, my head hurts and I feel bloated. The blood finally came this morning. At least I'm not pregnant.

Invited guest or not doesn't mean I'm actually wanted here. It'd be nice to go home with stories of accomplishment and connections. My photos might convince some people, but I'll know better.

And all the staring, each day, every day, like I'm an animal in a zoo. What do they see? An intruder or interferer, do-gooder, ignoramus, meddler? A listener, she's easy to talk to. But more likely, what does she want this time? And usually I do want something. What is she looking for: adventure, healing, danger, a spiritual home, a cause, a story? She's a thief—of land or culture, stealing their image in a photograph, or stealing a job for sure. The staring is wearing me down.

Time to go, leave this office, take my drama with me. Why have I stayed so late? A full-blown migraine pulses between my ears as the roar of a snowmobile grinds into my skull. I can barely greet

Tshinetshishepetau and Manikanet as they walk by me. A child is screeching and I want to scream, Can you look after your kid? Dark clouds hover, a dying violet and amber, and houses stand gloomily against them. Hands in my pockets, eyes focused down, I thrust myself forward. Two girls are burying their friend in the snow as a squad of boys runs circles around them playing tag. One of the girls is saying, What's your name, and *petute*, Come visit my house, a wide-open smile and zealous gestures beckoning, but I say, No, can't, sorry. And I feel rude and desolate and forlorn and guilty. I head for my tent, relieved that I decided to move back. The tent is empty, a cavern, a shield with no demands. But freezing. One of the Pasteen boys is there and has just split some wood. I point to the pile and wave a twenty wordlessly towards him.

Go ahead, he says. He nods at the wood as he takes the money.

I fire up the stove but then go straight to bed without any supper as village sounds outside my tent invade my dreams. I doze in and out, my thoughts like a sleepless river, icy and turbulent. Lethargy prevents me from rising to replenish the fire, though over and over my almost warm body is lured awake, then back into a half-sleep. I toss and turn and it is not just from the cold. I am without words, without comfort. Impotent. The deep song within eludes me.

It's daylight. The migraine has passed, but my body aches, drained, dizzy with fatigue, off balance. There is nothing to do but get up, start the fire, dread the day. I worm my way out of my sleeping bag as the ache of my migraine echoes back, a bouncing bruise inside my head. What to do with this day? There really is something wrong with me. I am hungry and restless and incomplete, grasping at something, anything beyond my reach. I'm not made for this work.

Tan etin? Pishum asks me when I stroll into the office. What's happening?

She knows.

You look sad, she says.

A tear collects and rolls down my cheek. She has seen me.

I have a bit of a cold, I mumble, fumbling for a tissue, avoiding eye contact.

I am unreachable.

I've just walked across the village, looking sorrow in the faces of people and in their downtrodden gaits. The stories of these same people inhabit the transcripts that I have read over and over, from one story to the next, one godforsaken story to another and back again. The arteries of these stories pulse with their particular rhythms, tones, and images, and they have sunk into and settled in my bones. I will never be freed of these stories now. Ever. My bones say, you may be lenient or blind, or open or scared, or tolerant, patient, or breaking. But I am none of these. What am I? I can't possibly show Pishum the austerity of my thinking. My undoing.

I can usually look into the distance, contemplate the essentials of things, but I've forgotten how. Ruminations about justice and meaning have lost their way, and the wind is just plain belligerent and all this land, forever gnarled up with trouble and worry and distress.

I feel so done.

XIV.

Oh my god, Mark and I are having a fight.

He'd called the Band office and left a message for me to call him back. The receptionist, Anniet, tracked me down, her message like a wake-up call. It hauled me out of my torment, hurled me into a fresh one. Why was he calling?

I just wanted to hear your voice, he says.

Me nerves. Like the Band doesn't have better things to do than to chase me around for a lonesome boyfriend. He's full of questions, like an interrogator.

How's the work? Did you figure out a plan?

Yes, we're doing it, it's happening.

He has no idea about Innu time, incremental progress, how the best thing is to just go with the flow. That's funny. As if I've been going with the flow these last few days.

You haven't called. I have no idea when you're coming back.

I called, remember? And what's the big worry?

You can't just go away and not be in touch, he says, probably from the cozy armchair in our living room.

Is it too much to just pick up the phone? he insists.

It is actually too much to be standing in the Band office reception area having this conversation. Anniet grabs a Winnipeg Fur Exchange catalogue, doodles scratched all over the cover, the corner of it ripped off. She opens it to a page of mukluks, a half-smile on her face, not even pretending to not listen.

Damn, Mark, there's a lot going on here. I was going to call if I was pregnant. I cup the receiver with my hand and whisper the last word.

You thought you might be pregnant and you didn't tell me?

His voice bellows through the receiver and Anniet's eyebrows are raised. I turn my back to her. Everybody knows everything in this town.

There was nothing to tell. I was just a little late, that's all.

That's all, are you kidding?

More guilt, another failure: I haven't considered his feelings enough. I'm biting my tongue, trying to measure my words.

Yeah, I've been busy.

My voice, under my breath, is controlled, calculated. I cup the receiver with my hand and move it away from my ear to avoid his response. A cigarette butt pools in the puddle from the snow off my boots. I want to say, This village has lost six kids, six kids are dead. My heart won't stop racing; my mind bounces between remembering and imagining. He's usually the one prone to the odd rage, low-level and dripping with sarcasm, for no apparent reason. We'll be talking about something banal—not that this situation is banal—and soon there's a crossfire of accusations. I could go there now, I want to, things could get worse; I want to blame him for everything. I put the receiver back to my ear.

Anna, where are you? Anna? Are you still there?

I'm sorry, Mark. But I can't do this here, right now. I'm at the Band Office. It's only a few more weeks. I'll let you know when I'm coming back. I gotta go.

You can't go now, I'm not done, he says.

Please, I'll call you back. Promise. And I hang up the phone.

Thanks, I say to Anniet, smiling an awkward smile as I head for the door. Good you were there. You saved the day.

No point pretending this call wasn't a threesome. She laughs, knowingly. Eavesdropping can be bonding. I can do this sometimes, create a sense of intimacy with someone, which you'd think would take a long time of being together. But it could happen in a moment, suddenly.

At some point I might be able to tell Mark about the dread over my late period, how I managed not to think about it, how I was feeling so up in the air, and despairing, and out of body and distracted. As far as I was concerned, I just could not be pregnant.

I don't know why it was so different from last April, when I was ten weeks pregnant. I'd wanted the baby so bad. Not one thought about an abortion. Mark was thrilled, and we were sure we could do this.

Barely through my first trimester, spotting drove me to the doctor for reassurance, a blinking heartbeat on the ultrasound. Mark insisted on coming. We saw it—a pinpoint beacon in a life the size of a pea—but it was a halting and uncertain pulse.

Take it easy, the doctor said under the fluorescent lights. Take a few days off work.

He recommended a blood test every day for a week to check whether my hormones were doubling every couple of days. He may have thought he knew something I didn't about the spotting and that heartbeat. I threw the requisition slips in the garbage. That heartbeat wasn't going to last. My gut told me. My breasts would soon be shrinking, my stomach would settle, my body would go into hormonal reversal.

Mark had been gaining a pound to each of mine.

In solidarity, he said.

In the days that followed, I wondered if his weight was leveling off too. Images persisted of a baby in a stroller, asleep in the cradle of Mark's arms, her first smile, dimpled hands pulling on my pant leg.

The cramps started with a dull gnawing. I was climbing the stairs to the bathroom when a contraction ripped through my gut. I clung to the banister to catch my breath. By the time I reached the toilet, a tiny diaphanous sac filled with a perfect invertebrate was nestled in my panties. The cramping continued; my breath was shallow. My cupped hand cradled the fetus, its diminutive limbs with fingers and toes emerging, veins running across its oversized head, ears like grains of salt, a protruding forehead. I wrapped it in facial tissue, placed it in a jar, and stuck it in the freezer. My version of events to Mark excluded the part about the jar. I told him about the cramping, my distress, the perfection of a life that is too small. As long as I could talk about it, I could stay closer to that strange rapture of creating life.

Mark's eyes had filled with tears.

Later that spring when Mark was at work, I retrieved the jar, opened it, and placed it on the windowsill. The sun's rays thawed the embryo so I could remove the tissue and find the sac once again intact and perfect. I swaddled the body, tiny and unbearably light, in an embroidered handkerchief and laid it in a small, round, silk-lined jewelry box. I dug a hole in the garden, placed the box gently in the ground, scattered soil over it, and transplanted a bleeding heart on top. I threw more soil around the plant's roots and packed it firmly.

Tiny soul. There was its foray into my heart, how death had passed through me. Did it even have a soul, was it a being if it wasn't sentient? And if not, why was I crying? Mark had found me standing there.

What's up? he asked.

Just transplanting a bleeding heart.

That night in bed, Mark snuggled up to me with his hand on my belly, where the swell would still have been, almost fully ripe.

"Miscarriage" is a strange word, I said.

What do you mean?

There are only two things you can miscarry: a baby or justice, like maybe I did something wrong and I have to pay for it.

You don't really think that do you?

It doesn't seem fair, I said.

I know.

But did he? And could he ever understand my state today, this last week, this place, the whole mess of it? Growing a baby in this well of grief. How could I tell him about it in anything but spurts and stops, conjure up anything but a disjointed collage, the whole shame of it.

And he gets to be angry because I haven't called. For some reason, my anger is always too shrill. You can think you know someone, and it's a mirage. You don't. You live, eat, sleep with them, shower and clean the house together, take a stroll in the park. Smell their shit. Everything. And there isn't a thing they don't know about you. That's what you believe. And you are wrong.

We don't speak the same language. We'll revisit a fight and he insists on letting me know what I'm thinking and feeling. I insist there's no need to blame, can we just own up, not project, try to really listen? Like the books and counsellors say.

I don't know what you're talking about, he says.

He believes in blame and restitution. Mark, my fixer-upper.

What are the chances he's watering my plants? Like he promised.

There's nothing like a good fight to put things in perspective. I left the band office with the wherewithal to walk over to Shustin, Kananin, Sepastien, and Napaen's houses to request a meeting for this morning. And sure enough, they all strolled in shortly after nine, so punctual.

Should we start with a prayer? I ask. Kananin, can you lead us?

We all sit up, people caught off-guard. We shuffle in our seats, energy shifting. I don't know where that came from, but it seems like a good idea to ask for help.

Mani tshitatamishkatin...Kanani begins. "Hail Mary, full of grace," a prayer from my childhood. The Innu words are a blur and I don't try to recall them, but my tendons know them, my bones remember. *Amen.* Kananin ends with quick sign of the cross. We all follow suit. We are gathered together.

How are we doing? I ask. We, although I'm not about to divulge my own recent state.

I only do one interview this week, Sepastien says, reaching in his pants pocket for a sheet of paper folded over multiple times that he hands over to me.

I go hunting, he continues. I have no money to buy food. I have my big family you know. I get only partridge, one porcupine and then I check my net, at least I get six trout.

He does have those eight children to feed, and a grandchild. Just the disposable diapers must chew up his cheque pretty quick.

I am nodding, listening. Not my turn at the mic. There is a defensive edge to his voice. A guardedness hovers in the room. What is she really asking?

His words sit with me: his family has been hungry. I say nothing, trying to let them in.

My niece sniff gas, says Shustin, like it's her turn next, her voice shaking. I have to stay with her and my sister.

She pauses and looks at me. The burden of my look is reflected in her eyes. I avert my gaze.

She sniffing more since the fire. Sometimes she run away and we have to go find her. She almost freeze in a tent two nights ago.

They might have lost her. They could still lose her. My gut is knotting up and there's a kind of scurrying in my mind. An anesthesia vies to get in, take away the weight of her words.

Kananin speaks up in Innu. There's more. She is looking straight at me with piercing eyes, like does she really have to answer to me? It was not the intent of my question, or was it? and I look away. My neck tightens. Shustin translates for Kananin. Napaen is rocking his chair, like he does. I am on guard, against myself.

She say her two grandchildren living with her sick now for two weeks. She take them to the clinic two times, but they don't get any better. She worry about meningitis; her grandson die from it last year. The nurses finally give the kids some medicine, so she think maybe they get better now.

These stories have catapulted me back into this world, out of my funk of this last week, which now seems so trite. A feeling of shame creeps in; a fog envelops me. My anxiety is moving over, making way for it. A white shame, an uneasy, desperate feeling, overwhelming, centuries old. A frequent visitor. Numbness is its friend and is not what you think, not the absence of feeling but something else. The edge of my own suffering, I was worried about me. Still no words surface and my silence rings in my ears. Napaen fixes me with a beady stare.

I went hunting, Napaen says, but from the look of him I'm pretty sure it was for homebrew and not caribou.

Any luck? I ask, finding relief in his impudence. My mind has managed to put its shoes back on and my voice has returned.

Then I have to stay home because of the rain, he says, trying again.

There'd been a bit of a drizzle on Monday, unusual for this time of year. That was four days ago.

Acid rain, you know, he says for emphasis with a wry smile, his eyes now with a glint. Poking me, a sleight of hand, putting me in my place, or so it feels. Has acid rain actually reached Labrador—its sulfuric and nitric acids coming from the west and the south, from my people, killing waters and fish, and only the gods know what else?

Kakeshau ishkueu, she's acting like the boss, he's saying, not with words, but with that look. He's teaching me about anger again.

This hefty man is hardly recognizable from the scrawny kid I knew not that long ago, his features now receded into a plumper face. He spent most of his childhood in a group home in Sheshatshiu. We occasionally met on the road when I lived there. In his teens he'd talk about nuclear bomb testing in Nevada and how fallout from the mushroom cloud had scattered all the way up here to permeate Labrador's caribou moss. And one time he told me how he blackmailed his uncle, like he was bragging.

Give me half your salary and I won't report you to police for what you're doing to your daughter, he told his uncle.

He's still smart, knowledgeable, and probably a little more law-abiding.

The questions are no good, he says, apparently not done razzing me.

I hesitate, and he knows he's got me.

These are the same questions suggested by the Elders, that he helped develop, debate, and translate.

How are the rest of you finding the questions? I ask.

I look Napaen straight in the eye, a mute challenge. Sepastien is the one to respond, animated and forceful. He runs his hands through his hair slowly and pauses. He pinches his nose with his index finger and thumb as he thinks and then goes on again at length, looking at Napaen as well, talking directly to him.

Enkuan miam, Napaen says when Sepastien is done, smiling my way, a kind of smirk.

I tell him we are the commissioners doing this inquiry, Sepastien explains. It is very important for our people. Everything must be discuss. No cover-ups and we have to talk to everybody. If the questions don't work he just have to ask about the fire. How do we stop these thing from happening? I tell him the media and government will hear about this and we need to do good job. If the government don't hear our voices this time, other voices will gather from all across Canada and other countries and government have to listen.

He's called all of us to attention, reminded us of our purpose. A modicum of relief circulates around the room, a burden lifting, and why was I carrying that burden anyway?

I've been wondering, should I help out with the interviews? I ask. We have so much ground to cover and not much time left.

They all seem relieved. This is hard work, sorrowful work, and harder yet when you know the people. That might even be a nod from Napaen, even if it's a cheeky one.

Talk to the *utshimauts*, Sepastien suggests.

He means the elected ones—yes, Manish is at the top of my list, but it'll be worth chasing down the odd informal leader too, the ones whose doorsteps are well trodden by visitors, especially when there's an issue in the village or camp that needs discussing. They're at all the meetings and ask the right questions and step in to short-circuit a racket when it arises, and they look after families when a baby is born or a loved one dies. A few of them aren't shy, and may even trust me, and they speak English. Like Katnen—even with limited vocabulary, she's figured out how to use it to her advantage.

How about Manish, Nush, and Matshikuaniss? Shustin says. And Shuash.

I write the names down. Shuash will be great. He knows me from the protests against low-level flying when I was taking pictures. He'd told the German Commanding Officer right to his face he could go fly his supersonic jets at a hundred feet over his own house and kids, while the CO's wife giggled.

Next week we all do interviews at the gathering, Shustin adds. People visit a lot in *nutshimits.* A good place to talk.

Will we have a meeting at the gathering? Or a workshop? I ask.

Ehe, ehe, Sepastien says.

Do we need to plan it?

Don't worry, he says. It'll happen, Innu time, Innu way.

Like the way we'd spontaneously come together at a gathering a few years back. There'd been an Alcohol Program meeting with a Uashat Innu family counsellor presiding. Would there be Innu games again this year? There'd likely be a women's meeting, and there was talk about a relocation meeting. That's why the gathering was being held at Natuashish, a prime spot to host a hypothetical village. There'd be a *makushan* and dance and all manner of socializing and visiting. A celebration of what should be, like one woman wrote in her questionnaire:

> *This is time of year. I really miss my late parents. They would be the first ones. Going out to NUTSHIMITS. In beautiful land. My parents wasn't just alcoholics. They both working hard in NUTSHIMITS. They both doing things together. They good as team work. I guess we raise good in ways we learn everything from them. Like sewing. weaving snowshoes. Etc. We don't need to depend on anybody when we are out on NUTSHIMITS. And we know how live off the land. I miss them everyday especially in spring time.*

When everybody is ready to go. Like soon we go to the gathering.

Breaking for lunch I head home, passing other walkers, pedestrians if they were in the city. Could Innu, who until recently walked the whole of the Ungava peninsula, be called pedestrians? The sun pokes its face out from behind a cloud and winks at me.

That was exhausting.

XV.

The whole village is hustling and bustling, and I'm all packed up: knapsack with a change of clothes, a bar of hand soap and toothbrush; sleeping bag and caribou skins; camera and extra film; notebook, pens, paper, flip chart, and markers. I'm the Flip Chart Woman—I never give up: *Mashinanikan Ishkueu.* I doubt that's proper Innu-aimun. My bag also holds an extra sweater, clean underwear, a pair of mitts and socks; moccasins and snowshoes; binoculars, candles and matches; a novel; a box of food and a couple rolls of toilet paper. Natuashish and the gathering are some twenty miles away on the mainland, at the head of Little Sango Bay.

I walk over to the big rock to wait for my ride. Against a shocking blue sky, a spiky edge of spruce outlines the top of the island out in the bay. Snowmobiles pulling komatiks loaded to busting zoom back and forth. Shustin arrives, her kids stuffed into their blankets in the komatik amidst the gear: tent, stove, tools and traps, a gun case, garbage bags of bedding, boxes filled with flour, teabags, Carnation Milk, sugar, margarine, Kraft Dinner, a couple bags of navy beans, and chocolate chip cookies. Shustin grabs my backpack, orders Napess to stand, and places my bag under him to sit on. She pokes the rest of my stuff between and betwixt the tangle of kids and supplies. She points to the starter cord on the snowmobile's engine.

Start her up, she says.

I grab the cord with both hands. This must be a test.

Stand back, I say. Or you might end up in the nursing station.

Let this be one of those machines that can be incited to life with an easy rip of the cord. With my best effort, I pull back with all my might to draw a weak, heartless burp from the motor. I used to do this as a kid, spent hours frolicking on snowmobiles with cousins on snowbound wheat fields. Avoiding Shustin's eye, I take a deep breath and pull the starter cord again.

Gahrooooom!

You could break somebody's jaw doing that, Shustin shouts over the motor's assertive rumble.

Now then, she wouldn't want my head to swell. She's sounding like Manish.

We drive over to Manishan's, then to Shustin's mom Mishta-Pinamen's and finally to Matshikuaniss's, a name that always elicits a tiny inner smile: Little Big Cheeks. With each stop there cannot possibly be another square inch of space for either stuff or human bodies, but loads get rearranged, more piled on, and people jump into the komatiks or onto the machines. Finally the three snowmobiles leave in convoy, trundling off in the bright new snow. The village behind us looks lonesome and dramatic.

We drive up over a hill and down, through a stubby forest, and onto a bay, where Shustin has assured me the ice is a good three, maybe four feet thick. Her snowmobile is big and strong, and she can easily leave the packed trail to give way to oncoming traffic. The snowmobile grinds and heaves in the deep snow while the komatik churns it up and blows it out as a cloud in its wake. Whether this was a Band Council purchase or a couple of months' salary, throw in occasional social assistance, the family managed to get a good one. Maybe they went hungry for a few days or weeks to get it. Worth it in the long run.

The wind has sculpted the drifting snow into a vast white ocean-scape and the air is sharp. My head bends to avoid the slicing wind as I hang on to Shustin, follow her dance as she throws her weight into driving, shifting from side to side as required to keep us upright and afloat. My hair and the fur on my parka frost up, my toes begin to tingle then ache from the cold. Soon they will feel numb. Back on shore we cross a marsh and weave our way between spindly and stoic trees, then through a thick colony of spruce, interspersed with pine and fir, tall and stately along the bay. We drive up onto a barren hillside overlooking another bay and Shustin turns off the snowmobile. She jumps off and points to a nearby pile of rocks.

A *kamiteut* is buried here, she says. That's his grave.

She points to a pile of rocks jutting out of the snow.

His name was Ushtinitshu.

The wind has blown the rocks bald. They conjure a moment of ceremony from decades ago, when the Innu still wore caribou clothing and lived in teepees. We're all quiet. Silence prevails in the shaman's honour. Shustin has removed her goggles and her eyes squint from the sun.

The night before he die, she says, Ushtinitshu play his drum and he sing.

She's brought me here for a purpose. She's not often forthcoming with stories.

He sing all his songs, she continues. There was no *makushan* or *kushapatshikan* or wedding, but he just sing and sing. He sing his hunting songs. He give them away.

How do you give away a song? I ask.

Maybe his friend come and tell him to keep some, but he come too late. The old man give away all his songs. And the next morning he never wake up. He pass away. He die. *Nukum* tell me this story. She say if the old man save some of his songs, maybe he live longer.

Wow, I say. A flimsy response. This is a world where a person can sing to beckon his death, where songs are a parting gift.

Let's go, Shustin says.

We hop back onto the snowmobile. Shustin checks on the kids in the komatik. Overhead a jet plane flies very high. There is another world out there. Passengers dressed in their travel clothes, hurtling through the air towards yet another world. Eating bad food. Avoiding each other or spilling their life stories. Maybe they've managed to make a connection, become a little more human in the way we are meant to every day.

With one last glance at the grave, a parting homage to Ushtinitshu, we're off. Shustin's hand is heavy on the throttle, and we soon arrive in Natuashish, a large flat expanse stretching out from the shore of a lake and surrounded by hills on three sides. Across the waters stands a range of imposing snowclad mountains, majestic. Before me stands a thicket of spruce and fir, and a few tamaracks and rare white birches are scattered across a long, even tract of land. Upon this starkly black and white landscape, a tent village has already popped up—fifty, sixty, maybe seventy tents erected higgledy-piggledy. There may be a rhyme and reason to their distribution, many calculated choices, but this is no provincial campground.

Shustin pulls up by a pile of fallen spruce and kills the motor. Sepastien and Akat have invited me to stay with their family. The tent isn't up yet. Shuni is stacking an armload of fir boughs into a tidy pile next to others. We unload my gear. I haul on my bearpaw snowshoes, and head for the woods behind the tent to do my business. I walk a ways, and as I crouch down I see something flicker on a nearby tamarack peering up from a tiny gully.

You need to look hard whenever you see something move, Sepastien keeps advising me.

A *uishkatshan* sits on a branch. I stop in my tracks, wait to stand, bum exposed. Rather than fly away, the grey jay flutters towards me, jumping from one branch to another until it is there right by me, only a foot or so above my head, trusting me.

Coo loo coo coo, coo coo coo coo! it says, welcoming me. Its bill is short and black. From up close, its plumage looks thick and fluffy—why it survives subzero winters.

Grey jays seem to follow me around. I have a soft spot for this bird, its back and tail a subdued medium grey, the underparts a slightly lighter shade, the whole contrasting with its head crowned black and white, like the nuns of my childhood. A beady black-eyed stare. This is no hawk or crow or eagle, in-your-face with gaudiness or power.

These birds might convince you of their mild manners, but they can be cheeky little buggers. One time I'd been lounging on a deck by a lake, and a jay had dive-bombed right by my face to scoop up a piece of blueberry shortcake half its size right off my plate. Trickster. Pilferer.

This jay is not scavenging. Its crooning is now a whisper song, a long medley of sweet notes interspersed with quiet clicks. I stand up gently as it takes off and lands a few trees away. It pokes its beak into the tree trunk, as if to move the bark aside, grabs a morsel of something in what must be a cache, and hops another few trees over.

Shustin told me once how birds converse: the robin sings for sunny weather and the white-throated sparrow sings for rain. I know that one: a perfect fourth interval, a high-pitched trilled oh-sweet-sweet-sweet-sweet.

Years ago at a summer gathering in Kanishutakashtasht, I'd seen Sepastien berate his son Matshiu after he struck a *uishkatshan* with a slingshot. We'd canoed to the mouth of a stream to check his net. We were close to shore. I wasn't sure what the scolding was about. I'd been impressed with the aim and speed of Matshiu's shot, although sorry to see the bird flounder midflight, regain enough grip to fly away, wobbly and wonky, but unable to recover its balance.

It was unusual to see an adult berating a child. This was hardly the first time I'd seen children shooting at birds or squirrels with a slingshot. Matshiu seemed sheepish, shrunken into his hoodie. He'd mumbled something, maybe he was apologizing. Sepastien felt compelled to explain the scene to me.

I tell my son that is a mistake to not respect the *uishkatshan*, Sepastien said. I say to him that sometime, I don't know when, but someday soon, there will be a big problem happen to one of us. A big problem. Something bad happen and it's because that bird is not respected.

A flash of my childhood mass murdering of frogs pops into my mind.

There was not one fish in the net when Sepastien checked only minutes after Matshiu's misdemeanor. I couldn't see how he might be to blame. But back at the tent that evening, Sepastien got a message over bush radio. The news was bad. His sister Matnin, who'd lived in Sheshatshiu for decades, was not well, her insides ravaged with cancer.

One of my neighbours when I lived there, Matnin worked for social services, but she was no bureaucrat. She spent much of her time ignoring department policy and protocol, trying to keep kids with extended family rather than sending them to live with strangers in faraway places. She cooked the most delectable caribou stews and salmon pies.

The doctor say she only have days to live, Sepastien had said, shaking his head but saying nothing to Matshiu.

I was heartbroken and wondered about Sepastien's foreboding, didn't dare ask. His sister died two weeks later.

I wonder about this *uishkatshan*'s powers, as a click of my tongue catches its attention. He spreads his wings and flies off as I head back, retracing my snowshoe tracks.

The camp is throbbing with life all around: gossip, a steady roar of chainsaws, the whacking noise of wood being chopped and split, smoke swirling from stovepipes, meat hung to dry, and trout frying. Children run and scream and laugh, bury each other in the snow or throw snowballs, stop to watch and learn something new. Shustin's mother, Mishta-Pinamen, sits on a red salt beef bucket smoking a pipe, taking in a few rays, waiting for the tent to go up to lay the stack of boughs next to her. The great storyteller, little Epa, scrapes a caribou skin, sitting on her grandmother's lap in the splendid sunshine. Next to them little Ben deftly slices through a log with a chainsaw, like it is not his first time.

Back at Sepastien and Akat's campsite, another *kakeshau ishkueu* has appeared. How did she get here?

Hi, I'm Deborah. From Indian Affairs.

Anna, I say as she extends her hand to shake mine. This is not really a shaking hands kind of world, but whatever. Her department has thrown money at this gathering and she must be here to check up on their investment. Her northern adventure. Should her grant be spent on spark plugs? How about flour for the Elders, a length of cord for a *ueuepishun*? What about Sepastien's snowshoes? Will she tell them to just itemize these purchases in their report? Will they be holding the meetings they promised or is this just a glorified camping trip?

This tent is not big. With Deborah, it will now be even more crowded, another body on top of the gaggle of kids and granddaughter. Sepastien and his generosity.

Is that a pleading look Deborah gives me? *Kakeshauts* sometimes try to latch on to me, like any of the goodwill or respect I've possibly earned up here might rub off on them. Or they see me as competition, as if earning the trust or affection of Innu people might be a contest. This is probably why Will, who has been parachuted in to work with the Alcohol Program after the fire, seems to be trying to sabotage our work, or at least present roadblocks. I like his style about town, his quick humour and easy rapport with people. But why the cold shoulder with me? I phoned him twice, and even dropped by at the centre, to try to get the stats the program compiled on alcohol-related deaths over the last twenty-five years. There's no easy banter or jokes with me.

The Innu will have to decide what they want to do with these numbers, he said.

Well, the Innu are the ones asking for them now, I said. They sent me to get them so we can put them in the report.

Like I told you before, I need to talk to my staff and board.

Finally, Sepastien went to make the request and sure enough, he scored. Maybe Will was annoyed at me because he hadn't been asked to do an interview. Like that was my decision. Like he'd been here long enough to merit that.

My heart sinks at the sight of Deborah's gear. Her mattress and military-issue sleeping bag will consume a couple of spots. We'll be that much more crowded. We're already eleven in the tent and she'll no doubt be assigned to sleep next to me. That'd be some of my space she's taking up and there won't be any kid curling into me for warmth, like a puppy.

She's probably vegetarian, a condition that always takes up too much attention, and time, and precious stove space. Some people prefer lentils and beans and brown rice over fresh caribou or char.

Give the girl a break, I don't even know her. But is she a public servant or a bureaucrat? Same job, different allegiance.

At least the inquiry is not being funded by governments. They can really suck the life out of a good idea. The Innu Nation lawyer managed to secure dollars from the Environmental Defense Fund, a crowd that believes the Innu are fit to figure out for themselves how to spend this money, how to conduct their own inquiry, who to hire.

Hopefully Deborah won't hijack any meetings, pontificate about Innu culture, how "we" have to do things "the Innu way," while the Innu sit there mute. *Kakeshauts* tend to arrive with their agenda, sharing only the information that will make most decisions a foregone conclusion. So seventeenth century.

I do it too, even with my best of intentions: talk down or like they are "other" or they just don't know how things work, make pronouncements on "the Innu,'" like they are all the same. Wishing they were just a little more predictable, or cooperative. Meaning what? Those thoughts seem impossible to intercept. Like changing your DNA. So much for trying.

How can I help? Deborah asks in her trendy teal jacket made of a high-tech fabric and insulation, with matching hat and mitts, neck warmer, and fleecy liner. At least it's not red, like the parka I'd worn the month I spent in *nutshimits* with the Ashinis. Red apparently scares off the animals, and it was the only coat I had.

We spend the rest of the afternoon setting up the tent. The boys have sawed down a couple dozen trees and shaved off all the branches. The resulting poles are placed along the inside of the tent to hold it up. A large one, tied to two poles crossed on each end, runs across the middle of the ceiling. On the outside, four strings reach out to poles on each side of the tent, stretching its canvas perfectly taut to prevent dripping from melting snow and keep us all nice and dry.

Matshiu seems to have come to life in *nutshimits*, wrapped in smells of smoke and spruce and fresh sunshine air, revved up by a spark of freedom. I can almost feel the contraction of his calf muscle as he shoots his body to standing—one graceful sweeping movement—and heads out on his mammoth-sized snowshoes to collect firewood, as unencumbered as if he were barefoot.

While the men continue to erect the tent, the women, including us two *kakeshauts*, head into the woods to fetch more spruce and fir boughs for the floor. Deborah has no snowshoes, so she's relegated to walking on snowmobile trails, and even then, she may sink up to her knees. She'll have fun trying to go do her business. I am not babysitting her.

We all return with boughs, some with armloads, others with mountains of them piled and tied onto a toboggan. Deborah's armload is impressive. Akat begins hauling the spruce boughs into the tent, scattering them pell-mell to provide a foot-deep cushion and insulation from the snow. We follow suit until they're almost all used up. She grabs a last armload of boughs and sends Shuni and Penatet to fetch more for the top layer. Deborah decides to follow them again. She's a trooper. Akat motions for me to follow her into the tent, so Deborah can borrow my snowshoes.

Akat and I each pick a spot at the edge of the tent and begin to carefully weave the boughs to create an even carpet over the loppy underlayer. She looks over to inspect my work.

Kapata, kapata, she says. *Nakatuapami.* I observe carefully, the bulging veins on her hands, knuckles swollen with arthritis, her index finger on the right hand bent northeasterly, broken at one time and never reset. She plants and coaxes the branch between a couple of others until it lies flat and secured. With eagle eyes she examines my next attempt to imitate her, and then nods.

Enkuan, miam, she says. Apparently, I've cottoned on to the task, but with no idea of how my new efforts are any different.

After many years, the fine intricacies of placing boughs correctly still elude me.

She says something else and Shuni translates.

She say you half Innu woman now.

I smile. Akat's standards are high. My friend Nush in Sheshatshiu, Sepastien's sister, used to tell me that I was "just like Innu woman." Outside, the men pack snow along the bottom of the tent to insulate and hold it in place. Matshiu enters carrying a sheet metal stove. To the left of the door opening, he hammers four sticks into the ground with the back of his axe to create a stand for the stove. He's carved out a wedge at the top of each stick on which he sets and secures the stove. He inserts a stovepipe, attaches an elbow and another pipe, and eases it through a hole in the tent, protected by a circle of sheet metal folded over the edges of the canvas opening to keep it from burning. In the front of the stove is a small door attached with wires. Matshiu opens it, throws in a handful of old man's beard, a few splints and larger pieces of wood, and rouses a frisky fire in no time at all. Soon we're all peeling off jackets and sweaters as the fire radiates its warm comfort.

No sooner have Shuni and Deborah returned than Akat points to a bucket and motions for Shuni to grab it.

Nipi, Akat says as she hands me a dipper and shoos us both out of the tent to go fetch water. We yank on our snowshoes and Shuni leads the way across the camp to a stream. We reach the water hole that someone has already hacked through the ice to expose a rush of shimmering water. I crouch to scoop water into my bucket. I aim the dipper at Shuni, pretending to sprinkle her.

Be careful, she says. You have to watch out for *Missinak^{u}*, she look after all the water animals.

Mee-ssee-nahkw, is that how you say it? I ask.

Yes *Missinak^{u}*. She have all her children under water. That is the place they play and grow up. Don't get too close.

Should I be scared?

Nukum say to me when I'm a little girl, never play around water hole. *Missinak*^{u} might catch you. She is angry and you can die.

I'll be careful, I say, my scooping now proper and subdued.

You have to say sorry too, Nukum tell me. You say: Sorry, God.

Sorry, God.

Shuni scoops one last dipper of water into the bucket and I cast a final reverential nod over to *Missinak*^{u} as we head back to the camp.

On the way Shuni points to my shadow, long and thin, leading me to the camp.

Everyone have a shadow that follow him all their life, she says. Even after you die.

She is full of information, and without a trace of her usual shyness. She tells me how rabbits run around on a starry night, but stand still when it snows, and she warns me against making snow angels. That too can lead to death and you have to apologize to God. My childhood too was filled with apologies to God, confessing my sins to the priest and reciting prayers for penance.

You know if you too lazy at the gathering, the people send you back to the village, she says.

I'll remember that, I say.

This is true things I'm saying, Shuni insists.

I know. *Tshinashkumetin uitsheuaniss.*

Thanks, my little friend. And teacher.

Akat is stirring a frying pan of stewed partridge when we arrive back at the tent.

Debbie, you want food? Sepastien asks.

My name is Deborah.

Kakeshauts are quick to correct people about their name.

Okay yeah, Sepastien says. But are you hungry?

Sure.

Akat scoops up a serving for her, a breast—the best part—and hands over the bowl with a large round *pakueshikai*, still warm.

Deborah takes the bowl and the bread. She seems uncertain what to do with the bread, shaped like a large, thick Frisbee. I motion for her to pass it over and break off a chunk for her, point to the tub of margarine next to the salt and sugar and teabags by the stove. I watch as she takes the first bite, wonder if she'll like the strong, sprucy taste of the partridge. She seems to and with great gusto chomps down the whole breast, lapping up the gravy with her *pakueshikai.* Akat hands over my plate, also with a breast, tender and succulent. Partridge is my favourite.

The kettle is boiled and dishes beckon. I wash and Deborah dries them. By the time we're done, night has fallen and Akat is lighting candles. She's counting on all twelve of us not to knock them over and burn down the tent. The candles glow soft, golden and gothic, on our tired faces, flames flickering a dance of light against the canvas walls.

Bedtime generates much to-ing and fro-ing, shifting and jostling, a steady chatter, children jumping on and over bodies, around candles. Not one word is raised at them as they desperately try to spend every last bit of energy they can muster before surrendering to the inevitable. Whenever the baby begins to whine in her *ueuepishun,* one or another of the children stop to give her a little swing until she settles. Akat works hard around their exuberance to lay a couple of blue tarps for extra insulation, blue tarps made in a Chinese factory town where the air lies low and thick, poisoning babies. I grab the other end of the tarp to help. She takes down the sponge mattresses that line the walls and places them over the tarps. More jumping up and down, up and down, bodies collapsing and piling up, squirming and giggling and standing again. Somehow, no one has fallen on the baby as Shuni changes her diaper. Boxes and bags are bundled up and taken outside to make room. I grab my bag of toiletries and repack my backpack, hating to surrender it to the great outdoors, hoping a bear or other petty thief doesn't snaffle it.

Deborah and I are assigned to the side of the tent by the door. It seems like more room than we deserve. She offers to place her mattress lengthwise to share it. Akat rejigs her mattresses and throws over a small one for the bottom half and I place my little blue foamie at our feet. Akat motions for Shuni and Penatet to sleep with us in our corner. Just enough space for everyone to snuggle and keep warm. The four of us stake our respective territories, lay out our sleeping bags and blankets and burrow in.

Storytime, Sepastien says. I tell you a story of when I'm a boy.

He begins in a hushed voice and the children's chatter stops in anticipation. The night is quiet, stretching out its arms.

When I'm a boy my family travel only by snowshoes, he says. In summer we are paddling in the canoe.

His voice is a gentle thrum of words. He is speaking English, for my sake and Deborah's. The fire crackles in the background as his story circulates groundless between worlds, disembodied words floating as if contained by the tent's canvas walls. This version is likely different from the Innu-aimun version, more self-conscious. The children have not complained about the English story.

The spell of Sepastien's words is broken when Akat cries out, *Ishkuteu*! She jumps out of her blankets. No one had spotted the sparks that have now burned a sizeable hole, right above our heads over in our corner. Akat trips over bodies toward the water bucket, scoops up a dipper, waves us out of the way, throws our blankets and mattresses aside, and flings the dipper of water at the creeping burn. She fingers the edges to snuff out the last embers, then bunches up a scrap piece of canvas, shoves it into the hole, motions us to make our bed and lie down again, and gingerly makes her way back around all the bodies to her bed.

Crisis averted, and Sepastien continues with his story.

In the winter we walk very very far every day, for many days, he says. My mother pull a toboggan that carry my baby sister.

I can picture a baby swaddled and tied amongst supplies on the toboggan, covered with caribou skins, and the family walking all in a row on the *meshkaia*, each carrying or pulling their assigned weight of supplies and gear.

The baby has started to stir in his *ueuepishun*, as if on cue, and Akat begins to sing a lullaby, a soundtrack to Sepastien's story.

Peu, peu, peu, she sings to shush the baby, the children and the wind under the full moon of this early evening.

I was a very small boy and I still help her, Sepastien continues. I follow her with a stick and push the toboggan. I feel like I am a big boy helping my mother.

I can see him chivvying the toboggan forward with his stick, too small to be walking amongst the men.

Sometimes my mother stop to feed the baby, Sepastien continues.

I embroider the spaces around his words, sense the baby's longing for the sweet, warm nectar of her mother's breast. She would be bending over, unbuttoning her coat and lifting her sweater to offer her breast to quell the baby's hungry cry.

This is the story Sepastien thinks the *kakeshau* women want to hear. It is a short story, a *tipatshimun*, barely a story, but still a good one. As he continues with his patchwork of boyhood memories—how he trapped his first beaver and couldn't wait to come back to the camp to share every detail with his grandmother—I want to take notes, so I can some day write about this boy with a quick smile and eager to please. Like Shuni, he must have been tall for his age, lanky, with a classic Naskapi face, patrician nose, tanned. Maybe he wore corduroy pants from the Old Davis Inlet church bins, and a canvas jacket and caribou hat, socks knit by his *kukum*, or is it *ukuma*? Like his son Matshiu, maybe his bangs fell over his eyes in a long straight sweep.

If I were to write these images down, wrap them in fine words, an emotion, a calculated order, would they ring true? Would my words be too parsimonious, maybe starved and gasping, soul-less. Could I avoid the sin of appropriation? I might have to stick to journal writing, write things down for my own eyes.

The sound of a deep inhale rises from one of the kids, a sure sign he's gone to sleep. Sleep is creeping up on me too. I pull my jacket down over my face, turn on my side, curl up and wait. The wind is awake, prying at the tent and hooting with the snowy owl under the sultry gaze of the stars.

My *nutshimits* sleep is filled with dreams, fitful and disorienting, wild in the wilderness. This happens every time. I hardly ever remember my dreams back home. Last night I started off in a prison. The guard walked into my cell with the blond head of a man on a platter. I was about to retch when I awoke to someone stuffing wood in the stove, the nausea stuck in my throat. Go back to sleep. Next I dreamt I'd taken Napaen home to meet my family, and he was climbing my Aunt Beatrice, who was a nun. He was scaling her body like a cliff. A different spectacle. Funny and a little less horrific.

It's been a busy night and morning never looked so good. The wood in the stove snaps and pops with the hot knots of spruce, as flames greedily gasp for air and the baby babbles in her *ueuepishun.* Outside, a chorus of birds warbles and cheeps, calling out good morning, and the sun dapples the tent with light and shadows as the canvas shivers in the breeze.

Snuggled in my bag, my feet are toasty in their wool socks as my dream world evaporates. Getting up will involve awkward small talk with Akat, my English words floating lifeless to their destination. We'll smile, shrug, nod, and point to compensate. The heat from the stove soon drives me out of my mummy bag. I rip it open and wriggle up to sitting.

Sepastien is gone, most likely to check his net, or maybe caribou hunting. Akat is busy, her tiny and taut body charged as always, constantly moving. We exchange smiles and continue in silence. I start to make *tekanep*—Innu pancakes made with oats rather than flour—as Akat changes the baby's diaper. Her hands know endless work: sewing and mending, plucking and cleaning, beading and stretching, washing and comforting, packing and unpacking, chopping and splitting, aiming and shooting. All this is done with a nonchalant ease. She stokes the fire, kneads *pakueshikai.* Her hair cannot be contained in her ponytail and she is constantly nudging her glasses into place with the back of her hand. She shapes her bread into a round disc and slaps it straight onto the stove. Last summer she'd buried her *pakueshikai* in a hole in the sand, built a fire on top to bake it.

I can feel her gaze on me as I stand and make my way to pull back the door flap and step out into the fresh air. A couple of dogs are charging around after each other, creating another generation, delighting in their abundance. A chain saw roars and a snowmobile rumbles by. At a distance the sounds of laughter and chatter float our way, a boom box on batteries plays a country and western song, a baby cries, real tears, and next door a mild argument rises and falls. Snow whiffles about, like a gentle hand over us all.

XVI.

I've no sooner finished my breakfast than Manish pokes her head into the tent.

The women are going hunting and you're coming, she says as she hunches down and steps over the threshold log.

She stands by the stove and inspects the pan of frying pancakes and pot of beaver stew cooking on the stove. She looks up at the hole in the canvas.

Looks like you almost burned down the tent, she says, matter of fact.

Saved by Akat, I say. Our shero.

We'll be gone all day, so dress warm, Manish says. Wear old stuff, not those.

She points to my caribou mitts that reach almost to my elbow and are trimmed with beaver fur and decorated with a beaded flower motif. A gift from Akat. I have another cozy pair, also leather, but nowhere near as impressive and from my world, where the dye that makes them burgundy is a toxic concoction that poisons rivers.

I pack a lunch and fill my thermos with hot tea laced with canned milk and sugar. Tea back home needs no sugar, but this is a cup of tea in the woods. Akat hands me a couple of tea bags.

Tshin make fire, more *nipishapun*, she says. She speaks like me, catering to my limited Innu-aimun. She knows we'll make a fire and I can make more tea. She hands over a chunk of bannock smothered in red berry jam and wrapped in a paper towel, to complement my roasted cashews and raisins.

Tshinashkumitin.

Deborah might have been invited but she's gone out, maybe for a walk. Too bad for her.

Akat and Manish are talking and laughing now. Probably about me. I throw everything into my small backpack and follow Manish out the door. I struggle with the harness of my snowshoes, a simple strip of caribou skin that straps around my foot and slips across the back of my heel. We head out under the bright gaze of the sun.

There'll be no meetings today. And if there are, we won't be there.

Four other women are waiting for us at the other end of the camp. Shustin has left her kids with her mom, escaped for the day. Emma wears a Grenfell boiled wool parka, a pullover trimmed with an abundant white wolf tail around the hood, a coat I've long coveted. Mata has on a striped hoodie under her unzipped coat, her scarf hanging loose, and an orange hat over a single braid tied with a beaded leather hair clip. I can see my reflection in Teinish's sunglasses. She's the only one wearing them; hopefully the rest of us won't get snow blindness. Manish, Mata, and Teinish have guns slung over their shoulders and diagonally across their backs.

You go first, Manish orders.

You're talking to me? I ask.

Yes, we're going that way, she says, pointing to a snowmobile trail. Lead us to porcupine.

You're kidding.

No, go on now.

Okay, I say, with not a trace of conviction.

The others acquiesce and we trudge off through the powdery snow that covers the trail, a clean wind whipping from the northwest, not a whisper of spring in the air. A vapour rises from this subzero air, so crisp, so dry the snow creaks underfoot.

It's hard to balance with these snowshoes on the narrow trail. If I step to either side of the snowmobile track, I'm liable to slip sideways and land up to my waist in snow. I hope someone has the wherewithal to spot a porcupine. I stop to wipe my nose. My cheeks are burning from the cold already, bright red in my downward glance. I rub my cheekbones and nose to warm them, but in vain. The women follow, chatter non-stop, and occasionally pile up behind me, tripping into each other on the heels of my clumsy steps. My harness needs adjusting again.

Not time for a break yet, Manish calls out from behind, and I march on.

The snowmobile trail has veered off to the right, but Manish shouts, *Kushkunu, kushkunu!* Go straight, go straight! Into the woods we head. Manish even has me breaking trail! Tree branches of pine and fir and spruce droop all around us, laden with snow. Sunlight slices through the trees and strikes the white mountains to the southwest, sharpening the shadows that show off their creases, patches of trees, a coulee snaking its way down.

The women continue to tag behind me, fledgling Warrior of the Woods, watching my every step, careful and deliberate. A subtle swing of my bearpaw snowshoe; that's how it's done. The trail is ancient, narrow and unobstructed, and below the metres of snow must be a covering of centuries-old moss. I'm learning a different history as I walk on this land, a story without words is settling into my body. The women's chatter comes in spells now, punctuated with the inevitable laugh.

Prtrtrtrgrutruprahsututut, one of the women lets loose a loud and impressive fart. A low but high-voltage fart with a side order of rotten eggs.

Partridge, *Matshishkapeu* say there many partridge around here, Teinish cries out.

She is translating for *Matshishkapeu,* the Fart Man, Spirit of Flatulence.

Mauats mauats. Matshishkapeu say *kakeshau* woman need sex real bad, Mata says to a squealing streak of giggles.

Some people are brilliant interpreters.

She's right, I say. But we might have better luck finding partridge than a man around here.

Another round of laughs, more subdued.

Matshishkapeu is a lovable kind of character. He pitches up spontaneously—there's no need to hold in your farts around here—and you never know what he's up to. Apart from being a terrible tease, he might comment on the weather, the hunt, or what someone ate the night before. He might point out that the person who just farted is an alcoholic. He can sing, mimic, settle an argument, or predict the future. Sometimes he can be cryptic. The interpretation tends to be as quick as the outburst.

One time in the middle of a public meeting, people were arguing about whether the community should protest to shut down the new housekeeping course being offered by the college to teach Innu how to clean their houses properly. There was the insult and the issue of no running water and training allowances that would be lost. Things got pretty tense, emotions high; the discussion was heating up when Mishta-Pinip farted. Whatever Matshishkapeu's contribution to the discussion was, everyone laughed heartily and the tension in the room dissipated. A week later the course was cancelled.

Mostly *Matshishkapeu* is a funny guy, but he's not just a comedian. He's also *utshimau*, powerful, more so even than *Katipenemitak*, the Caribou Master. This is what I read in an anthropology article. Farting is a form of divination, the researcher wrote. The Spirit of the Anus is not to be crossed, ever, or he will curse human or animal with a painful, even deadly case of constipation.

Today's cold weather can also cause constipation. Cold is nothing new to me. The cold from my childhood prairie winters is my heritage. It hasn't fazed me yet, even if my warm breath has formed ice crystals on strands of hair that have escaped from my hat, on my eyebrows too, and my spit freezes mid-air. But my fingers and feet are starting to feel numb. Don't eat the snow even if you're parched. Stop and stretch your fingers and toes, slap your hands together and pound your feet down into the snow. Hard. Get the blood flowing. Keep walking.

Pineu! one of the women shouts behind me with no attempt to keep her voice down and not frighten the partridge. *Matshishkapeu* was right. I turn to see Emma pointing about twenty feet away to a spruce partridge on a snowy branch sitting pretty and still, looking so much at home and burbling sweet nothings to us. Emma grabs her shotgun, aims, and pulls the trigger. A stark, high-pitched, deafening blast cracks open the silence. Missed. Emma laughs self-consciously and aims again.

The partridge has not moved, not just oblivious but as if awaiting its destiny, as if it exists on that branch merely to serve as our supper. Shot after missed shot, the partridge continues to sit until finally the bullet pierces its heart. Emma walks over as she hauls off her hunting bag, scoops up the partridge, and throws it in.

Jumping up and down helps to keep warm. The women decide to take a cigarette break and I keep jumping up and down, pause a moment to take a sip from my thermos. The women exhale the cigarette smoke, each puff like a little balloon of fog. All around, little text balloons like in comics shatter into a million pieces from the cold.

Keep going. Manish is still ordering me around, and we continue further through the woods, the posse on my tail. Despite the cold, my snowshoes feel more secure and stable. My stride maybe even confident.

These snowshoes really are the perfect technology, I say to Manish who is now directly behind me.

Yes, we are a simple savage people living close to the earth. Using the natural resources of our tribal territory in a sustainable way to carry out our primitive way of life.

Shag off, I say. You know what I mean. Weren't you going on just last week about all the skill that goes into making them?

She had told me how her *ukuma* had shown her how to fill a snowshoe with babiche, and she had shown me, beginning with the toe hole at the corner of the crossbar weaving in and around, over, and under into a latticed triangle, until it was completely filled.

We continue on our way until the sun has travelled almost halfway across the sky and the cold has slowly and with great determination crept in to occupy my body. I've led the women to six partridges, but no porcupine. Could be because I'm not that partial to porcupine.

A voice calls out from behind me. Is that *mitshim*, she said? We are stopping for a boil-up, a snack and the most welcome hot cup of *nipishapun* in the woods ever. My thermos is long empty and I want to shout out, Finally! I want to say, Let's make the biggest damn fire we can. I want to jump up and down again and make the biggest damn fire ever. My body is cold. Forgive my cold body. There is the question of frailty and mortality. We won't have to burrow into the snow after all. We *will* make the biggest damn fire. Cells have burst. Frigid here. Burning there. My cold cheeks must have gone from red to white by now, and tomorrow they'll be black from frostbite.

We spread out in different directions to fetch wood—mainly dead branches and old man's beard. Shustin coaxes a flame to life with her cigarette lighter. The fire spits and swears, flames conflating and licking hungrily towards the cloudless sky, coils of smoke spiraling higher. Manish hauls out her kettle, and after filling it with snow many times over, we manage to get enough water boiling for each of us to have a small cup of tea. I pluck my bannock with partridgeberry jam from my backpack and wolf it down, along with my cashews and raisins, many falling into the snow because there's no way I'm taking off my mitts to eat. The beef jerky and canned wieners the women chow down make me salivate. We all hover as close to the fire as possible, my hands inches away from the flames.

Takau, I say.

The women all nod. I have spoken a word, cold, when the thawing of my fingers and toes calls for bellowing. The pain is throbbing, like a hammer striking down on them. I step away from the fire to slow down the thawing, but then rejoin the tight circle. We need to store up heat for the rest of our journey.

Time to head back, Manish says.

Having only just reclaimed my extremities, I want to remain with the fire, warn the women to stay for their own sake, but I follow Manish's order and head out, once again in the lead. One step in front of the other, and as we retrace our tracks I feel better, surprisingly fresh and refuelled. I have found my stride. I've got swagger. Scanning the treeline, there it is, a porcupine clinging high onto a gaunt spruce trunk along a craggy rock face.

Kakᵘ, I cry into the wind.

We all stop and stare as the porcupine's round body tries to scoot its way higher up the tree, but is soon defeated by a small branch in its way. Manish is reaching for her gun. She is the chosen one.

It's a male, Manish says.

How do you know? I ask.

Its tail is longer. It's not very big, but not a baby.

The porcupine looks directly down at us, at me, like his eyes are holding mine fast, forcing me to look full in the face at what we are about to do, what all life does. I'd merely observed earlier as the partridges died, but with this, my first sighting, I'm spooked. I eat meat but I've never shot an animal. The porcupine continues to hold my gaze and I am staring at my own death in his eyes. I'm afraid. I know not what lies beyond. "Other direction buddy! Quick, slither down, or you'll end up in a pot!" I want to tell him, but that would not be appreciated, and besides, my skills as a porcupine whisperer are dubious.

Manish aims. Her face is tight, her eyes focused, and her breathing hard. She shoots and misses. My ears are ringing. The smell is metallic, acrid, a hint of sulfur and urine and ammonia. Even with the sound of the gun blast, expected yet still loud and sudden, my solitary little friend stays immobile. I expect him to slide down the tree, but he too sits, like the partridges, breathing silently, offering himself with no protest. Maybe he's not meant to die. Maybe someone has shown disrespect and *Uhuapeu*, the Porcupine Spirit, is angry. Maybe a dog in the camp got hold of a porcupine bone. The Spirits want to protect themselves, and privileges could be withdrawn for years. People could run out of food.

One more shot and finally the porcupine tumbles down into the empty stillness of the snow below. Manish snowshoes over to it and I want to go too, to touch the little guy and hold him, feel his weight in my arms, examine his mess of quills up close. I am unsettled, as if I had pulled the trigger. My heart pounds in my chest. I feel every beat. A small storm of uncertainty, grief, relief, and remorse rises in me slow and steady, a soul-wrenching awe in the face of this encounter, a thread of life snipped. A voice inside of me is howling.

I inhale and close my eyes for a brief moment. When I open them, Manish is tying a rope to a front and back leg, short legs, the soles of his paws hairless. Beady black eyes stare blankly now from his wee face, framed on each side with two tiny ears. Black and white quills spring out of his body like a David Bowie haircut. The women watch in silence. A whiff of his smell stings my nostrils—a cross between human sweat and blue cheese. Manish swings the bundle over her head to carry it across her back like a bag. Blood drips onto her coat.

She points the way to signal it's time to go, and we continue on our *meshkaia*. The sky is still blue, break-your-heart blue, and unblinking.

Until now, my only encounter with a dead porcupine was seeing roadkill, driving by in a car, a peripheral sighting of the creature left to rot and waste on the shoulder. My siblings and I made a game of it: who could spot the largest number of dead animals?

Maybe the women, too, are contemplating beginnings and endings. We are living something larger than ourselves, taking life to live. This is honest food, not pumped with antibiotics, millions of animals across our continent unable to move, jam-packed in their own excrement, never to catch a moment's glimpse of the sun.

The women have quieted, no more repartee and ribbing. The only sound is the faint squeaking of our snowshoes on the snow, the crushing of ice crystals against each other. We are walking on land that is centuries, millennia unchanged. We are in *nutshimits*, "in the bush in the country" my friend Nush always used to say to *kakeshauts*, like either part of the phrase on its own does not suffice, neither translation really cuts it. People speak of *nutshimits* with such longing and love, as if this land was a place of comfort and healing and sustenance. The wild beauty of this walk feels safe and tranquil, but this land is scary, fierce and austere, uninhabitable, not a place to be alone. So bloody cold.

Dusk approaches. The last rays of the sun are chasing us home, and the full moon, like a perfect, cool pearl, is rising in a purple-pink sky to welcome us back to the camp—the sun in the west, a muted red ball. All I want now is to come in from the cold. My fingers and toes have long stopped screaming in pain. They barely even remember the pain. All I want is to lie down and go to sleep, cradled by the land. Maybe it is not so unforgiving. I have put on silence and ice like a coat. I walk in emptiness.

We finally reach the camp and pass by Manteshkueu and Mishta-Pinip's tent. He sits on the threshold taking in fresh air. Manish stops and hands him the porcupine. Innu protocol: the porcupine is gifted to the first person the hunter sees back at the camp. I'll not have to endure the oily, smoky burned-bone smell of porcupine stewing that would fill up our tent and drive me out. Its bones look frighteningly human. Hopefully *Uhuapeu* can't read my thoughts.

XVII.

Last night, I was nodding off even before I'd finished washing the dishes. Akat sent me to bed and I fell asleep before the children. A herd of caribou outside the tent would not have kept me awake.

This morning, my body is achy and stiff as I roll over in my sleeping bag. Gangrene has been averted, although my cheeks are tender and the flesh feels hard where the skin is probably black. I peek out of my bag and everyone is still asleep. It's barely dawn. I crawl out, pull on my extra sweater and my parka, make my way around bodies to the stove, and light the fire. A breeze ruffles the canvas walls while the sun casts tree shadows. Still, no one stirs. I need to *shishi*, so I head out of the tent, slip on my snowshoes, and make for the hill on the south side of the camp. The sunrise awaits. Voices waft from a distant tent, and the neighbour's dog barks half-heartedly at me.

Shush, I say, not wanting my moment of solitude invaded.

My dream from last night follows me. Another vivid dream, powerful but gentle for a change. My father showed up again, sober this time. It seems I'm seeing him more often these days than when he was alive. I was walking in the woods on one of my usual grief-trudges and there he was, sitting high up in a spruce tree, his legs wrapped around the trunk, not unlike yesterday's porcupine. I wasn't surprised to find him there or in that strange position. We chatted but I can't remember about what, and then he was gone. Poof, just like that. I looked around, but there was no sign of him, no prints in the snow around the tree where he'd sat.

I'd stared a long time at the spruce, watching the light sift through its branches as they swayed in the wind. Slowly, with each gust of wind, the tree began to transform, to morph into the shape of a man, small branches on the top bending down and around to form a head, and below a burly chest, the trunk dividing into separate legs. Hollow inside his body of branches, Spruce Man stepped forward, towering over me. I wasn't frightened, only wonderstruck, like the feeling I'd had yesterday when the porcupine was shot down. Half asleep, I blinked to see if Spruce Man was real and there he still was, larger than life. He'd walked right by me, heading for the camp. I followed him, the breeze gently blowing around me, a tranquil and beneficent breath.

I'm feeling plucky on my way back to the tent, like I might just burst out of my skin. My morning stiffness has dissipated. The sun has barely risen—an expansive swath of pink permeating fair weather cumulus clouds—yet the snow under my feet is crystalizing already, sinking slowly into the ground, spring creaking at its seams to manifest itself and bring new life. The promise of a warmer day than yesterday. The sun swells over the horizon now, fully awake and prepared to shoo the clouds away.

You're stealing our dreams, Sepastien says, when I ask him for his interpretation.

What do you mean? I ask. Maybe he's teasing me, he who likes to constantly point out how our worlds are not the same.

Maybe an Elder can help you, Sepastien says, tell you what it means. Manteshkueu, Akat's mother, is very good to know about dreams. We can ask her after breakfast.

I scramble eggs and fry up bacon that I've brought, dish out the food, and the whole time Akat and Sepastien talk in hushed tones. The kids grab a bite and head outside to greet the day's adventure.

Dishes can wait and the three of us head out for Mishta-Pinip and Manteshkueu's tent. We walk by Manish and Pien's abode. She's holding the two back legs of a caribou lying on his back, while Pien skins the animal. Blood has splattered across their pants and coats. The caribou is mostly naked, with his fleshy red thighs and lean, hollowed torso, guts removed. Tshakapesh, who must be about eight, sits nearby watching intently. He flashes two red hands at us, covered in blood, gorgeously crimson. Kuekuatsheu, not much older, hovers, intent on helping. It's possible that's a smile Pien just shot my way.

Pien did good yesterday, Manish says. Better than us.

We got eleven, Pien adds, not a hint of boasting in his voice.

Sepastien and Pien chat on, no doubt dissecting every detail of the hunt, until Akat prompts us to carry on. A handful of kids are playing outside Mishta-Pinip and Manteshkueu's tent, dressing a snowman with a scarf and mitts at the end of stick arms, spruce branches for long hair, like dreadlocks. I half expect it to come to life, like Spruce Man. One of the boys sports cool sunglasses and a tuque with the Labrador flag. He sticks his tongue out at me, then flashes a giant smile. I fake-punch him in the arm and pop my red beret on the snowman's head.

Akat pokes her head through the doorway to announce our arrival and we all step into the orderly tent, manoeuvre to find a spot to sit. Mishta-Pinip and Manteshkueu sit side by side on a large trunk near the stove, both in short sleeves; his shirt is plaid, hers Wedgwood blue with white flowers and leaves. A teakettle grumbles and boils, and Manteshkueu passes out cups and dippers, points to the *kashiuasht* and *tshitshinapun* for us to help ourselves to a cup of tea.

Akat explains our purpose. With no prompting from me, Sepastien takes over to describe my dream. Or so I imagine. It appears to have made an impression on him. He goes on, and I don't remember it being so elaborate. Manteshkueu and Mishta-Pinip listen intently and there is much discussion back and forth between the two Elders.

Every so often they look my way, expressionless. Mishta-Pinip is shaking his head as he slips a cigarette into his mouth. Not a word of translation yet. It would've been nice to be able to tell my own dream.

A young man sticks his head in the tent and hands over a couple of partridges. Manteshkueu takes them and begins plucking one as she continues to talk, deftly grabbing handfuls of feathers while the *pineu*'s skin remains intact.

I'm still waiting for them to pronounce on my dream. Two cardboard boxes, one for food and one for dishes, sit next to the stove along with a box of Purity crackers, a bag of flour, a yellow tub of Imperial Eversweet (indeed) margarine, a metal bowl with an uncooked *pakueshikai*. A large lantern flashlight and long strips of caribou meat hang from the crossbeam along with mitts and a pair of lumberjack socks, grey wool with white toes and heels. A hefty pile of wood junks is stacked tidily behind the stove. The *eshpishatshimeuan*, made of a couple of sheets and hung at night like a tent inside the tent to contain body heat, has been pulled and tied back out of the way. A beaver skin, stretched on a frame, leans against the back wall.

They keep talking. Maybe they've changed the subject altogether. Why would my dream warrant so much discussion? But then again, when I've asked my friend Annie to interpret a dream, she usually needs time to think about it. She's my dream guru back home. She would tell me my father in my dream was a part of me, and Spruce Man too. She'd ask me about the different parts of the tree, the surroundings, the weather, my feelings during and after the dream. And I'd tell her I was happy, and curiously uncurious about why my father was up in a tree, and how amazing Spruce Man was, and how I'd follow him to the ends of the world.

We might ponder the meaning of "tree." Dissect all the expressions and idioms: go climb a tree, and I could be out of my tree, or find myself up a tree. I can't see the forest for the trees and money doesn't grow on trees. There's the Tree of Life and the Tree of Knowledge and the Family Tree. Tree as totem and the tree as maypole. May

Poles would be part of my heritage and Annie might get me thinking about our medieval ancestors, how they would've gone in search of the perfect tree, chopped it down, peeled off the bark, decorated it with ribbons, and had girls dance around it, bathed in sunshine, ushering in spring and fecundity. And there's the Christmas tree, and the tree—or maybe two trees—that make up the holy cross of Jesus crucified.

Root, trunk, bark, branch, leaf: trees are the earth's lungs.

So what does it mean? I ask.

It is, after all, my dream they're discussing.

They all look over at me, as if reminded of my presence.

I'd like to know what you think it means, I ask again. My dream.

It's an important dream, Sepastien says. Manteshkueu say that.

That might be a look of annoyance on Mishta-Pinip's face, lines etched across his contracted brow. Or could it be puzzlement, or worry? I'd heard Tshinetshishepateu speaking at a meeting about the school, about how young Innu were no longer dreaming, and this was why they were losing their way.

Manteshkueu is speaking again. She's just stood up to flip the *pakueshikai* in the frying pan. She holds both of her hands together, points them out, and up to her lips, then rubs them together, waves one of them my way. Then she holds both out, palms up. Wrapping her words into an offering.

Maybe she's thinking that I am like an Innu child. Children, I've been told, are too immature to talk about their dreams, and doing so can bring bad luck.

She say your father is lonely, Sepastien translates.

He didn't seem lonely when we were talking, I say.

If a person pass away and come in your dream, it mean maybe he want you to go with him, Sepastien says.

Go with him where? I ask. My father disappeared in my dream.

How could I follow him? It was the tree I wanted to follow. Surely it couldn't be like Manish's story about her aunt? How the old woman had told Manish she was taking her son with her when she passed, and how he died less than a month after her.

Manteshkueu say you need to respect the tree, and your ancestors. Very important.

Respect the tree? I ask. What tree?

A dream is not to play with, Sepastien says.

Who's playing? I think. And I want to say, I thought this was a happy dream.

Manteshkueu has just disemboweled one of the partridges, placed the heart and gizzard on the lid of the margarine tub. She grabs the other scrawny bird and cuts along the crop, where spruce needles and other digestables reside partway down the gullet before entering the stomach to be macerated and absorbed. The crop is blocked with spruce needles, green and pungent. No berries at this time of the year, only in the fall and spring. These partridges are reconstituted spruce needles and berries, a kind of revisioning of spruce needles and berries. The wispy feathers, smeared in blood, are all versions of the same thing. So what does that make me?

Manteshkueu wraps all the feathers into a sheet of newspaper and places them in a plastic bag.

What else did Manteshkueu say about my dream? I ask.

She know what the dream mean for Innu, but maybe not in your culture, Sepastien says. Maybe it is for you to try to know it, what it mean to you.

Respect the tree, in my world? I am a tree hugger, but my Spruce Man might be asking a lot of me coming from a culture that wantonly destroys trees. Thousands of hectares of clearcuts all over Newfoundland visible only from planes, hidden by small strips of forest so they can't be seen from roads. The earth skinned alive in a godless world.

Sepastien's kind of right. I'm fascinated with my dreams, carry them around when I'm awake, but I contemplate them with my head cocked, one eye closed. Dreams are a random world, strange and madcap, scary and freaky—a little too close to the world that had my grandmother strapped to a hospital bed, electrode pads attached to each side of her head, a rubber tube between her teeth, while the doctor pressed a button to send electricity coursing through her brain. I was little when I was told she got taken away because of her Nerves.

Dreams may be mere electrical impulses in our gray matter. But we sleep for one-third of our lives. If I live to be seventy-five, I will have slept a total of something like twenty-five or more years. That's a very long time, yet we give little credence to this parallel life.

And respect my ancestors? Really, I love some of my people, I do, but Manteshkueu doesn't know my family. I left home and I'm not going back.

It doesn't look like she's going to tell me what she knows about my dream. What she's said is, pay attention.

It would be nice to believe that my dream could be my power, a deep place of knowing where the dead can speak, trees too, a direct channel to the spirits and gods. In the Innu cosmos, dreams are what it means to be alive. A believer who dreams of playing the drum three times has the right to play the drum awake, and while playing he can be drawn back into his dream, a dream now sweeping in its powers.

I won't find any power in my dream here and it looks like we're done.

Tshinashkumitin. It's a feeble thank you.

The blue sky outside is uncompromising. They are upset over my dream, or maybe my request? What would they have said about my decapitation dream? Let's forget about that one. I grab my beret off the snowman as I walk by. I might need it to study my dream. Find a tree to lean on. For comfort. Immersed in their world, I'm still stuck in mine. Tears well up but I won't succumb.

That was no stolen dream. What I know is that before coming here, my father's passing left me wondering about the dead, how they can take up a lot of space, too much, by their absence. They become too important to the living, just by dying, and it's too late. I keep stumbling into this truth here.

My dream whirls and backpedals, moves on and settles, and my Spruce Man wrapped in sunlight has already begun to melt and trickle away, like the mid-April snow mountains all around.

XVIII.

Easter mass is already underway when I stroll into the *shaputuan*. The ritual takes place at every spring gathering in this massive tent. A crowd of faces look my way and watch me without curiosity as I walk over to perch myself next to Manish. They must be used to seeing me around and no longer find me that interesting. Two stoves in the middle radiate heat all around, welcoming us from the cold.

At the back of the tent, Father Adrien stands behind an altar made of two-by-fours and plywood draped with a starched linen cloth embellished with embroidered crosses and lace. Next to him is a wall-hanging pinned to the tent canvas, made by Mishta-Shanut. She's cut small pieces of caribou hide into different shapes and appliquéd them onto a piece of white duffel wool. They depict a man carrying a canoe; a tent, river, and hills, trees; a dog, scaffold, and sun; a woman pulling a toboggan; and above her an imposing caribou across the sky, like a Spirit suspended.

Next to the collage, a drum hangs on a tent pole. The *teuikan* is made of birch and caribou skin, crossed with a snare whose resonators are made of tiny bones from a caribou fetus. It is the instrument of the *kamiteut*, who sings and drums awaiting a message from the Caribou that it is ready to offer itself to the people.

More than one God is attending to our prayers today.

And the ghost of Father Pederson from not so long ago is here, storming into a tent to grab the drum from Tshinetshishepateu, calling it the instrument of the devil, saying there'll be no drumming, no singing, no dancing. Get out.

Father Adrien is more kindly, beloved, even if Manish doesn't want him at meetings. His propensity to spirits of the alcoholic variety is tolerated, overlooked. His occasional bluster is unconvincing. Over a white pressed cassock, he wears a vestment of smoked caribou hide, decorated with bric-a-brac and beads, not unlike a ceremonial robe that might have been worn by a *kamiteut.* He makes the sign of the cross and begins to recite the mass in Innu, a monumental task of memorization. His words are over-articulated, but they carry the same mechanical inflections of the liturgy, in whatever language. Sepastien's son Matshiu is the altar boy. The young hunter, also in a cassock but a few sizes too small, swings the thurible three times, frankincense and myrrh, three holy smokes.

The profound ennui that occupied my body during mass when I was a girl is strangely absent. All the restless sitting and kneeling and standing, shifting my weight from one leg to the other, wondering how knock-kneed I looked from the pew behind me.

The women are singing an old hymn in Innu, not one of the more contemporary folk melodies from the post–Vatican II mass of the 1960s, when Latin and mantillas gave way to guitars and go-go boots. The hymn has its own tempo and rhythm and language, a melancholy filled with longing. The sound is full-bodied, complicated, penetrating, almost metallic, made more sonorous with its discrete microtones. The voices draw from the *nikamu*, a song to the Spirits and Masters, received in a dream that could make sustenance, a cure, life itself, possible.

It makes for very fine church music. The wind ripples the sides of the tent to accompany the women's song, like the strings of a harp. Father Adrien kneels; his knees can be heard cracking as he crouches down. He places his hands together in front of his face in silent prayer.

My mom was the one who taught me my prayers, barely more than a toddler kneeling by the dryer on the cold basement floor, while she folded clothes. She was multi-tasking. Later my prayers were about her.

Please God, make my mother happy.

Being Catholic no longer troubles me, although memories of my grade one catechism class persist. Sister Paul stood in front of the class every day to warn us about all that would befall us if we continued to be sinners. Mine was a childhood filled with sin, including the shame of "original sin." Forgive me Father, for I have sinned. Every month I'd enter the claustrophobic confessional and reveal my sins. Disobedience was the most common and there were lies I told; reading my book when I was meant to be vacuuming; stealing penny candy; thinking bad thoughts, like you could control those. Sometimes it was hard to come up with a list, but a list I had to have. Venial sins were small black spots on our souls, and mortal sins blackened the whole of it. Spots somewhere inside my belly. I was not allowed to strive to be popular, pretty, smart, successful or beloved. Vanity was a sin. Good girls never talked back, could not be priests, were to blame if the boys pulled their pants down.

Sister Paul was all about sacrifices, about guardian angels looking over our shoulders like spies, and punishment with hats made of bristol board, *LAZY* emblazoned across the front. If we didn't keep our cursive writing within the lines, she rapped our fingers with a ruler. She smelled of cold storage, musty, like she needed airing out. She showed us images: God as an old man floating in clouds surrounded by cherubs, the inferno of hell, Jesus resurrected ascending towards the heavens from a cave. I really wanted to serve God intently, be good, pray, and when I received communion, I tried hard to keep my tongue just right so the host would not stick to the top of my mouth, which I was told, would result in Jesus, the flesh and blood of God, escaping. It was a struggle being good because the devil was relentless. He could be with everyone everywhere all over the world all the time, like Santa.

My brothers and sisters, I beg you in the name of Jesus Christ, Father Adrien has switched to English for the homily. I beg you to put your faith and trust in Jesus. Come to know him. Let there be no debate because Jesus is Lord our God. Today we celebrate the triumph of good over evil and light over darkness.

Jesus has never been the problem for me. He hung out with fishermen and prostitutes, and that scene in the market where he kicked the tables over—I wouldn't mind trying that out myself. Jesus wasn't looking for pure and perfect, certainly wasn't nasty and all judgie. But he should have had women apostles, and did his mother have to be a virgin?

I do still pray, although it's not clear to whom. I'm a religious none. Sometimes I wonder about my Celtic roots, the ancient tribe of my ancestors when they may have lived much like the Innu, not that long ago in the scheme of things. I've flirted with the odd pagan ritual—women gathered to celebrate the solstice, dancing around a bonfire on the beach, chanting to the full moon. It's likely my ancient grandmothers honoured an earth mother and her fecundity, all giving and beautiful, eternal, still untouched by human excesses. Not yet defiled by mining, burns, chemical poisoning, wars, clearcutting.

My blood might be laced with the knowledge of these grandmothers, their magic and spirits and secrets. Somewhere in my DNA, in my bones, is where I know that I'm miscarrying before the doctor does, or someone is deathly ill before diagnosed. Even as a girl I knew that my grandmother was the sanest of us all. These are not powers I care for.

On this earth the Innu and my people could have been the same, worshipping the same sun and moon? All those witches burned at the stake for their un-Christian rituals, divinations, magic and herbal potions, some of them could be my ancestors. Madeleine Dubois, my family's fille du roi—witch pyres ablaze in France—was she complicit or a rebel? Did I get the rebel gene from her?

What did Madeleine make of the Innu? She might have traded with an Innu woman, a kerchief or a needle for a couple of partridges.

She could have made a friend—someone like Manish. Maybe Madeleine learned some Innu from her new friend, or maybe she gave her smallpox? They could have traded stories, like the one about the great flood, how it was *Kuekuatsheu*, the wolverine, and not Noah, who built a big boat and put animals from all species inside it before the rains came and flooded the world. Did her friend wonder why our god did not respect her gods?

An Innu hunter might have caught Madeleine's fancy? Maybe they wanted to make a baby. What is certain is that my people stole land, in the name of God, the Church, and King. Tshinetshishepateu still carries that story from four hundred years ago. His grandfather recounted to him that once the *Mishtikushuats*—those who arrived on large wooden ships—had settled the land, they waged war and stole women and children.

Is collective amnesia treatable? My family's story, unsanitized, can be imagined more than gleaned, and excavating microfiche or yellowed church documents won't provide any redemption. We killed each other in battle.

You may now offer each other a sign of peace, Father Adrien says.

Peace be with you, Manish says with an ironic smile, turning towards me with her hand outstretched, disrupting my trance. She squeezes hard, jesting. Ouch. I turn and shake a few other hands. There is eye contact and a handshake, words exchanged. It's always so awkward. Are you feeling it yet? All around me, people are muttering as they hold each other's hands, and peace be with you is sounding an awful lot like wisecracking. Laughter as sacrament.

Father Adrien breaks the host and holds a piece of it up towards the sky.

Oh Lord, I am not worthy. Only say the word and my soul shall be healed, he is saying in Innu. I can't recite Shakespeare but I know this liturgy by rote from my childhood. Father raises the chalice and continues with his clumsy Innu.

Manish stands up next to me to follow others making their way to Father Adrien for communion. My soul falls short of the required state of grace required for this ritual. It is filled with mortal sin, like pre-marital sex and taking God's name in vain, and I haven't been to church in ages, but that hasn't stopped me before. When in Rome, do as the Romans do. I join the procession.

The body of Christ, Father Adrien says, as I stick my tongue out to receive the host.

We are breaking bread to celebrate our union with God, consuming the flesh and blood of his very son, and of all the sumptuous breads in the world, the Catholic church settles on a thin, dry wafer. In this ceremony, there's no getting carried away by the spirit, no speaking in tongues or euphoric evangelical soul singing. It's a far cry from the sweat lodge ceremony I participated in last summer up on the hill above the airstrip.

Fourteen of us had crawled one by one into the lodge, a dome the size of a four-person tent, covered in canvas, blue tarps, all manner of blankets—wool, army, plaid, and a couple of caribou skins thrown into the mix. Its door faced east. Layers of fir boughs, *shtapakun*, served as a cushion to sit on. Sepastien had carried a pile of red-hot stones, Grandfather Stones, with a shovel from an open fire of quivering coals. One by one he'd placed the stones into a pit in the middle of the lodge. We all took turns smudging ourselves, fanning the woodsy and menthol smoke from a bowl of burning sage first toward our hearts, then over our heads and all around our bodies. We were cleansing ourselves, clearing away negative energy, inviting peace and harmony into the lodge.

It's so easy to conjure the whole thing up again. I entered the sweat with apprehension, a fear of suffocating, claustrophobia. And the leader, Simon, a medicine man from Alberta, made me nervous. He took off his black faded biker jacket; he seemed so young, not much older than me, mid-thirties maybe. He never thanked anyone for their hospitality, nor did he acknowledge that his sweat was not the Innu way. Tapit had pointed out these shortcomings to me, but any misgivings I had did not deter me, and there I was with Simon, who was keeping all of us on our toes, especially me as the only *kakeshau.* His eyes scanned our group and his gaze stopped on me. It felt like a glare, like he knew every embarrassing moment of my life. Yielding to his scrutiny, a mixture of shame and strange relief surfaced.

Are you on your period? he asked me in an accusing kind of voice, like it was something I might hide from him. Was he trying to get rid of me?

I'm not, I said.

Manish had already checked with me before we entered the lodge.

When it is the woman time of month, she is very powerful, she said. The blood connect with the earth and she have too much power in the sweat, no balance for the men.

This was a way better take on menstruation than the bible, which says that a woman bleeding is unclean for seven days, along with anything she lies on, sits on or touches. But Simon's question had not helped me warm to him. It wasn't his youth that bothered me, but the glint of rage in his eyes. Far be it for me to judge any Native person for their rage, but could he deliver on the healing?

Each of us settled into our spot in the circle and Sepastien, who sat by the door, reached outside to grab the canvas flap. He pulled it down and all light was extinguished. We were engulfed in a pitch-black cave, not a hint of a glow from the rocks and dark enough to make a person believe that light no longer existed, that the moon and the stars outside were forever snuffed out. The air closed in on us. There was no way out, except to ask six people to crawl out of the lodge ahead of me, to make a scene. My head was already spinning, but with a few slow, deep breaths, in and out, in and out, I settled in. Desire took over.

Simon had started by saying something like, This ceremony is to give thanks, to heal, to seek wisdom and purify our mind, body, and soul. Sepastien translated for the Elders.

There are people who are not from this tradition, Simon also said.

That would be me, and the Innu who have their own sweats?

Sepastien had convinced Akat to come and she was sitting next to me. It was her first time too, but she radiated calm, a kind of amused and curious energy. Wafts of tobacco filled the darkness, and Simon began to sing, a chant from another language, not Innu-aimun but related. Everyone joined in, a chorus of beautiful and fervid voices, something to concentrate on.

You will be uncomfortable, Simon said. You're supposed to be uncomfortable. The ceremony is about suffering. When your body suffers, it is purified.

Oh great, I thought, as I sat with my arms clutching my knees. There was no space between any of us; we were as snug as possible.

An otherworldly growl from Simon filled the lodge, the sound of what might be a hibernating bear just waking up, like a whoosh-snore summoned from deep within a boreal forest den.

Give all of your bad energy back to the earth, he said. This is the time to think about why you're here. What do you want? Who are you suffering for? What intentions do you mean to carry out in your life?

There'd be no rote prayer repeated for millenia or any cursory sign of the cross. My reasons for being there or for whom I was meant to suffer eluded me. The excruciating heat was getting our minds out of the way so we could do the work. But I wasn't ready for this journey within, for what I might find or not. In that impenetrable darkness, the ground beneath me was slipping away. Droplets were forming on my forehead, dripping into my eyes, and the saltiness stung. I wiped my forehead with the back of my hand.

Simon poured water over the rocks, the Grandfathers, and they sizzled and hissed. They were alive and they were stirring us to our core. The rising steam assaulted my throat. Breathing was hell, a deeply dark spiralling tunnel of heat and spirit taking us to some other dimension. I couldn't stay but I couldn't say, Let me out. I couldn't move, or I might pass out. Miserable yet ecstatic, I slipped lower, deeper. I put my hand in front of my nose to filter the searing heat. I could not be the weak *kakeshau.* She didn't last very long in there, did she? There was no escape. I could do this. I had backbone, stamina, I didn't cower from pain, but now we were all meant to speak. It was like confession, but in front of a group, many people. Therapy sessions always made me cry, but this—the floodgates were about to open. There was my mother and her sorrows, my loneliness and Mark. An image of him appeared: he was walking with his head down, hands in his pockets, pacing up and down dejectedly. It was very hot. So hot. People took turns speaking in Innu. It was a miracle they could speak at all in this heat.

Undone, the heat was breaking me; open, my heart racing, my throat seizing. It was my turn and I let the words out.

I'm sad. Very sad. And thank you. Thank you, I repeated.

These measly words were all I could muster, but they had exposed me, small and white. My mind was in overdrive, thoughts gushing, a thunderstorm of feelings, joy, pain, rage, my simmering fear let loose, about to boil over. I had stumbled into something more terrifying—a longing for love too deep, scalding, and tender for this world—something more personal and more profound than anything I ever wanted to know or do or see. But I did want to know. It finally made sense to be scared out of my mind. Such love seemed part of being as alive as possible in the deepest way. I wanted to go further. Badly. I meant what I said. Sad, oh boy was I sad; the word had found its way out.

All my life people told me I had it good: white, two parents, nice home, orthodontics, a trip to Disneyworld, a debt-free education—the world is your oyster, on a silver platter. How to explain all my sorrows, for whatever reason, maybe no reason at all? When I went to a counsellor to talk about my past, I discovered a different kind of violence, everything repressed as if stashed under the grey-mottled Arborite table in the kitchen of my childhood. The pain had no name. Nestled in, ensconced, curled up in a nice ball, it was as real a pain as could be, but unidentifiable, the other side of white—amorphous, like air. I could yell it into the sky and wait forever for its echo. It evaporated.

Simon poured more water on the rocks, the steam intensified, and my desperation for stories that fit my wretchedness revealed itself. I'd been denying it, making light of it. My exterior is a good-natured cloud floating by, but a girl inside of me huddles in the corner, thinking she has no right to be here. No one will listen because my life looks too good on the outside, too white, too innocent, too pure.

You people think you're not oppressed, Manish said to me once. If you're not oppressed, then why everybody so uptight? What's that about?

Simon had started to chant again, and the vibrations pierced my mind, laying me bare. Tentacles of sage smoke circled and entered into me, whorling through my thoughts. My brain was trying to cling to its ways, but the smoke called out, This is another way. I was battling demons, all their clutter and misery, a woman indifferent, obstinate, rebellious, and needy. Self-hating, careless, cold, anesthesized, I was a woman who craved and shirked her own power, or lack of it.

I thought I was feisty, that I was someone who jumped in, wasn't afraid. But I could barely see this woman. There was a baby, left to cry in her crib, screaming at the top of her lungs. A toddler falling down the stairs. A little girl. She was visiting the priest's house with dear aunt Sister Beatrice, assigned to be his housekeeper, and the priest said the child needs a bath and he put her in the tub, and he was washing her, and he was rubbing, rubbing her so hard. You want to be clean down there, he'd said. We'll make it pure. Pure. And it was sweet but it hurt too, and the girl was so little yet knew deep in her bones that it was bad, really bad, and she couldn't tell another grown-up. Instead she divided herself into different parts and at night she watched them all fly to the corner of the ceiling, and the bells tolled, they wouldn't stop. Her head hurt and she learned to cry more quietly.

Stop crying, her mother said, or I'll give you something to really cry about.

My thoughts collided with each other around the hot circle of breaths, each thought with its own weight, groping to believe there was no reason to be devastated, really, was there? Don't worry, be happy. The weight came with an armour, a saving-face kind of armour, privilege, an uncompromising belief in the unspeakable. But the wound was open now, a deep festering at the heart of who I was. Me at the centre.

Where have I been all my life? It's hard to feel privileged with all that shame and trauma.

Beside me Akat still exuded quiet and calm, as if this sweat was the sort of thing that happened all the time. Our knees were touching. She didn't seem at all worried about her first sweat or what she'd shared in the circle, but she must have wondered why I started crying, sobbing, hyperventilating. She reached her arm around my shoulders, drawing me close to her. My nose was running, mucous spilling down over my mouth, onto my knees and to the ground. Finally my sobs quieted. Breath in. Breath out. Everyone else was breathing with me too. Deep inside, a speck of light that was not me at all, flickered.

The canvas door lifted finally and starlight poured in, gracing us, as my sweat-drenched body crawled out into the cool evening air, feeling at once unfastened and light. It was like a huge weight had lifted from me; my endorphins were dancing. Simon reached over to pat me gently on the back as I walked by.

On my way back to the sisters' house that night, I'd stopped by a tree to rest and catch up with myself, attempt a kind of reassembling. But it was too soon. I had to stay with the mayhem and wonder what force it would take to propel currents of hope and trust and hallelujah through my fragile bones and the small device that is my heart. The tree was there to support me as a red beam of light began to hug the horizon, and soon the inky sky was bathed with shimmering swaths of green. It was like fish were swimming across the sky, swirling and swaying, morphing into yellow and red, and then like an artist had gone wild, sweeping her brush up and down across the firmament, leaving the sky ablaze with her colours. It seemed hardly a coincidence that the aurora borealis was there that night too, to wrap its arms around me and lead me home. I'd thanked the tree for its support, running my hand down its trunk, rooted, solid.

Go in peace, Father Adrien says, repeating his final blessing in English as he waves his right hand up and down, from side to side, blessing his flock with a sign of the cross. The mass has ended. We're being dismissed.

Thanks be to God, rises out of me from nowhere. I'm still caught up in the sweat and what followed, how my feelings of fragmentation and euphoria didn't last, but the memories did: all that became clear, the things I had wanted to know and those I didn't. They can still stir my mind up into a whirling dervish without warning, like just now. What to do about it all is still unclear, almost a year later. My parents are only part of the picture, and they did their best. There's my grandparents and beyond. Before this, I thought the worst I had done was shop at Hudson's Bay, but now its basement is exposed, its bowels filled with lies and fears and horrors nobody knew. Mine is a world that takes and takes, that changes and rearranges, interprets and reinterprets, until everything is meant to be reasonable, but it's all tangled up and we've lost the thread. This is why we tolerate what we tolerate. It's all hidden away, all connected, but we're severed from ourselves and each other. A department store is my culture. Starting with the fur trade. It's as scary as Fanon imagined and our minds are occupied territory.

All this time, my obsession with the Innu story has obscured the truth. We are on stolen land with its treaties, the Indian Act, reservations, children kidnapped and sent to residential schools, and that's just the beginning. Innu land has a story that belongs to me too. Where do the lies begin and where do they end? They are inside of us and outside too. There's a disinherited Métis where mortification and subjugation reside. A ghost inside of me is looking for its clothes. Tapit is accused of exaggerating whenever he extolls the evils of the government's "genocidal policies," but he's right. People say it never happened, or get over it. The Holocaust is real—six million people murdered, the gas chambers and concentration camps—but what happened here, and keeps happening?

Survivors surround me. Simon talked about being uncomfortable in the sweat. Shame is my discomfort: to walk around the village with its rows of shacks as some kind of payoff, to see what has happened to people, to the children. My government did this and what unmentionables did my ancestors commit? There are memories in my cells that go far back, sit inside me, diminish me, bring me more into myself, shut me down from what might help me, make me forget my purpose. I want to point the finger at someone, at some tangible thing. I didn't steal land, I didn't steal children. I want to defend myself, to deflect, to cry. No one's trying to hold me responsible, but I'm not off the hook.

Take the land, it's yours, I want to say. But soon the troops will move in, as they are wont to. They've moved in, settled right in my mind.

Once we realize we've all been dispossessed, then we have a place to start from, but how to talk about it? This place has wrecked me, its grief, and it keeps hitting me over and over as ugly as I feel inside. Heartbreak is not respectable in our culture. We celebrate winners, or at least bravery and resilience, but we run from broken people. Their suffering is painful to watch. Do the broken need to make such a spectacle of themselves, weeping their giant tears? It doesn't matter that most of us suffer our own heartbreaks, that we know the grip of grief. As public behaviour, it's embarrassing. There's also the small point that maybe we should do something about this mess?

I've done stupid things and I've made mistakes. The nerve of all of this is raw and maybe it will always be raw, but somewhere there is kindness and generosity. I want to be in that place, at risk of falling into the abyss and yielding to the depths of compassion. Contrition can sting us into a kind of surrendering, awkward, discomfiting love.

That homily. You'd think Father Adrien might have talked about the fire, hope and resurrection and all that.

XIX.

Afterwards, people linger, standing and shuffling around the *shaputuan.*

If you want to stick around, Father Adrien says, we have a special guest here who will be speaking to people about how to help the children. We know our children are hurting. I'm sure everyone can benefit from this meeting.

There's no sign of Deborah.

Meeting? I look over at Manish. Now?

Yeah, Manish says. About band business and the inquiry.

Thanks for letting me know, I say with just a hint of sarcasm. And where's Deborah?

Missing in action, Manish says with a grin.

Both of us plunk ourselves down again. Not sure why I'm looking out for Deborah. Hopefully Manish will translate for me. Some people head for the door, others are stretching, as new people trickle in. Everyone stakes a spot. The orientation of the tent shifts into a circle, and a buzz of idle chatter rises. The turbulence inside me from the sweat rises again. Breathe in, breathe out, breathe in, breathe out. What I really want is to head for the hills, find a little space, a small clearing, a tree to lean on, some relief.

Mishta-Pinip has made himself comfortable, lying on his side on the boughs in front of the altar, looking pretty chill. A few people stand at the door, but most are now sitting layers deep along the sides of the tent. Meetings in a tent are intimate, people leaning close into each other, couples, women, men as well, unselfconsciously nestled in; a head on a shoulder, a side, a belly.

Tshinetshishepateu and Manikanet rest on their haunches across from me. Manikanet is dwarf-like. Decades have shrunk her, but she remains sturdy and muscular with a weather-beaten face and gnarly hands. She always seems alert, from smoking and coughing incessantly. Or smiling, like now, drawing me into the moment. I smile back. Tshinetshishepateu also peers over at me with his thick glasses. His smile is in his eyes. His hair reminds me of Elvis Presley's, but not recently coifed, amazingly black for his age, with a streak of white across his bangs. His hands are muscled and callused from hard work with axes and ice augers, chisels, oars, and crooked knives, scarred with gill net cuts. The two are in their eighties or nineties or could be a hundred—nobody knows. They were born in Innu time, before calendar years, before they existed in church and government records. They had a hard time getting signed up for their old age pension, likely missed a decade of cheques or more.

Tshinetshishepateu opens the door of the stove, stokes the fire and replenishes the wood. Unlike many who seem to question or resent my presence, Tshinetshishepateu has always been gentle and accepting, never forceful or demanding. Not with words, but by his demeanour. He has that detached look you see in people who know a hundred times more than anybody around them, but since nobody cares to ask or notice that he might have something to offer, he just smiles, bemused. Rather than elbow his way in, he watches over the rim of his glasses with a curiosity about what might happen next. He strikes me as humble, never judging the confusion around him or even paying much attention to it at all, but always looking to learn something, some new pattern in order to make sense of this new world, which the *kakeshau*, whoever they are, might have brought with them. That's the vibe he sends. It never occurs to him that he might be a big deal. As always, he's calmed me down.

Manish is talking and her words are sprinkled with *Mamunitau Tshitaiauimuanu* here and there, reporting on our Gathering Voices. The sun's dappled light through the trees is reflected on the tent's canvas. People are paying close attention. She speaks intently as she plays with a bough on the floor, running her hand along the grain of the flat needles and down the stem. She tucks it further into the carpet and motions for Sepastien to speak. I assume he'll give an update on how the process is going, and he'll extend an invitation to anyone else who might want to contribute.

Deborah has just walked in. The air draws in and leaves a slight chill. I can feel the cringe. A *kakeshau* is joining us. Another white person, a stranger. We should be called pinks. White is processed food, unnourishing, white bread, mayonnaise, mashed potatoes. A white picket fence, a whiteout, white knuckles. Deborah heads my way, to sit by me. Manish elbows me. Sepastien looks over, but only barely skips a beat. The moment passes, unlike what often happens when an Innu walks into a room of *kakeshauts*, and there is silence. The very particles of air are reconstituted to declare, You are making me uncomfortable, or worse. It can be in passing, in a bar, a store; the sang-froid lingers. There is an elephant in the room that can't get out, and you can't quite put your finger on it.

I didn't know the meeting was happening, Deborah whispers as she sits and crosses her legs. Do you think I can get on the agenda?

Don't ask me, I say, but Father Adrien did tell people you'd be here.

Tapit has just stood up, and he looks pumped. We may be in for one of his soliloquies, delivered with his professorial tone, spiced with philosophical flourishes and anger, his own brand of anger, somehow not bereft of kindness.

You want to help our children, I've been told, he says. This one's for Deborah. She hasn't been introduced, but she's on the agenda.

You need to know that the children here are not children, he goes on. They have been robbed of their childhoods because their parents and grandparents have been abused and beaten simply because of who they were. The cycle lives on.

His English grammar is correct, and he speaks with the hint of a British accent, probably picked up from all his travels to Europe advocating for Innu rights.

When people of a race or culture have dealt with forced assimilation, have been traumatized and colonized, he says, you get people who are wounded. I say that in a clinical sense. The Innu history of colonization is a brutal one, like that of our brothers and sisters across this continent.

It's a full-on lecture, like Fanon might give. His face is tanned from the sun of long spring days, the skin lighter behind his sunglasses. A scar runs the length of the left side of his face. There must be a story behind that scar. Tapit is a friendly man, thoughtful, unguarded, generous, often jovial, even with the cynicism and occasional angry, scary outburst. One of his missions in life seems to be to educate the *kakeshau* that cross his path. His speeches are more or less the same, guiding his listeners with tales of his life: childhood violence, sexual abuse, hunger, cold, the ravages of alcohol, fear, self-hatred, attempted suicide, suicides of relatives and friends. One time he told me to go home. We were talking about colonization. He meant France, like after four hundred years it could still be home. What could I say? I tune out a lot now, although there was a time when I hung on to his every word. Like Deborah today, on full alert.

Your people have done this to us, he says. We've been disinherited, dispossessed, starved, infected, raped, displaced, brainwashed, mocked, and sequestered.

It's a lot to take in, and what does "sequestered" mean?

And now you're here to help us, Tapit goes on. You expect us to trust you. And if we don't agree with your help, who's to say you won't start throwing stones at us like they did in Oka last summer? Or that you won't send in the police, or troops, like what happened when we protested against NATO at the airport in Goose Bay. You want to help us, you say.

His words are stirring up the tumult of my sweat again. Deborah stares at the ground, expressionless. I was just there: heart racing, feeling small and bad, wanting to slip away quietly. Tapit is about to go on, but Mishta-Pinip cuts in full throttle, talking fast and loud, his frailty evaporated. His interruption exudes impatience, and several Elders exchange sidelong glances and grin.

What's he saying? I ask Manish.

He say this time we are the ones to decide. We are the ones to build a new village here.

Deborah's relief at the sudden switch in the agenda is palpable.

Mishta-Pinip is done speaking and leans on his cane to stand, rousing everyone to their feet.

What's happening? I ask Manish

Come on, she says as she stands. I follow her and there's a bottleneck at the door. People elbow their way out. There's a jostling for rides as people jump onto snowmobiles. I scramble into Manish's komatik just as she takes off. Kids run for the hill where they've been sliding the last few days. Manish roars around the tent and steers toward the same hill, a procession on her tail.

We reach the top where the wind blows a wild bluster. Snowmobiles pull up one by one, the crowd grows, all abuzz, voices a blend of shouting and laughter. A number of Elders sit on machines and kids scamper around playing tag. Eyes scan the wide expanse of land below. Mishta-Pinip continues from where he left off in the tent. He points directly below the hill.

That's where the school will go, Manish translates. The clinic across the road.

And everyone has jumped in. The store should go there, with a hotel attached to it and next to the band office. The arena there, by the school and across from the church, the garage behind the store. Voices overlap; thoughts spill and intersect with opinions and stories, a cacophony. The children have stopped running and listen intently. The healing lodge will go outside the community, on the way to the airstrip, across the pond to the west where all the red berries grow. An arm points north, tracing a route northeast; it'll be a job bulldozing a road from there to the wharf, where the waters are deep enough to accommodate large ships. Families are already staking their territory, homes in clusters according to clans. This is dreaming awake, messy and lively, dreaming big. They must be counting on their gods to intervene.

Mishta-Pinip climbs back onto his Ski-Doo and the crowd begins to disperse unceremoniously. Machines rev up and circle around to make their way down the hill back to the tent village.

Are we still meeting? I ask Manish.

Nope, she says, all done. You can make a motion to close and I'll second it.

Very funny.

Deborah has just arrived on foot, out of breath. She didn't manage to hitch a ride. Manish takes off.

What happened? Deborah asks.

They got plans, big plans, I say. For a whole new village. They just mapped it all out. Their idea of helping their children, I guess.

Deborah is smiling, amazingly composed.

I was going to propose they organize something like a craft project for the youth, she says with a whiff of a snicker. This woman may be catching on.

With movie nights, leadership training, maybe safe sex education, a drama group, I say. You've got money for that, right?

We laugh.

Good luck with that, I say. Although they might come up with some of those ideas themselves. In their new village.

Deborah scans the horizon, her hand over her eyes like a visor, like she might spot what she's looking for. I know that feeling.

Just give them the money. And come back, I say. Sometimes it takes a few visits to get that meeting. Unsolicited advice, but she nods in agreement.

We're back in the *shaputuan* for the *makushan*, the feast of the caribou, our last night at the gathering. I spot Deborah sitting next to Tapit. Her eyes sparkle while she listens and tries to polish off what looks like a pound of *pimin*. She won't be hungry for days. She'll eat the whole thing out of politeness, although she's not really meant to.

For the last couple of days all around the camp, the men and their apprentices have been preparing for the *makushan*, crushing the caribou bones to boil them and separate the very rich bone marrow, the *pimin*, that rises to the top of the broth. The women have also stewed caribou meat and baked *pakueshikai*.

Tapit must still be instructing Deborah, informing her that the caribou is at the heart of life and survival. The caribou is law, the whole of the caribou is sacred, the *makushan* is mass, communion shared.

When we're done eating, Tshinetshishepetau will rise, play the drum, and sing. It will sound slightly off-key to my western ear. I expect Deborah will join in the dance, as the deep voice of the old man will resonate and alternate between high-pitched and nasal beats. Rising and falling in calm repetition, the beats will draw all of us into an interior collective two-step, gathering all our heartbeats into one.

XX.

Back in the village, the team has organized a workshop for school kids at the mission. We're waiting with our flip chart paper and markers when they pile in, rushing pushing strutting until the hall is overrun and buzzing with their fiery energy. Grades 4 to 8, they're a wild mix of curious and shy, brazen and demanding as they laugh and shove each other. I see perfect teeth and rotting teeth, smeary faces, psychedelic and camouflage and two-toned jackets. One kid has a runny nose, a white-and-red crocheted tuque with *Davis Inlet* emblazoned across the rim.

We can't do this workshop at school, Sepastien had said, and insisted, no teachers.

We'd all nodded in agreement. This workshop was not about correct answers. But how would we manage without the teachers? Shustin and I sit in a corner while Kananin calls the scallywags to attention. The children settle quickly.

Good thing Kananin used to work in the school, Shustin whispers. Now the children are all mumbling in unison, not even the tiniest misbehaving. She must have asked them to say a prayer for their friends who died. More than likely they're reciting "Our Father." I keep hoping for an Innu prayer, calling out to the grandmothers and grandfathers, the ancestors, the Animal Masters, asking for their help, to show us all the way. To lead these children back to a place where life and death make sense.

Sepastien takes over and the children are riveted, fixed on his every word. *Ishkuteu*, I hear, fire. They're all still wearing their jackets and Ski-Doo boots and moccasins and hats, for a quick getaway maybe.

They avoid my eyes. Who is that *kakeshau* woman? Some of them would have sat in school next to the kids who are gone now, their empty desks a merciless reminder.

Sepastien continues to expound. He must be directing them to think about what it's like being a kid in Utshimassits. They don't know about how things have changed since settlement. But what's good about village life now, and what are the bad things? And what's good and bad about being in *nutshimits*? We want them to draw their answers. Hopefully he's told them why we're doing this.

Now he's pointing at me, and in a split second the kids are surrounding me.

I need paper, the kid with the Davis Inlet hat says.

Me too.

And me!

Me!

How about me?

I rip off sheets from the flip chart pad and hand them over with a random assortment of coloured markers.

Can you say the instructions in English? Shustin asks.

It's more than likely not needed, but I do as I'm told. With any luck my words correspond to Sepastien's. I write the two questions down on a sheet of flip chart and tape the sheet on the wall.

When you're done, each group will present their picture, I say.

There is some jostling and negotiating, and the kids go off in groups, plop themselves hither and tither around the room, sheets of paper and markers in tow. A couple of groups sit on the floor where they've found a dry spot. They get right down to business like they've been waiting a long time to do this.

Tshipesh, a boy I recognize from the gathering, takes the lead in his group. He points his marker in the air as he speaks. Hard to know if he's sharing or prompting. His baseball cap sits backward over his long, straight, jet-black hair, and a racing stripe runs down the sleeve of his jacket. Heads huddle around the sheet as he begins to write stuff down. Another kid with spiky, punk hair draws on the other side of the sheet. The artist needs no words.

Sepastien, Shustin, and Kananin have each joined less enterprising groups. We'd decided I would lay off, as the kids might take me for a teacher.

Concentration continues to still the room. Most kids seem oblivious as I snap pictures with my camera. Except for Kananin's group. They pose, a string of huge grins beaming in a semicircle with beautiful Kananin in the middle. In another group, each child has pulled a chair up to a table and claimed their own territory on the sheet in front of them. No talking—they draw in their own private world, stay focused even when the camera points their way and captures them on film. Another group sits on the floor and the conversation is quiet but animated. One girl raises her hand, bouncing up and down on her bum, as if in school and desperate to share her answer. She knows. She knows.

Tshipesh is waving his hand at me now from the other side of the room.

More paper, he says.

I am delivering another sheet when Shuni and a friend from her group sidle over to me. Both have perfect bangs falling just short of their eyes. They're wearing identical sweatshirts with the Band Council logo, same as the one coveted and stripped off Samish at the party a couple of weeks ago. They agree to pose, and stand close, arms around each other's shoulders.

Auei tshin? Shuni's friend asks, wide-set dark eyes smiling at me. Curious.

Anna. *Mak tshin?*

Nanishi, she says, introducing herself. You speak Innu?

Apishish.

Nanishi shoots a rat-a-tat of questions my way, while Shuni stands beside her with a half-smile. Where's my husband? Have

I been "on" the movies? The predictable Where you live? and Do you have baby?

Do you like here? Nanishi asks. Shuni is watching to see my reaction.

Ehe, I keep coming back all the time, I say.

Yeah, I see you before.

My response is evasive. These girls can't know what it feels like to be here and not from here, to arrive and then leave, and come back again, and it's hard to explain why. There's no pressure to fit in here. Would they understand that it's easier to be an outsider here? It's okay to be eccentric.

Are you teacher? Nurse?

Nope. I'm helping Kananin and Sepastien and Shustin with their work.

What about when you's a kid? What was the good and bad things?

The question catches me off guard. I won't be sharing memories from the sweat. Stick to my old narrative, it was bad enough. What could I tell them? Mine was a childhood of amorphous years when life was implacable, and everything was prairie dust and blue sky, forbidden and forbidding, unforgiving and forever.

I could tell them about our cold winters, getting rheumatic fever, our home by the river, how I had to cross train tracks on my way to school and sometimes when it was stopped I crawled under it to get to the other side. Have they ever seen a train?

The good, let me think, I say. My friends, skating, swimming. Books, I really loved reading books. And the bad?

I pause.

Hmmmm...school and mean people, you know mean kids, bullying...and people drinking too much, that was bad...And the word "no," I never liked that word. People said "no" a lot when I was a kid.

The girls probably don't understand the 'no' part. Kids seem to do pretty much what they want around here. The girls are looking at me like they want more, and memories are flooding back: how I loved pickles and olives, sunsets, thunderstorms, playing baseball, chasing gophers, catching fireflies, reciting limericks, watching TV standing on my head, my doll collection, my zillion girl cousins. The list goes on: the tree house at the cabin, playing poker and Scrabble, riding my brother's horse, my mom's cinnamon buns. And later as a teenager I was obsessed with Crosby Stills Nash and Young and played Chopin waltzes on the piano with great gusto.

Stories were the best, my favourite, I say, I really loved books so much.

I'm not very good reader, Shuni says with her nose turned up. What about another bad thing, tell us.

My mom being nosy, I say. She was like a spy. She knew everything, especially when I did something bad.

I don't tell the girls the only time my mom let down her guard, like she no longer needed to protect me from myself, was when I was sick. The nagging stopped when I had rheumatic fever. My asthma provided respite. Mom would create a steam bath in the bathroom, run a scalding shower against the tiled walls and porcelain tub, put my head by the open window, hold me as the steam eased its way into my nose, down my sinuses and throat, into my chest, and after a while the phlegm would jiggle loose from my lungs and I'd stop barking like a seal.

My parents' domestic little cold war was pretty bad. There was creepy uncle Bébé who you just knew to stay away from. He was probably trying to live down that nickname. He liked to flaunt a medal he stole from a Sioux grave, make up stories about its ghost and scare us. There was the year my breasts grew and the boys called me "Falsies," and around the same time my cousin Louise and I were so mean to Jimmy, a Métis boy. We'd do things like sticking not one but multiple thumbtacks on his desk chair at school, stifling our giggles to avoid the teacher's wrath when he sat on them. Alice was Métis too.

You are not to go to that girl's house, my mother said.

Why not? I asked.

Because I said.

She wouldn't give me a reason, but I had learned why. This lesson was not in the curriculum, but it was of great import. Alice and Jimmy were Métis and I was white, and this distinction came with rules about who we could associate with, who was most likely to get strapped and put in detention in the dark closet, about where we lived and whether we got to eat every day, the clothes we wore, the music we listened to, and what we could become when we grew up. The way we were.

And there was the actual curriculum all three of us learned—probably not much different from what the girls are learning: that Canada was the true north strong and free, how Cabot, Cartier, and Champlain sailed the ocean blue to the "New" World. We also learned that Indians scalped missionaries, and Louis Riel was a crazed man executed for treason. Alice and James must have got a different history at home, like maybe how Riel was a hero, a democratically elected Member of Parliament, even if he was expelled twice from the House by some forgettable Ontario Orangeman.

The tribalism of my childhood was rampant. We were either Limeys, Polacks, Galiceans, Krauts, Savages, Chinks, Kikes, Frogs, or worse.

Would I score points if I told the girls how I sassed teachers and got kicked out of class more than once? There's the story of my birth, how there was a blizzard and my mom never made it to the hospital. It was during the Hungarian Revolution and the priest had asked people to billet refugees. My mom was pregnant, big as a whale, living with two strange men who would walk around the house in their underwear. Apparently, I was in such a hurry I ended up being born at home—a fact told like it was adding insult to injury. My mom likes to repeat the story, as if somehow it explains what has become of me.

The girls wouldn't get it. I don't either.

When I first came to Labrador to live with the Innu, I thought I might be free, free from my stories. No one here would know me and I could tell them as much or as little about myself as I wanted. What a relief to be away from friends and family. Could I be more truly, wildly, messily who I was, rather than who the world wanted me to be?

Do we get to change our minds about who we are? My parents never told me anything about that. They told me what I should do, but not about how to do what I wanted to do. And there was also the school to help me unlearn to be me.

It's not easy to stop being who I'm not. Up here on some level I was hoping to touch down, become visible, figure out how one pole of experience is caught up with the other, and know deep inside my body how to live in a world gone terribly awry. And it might be working. I am a stranger in my own country now. Ever more. It's not that I don't have friends or a community or that I don't love my mother despite it all. I'm the outlier, but I've learned I get to change my mind, figure out each and every day what I no longer agree to.

The girls look like they might need to escape my silent brooding, like they might go back to their group, or leave altogether.

Do you have a boyfriend? Nanishi asks instead, noticing that I've resurfaced.

Yeah.

What his name?

Mark.

Are you marry him?

No.

Why not?

Mmm...I don't know.

He good looking?

No, not really. Cute maybe, in a nerdy kind of way.

Things have livened up around us and it may be time to regroup.

I'll send you a copy of the picture if you give me your P.O. box number, I say.

I hand over my notebook and a pen and they each scrawl down their information. They have no idea how beautiful they are, both of them. It's not that they look exotic or novel; it's not a physical thing. No, they're beautiful in the most elementary and innocent way: young and full of life and courage, as well as some unnameable sorrow, and still standing. And a little saucy, like I used to be. I snap their picture one more time and they just keep on smiling at me, as though they know this has been a performance and are amused by it.

The groups have dissolved, and as quickly as the kids were hushed, they're creating mayhem. Two boys are ripping sheets of flip chart paper, bunching them up, and throwing them around like snowballs. Girls and boys leap over and into chairs in what looks like a riotous game of tag. One little rapscallion knocks a table over. I hold my camera close to me and gather the sheets with drawings and words, roll them up into a tube for safekeeping. I help a boy off the floor who has literally just bounced off the wall, flown airborne, and dropped. Two boys are fist fighting. And then, as suddenly as the bedlam started, a little crowd gathers at the door, and one after another they begin to slide out, disappear in their jackets and boots. Sepastien calls them back. He looks over at me and shrugs. Soon the hall is empty, except for us.

That's it, he says.

So much for the groups reporting back to each other.

We did it, Shustin says, and the three of them explode into a nervous laughter. We've just been spun, like a top.

I think we call it a day, Sepastien says.

I grab my jacket, hat and mitts, and camera and head home with the roll of kids' drawings tucked under my arm.

XXI.

Back at my tent I unroll the sheets of paper one by one and lay them out on the floor. The line drawings are mostly simple and spare, some more stylized and anime. A stick figure with long spiky hair claims, *Is good to be cool*. Skulls and crossbones, daunting cans of gas, bottles of alcohol—one with *50%* on the label—and large grotesque heads without bodies dominate the drawings at first glance. One kid has written, *Things I don't like: 1. vandalism, 2. Lists, 3. irony.*

In the drawings of community life, chaos rules. Nothing is as it should be. No order or equilibrium. The heads look ravenous and frightening, like some kind of *atshen* or man-eating monster, and words like *GAS SNIFFERS* and *DRINKING* are scrawled across the page. There are unhappy faces, people with bags jammed in their faces, and others seeing stars. On more than one sheet, small hands have drawn dead people splayed on the ground, larger than life.

My eyes dart from one drawing to another. Some tell a story. *See me drink. See me drive. See me die!!* with corresponding line drawings. One of them has a numbered sequence of events: 1) *children left alone*, next to a drawing of two kids sleeping in a bunk bed beside a woman with a bottle; 2) *woman beaten*, with a stick man punching a woman, one eye a large black circle, the ground strewn with bottles; 3) *badly beat up*, the woman lies in a hospital bed on life support, with a tiny and solitary visitor; 4) *death*, a coffin with a cross on it, next to a lineup of stick people who appear to be running away from the casket.

In contrast to the community drawings, there is peace and balance in the world of *nutshimits*. Things are where and as they should be. Stars shine in the night sky next to the moon and not around people's heads. A bunny is cute with its whiskers and lopsided ears. It's a place where a child has printed *Families stay together* and *father fishing with the children and cutting wood*. The sun is shining, the woman with the happy face is running into the tent, the hunter got his beaver, the dogs pull children on a sled, and the people and tents are protected by trees. In this world, the kid with the spiky hair is paddling a canoe.

Only one thing is askew in these *nutshimits* drawings. Within the smoke escaping upwards from the stovepipe of one of the tents, are the words *Way of life*.

One drawing appears more like scribbles on first glance, but quickly comes into harrowing focus. Big and small people with glum faces stand idly around a house. The scribbles fly out of the roof. They are flames and below these and between them inside the house are small people with *help me* and *help me* and *help me* in text bubbles. A small person standing next to a gas can and away from the house, is also calling out *help me*.

The drawing brings me face to face with the naked truth. A child, with a marker in hand, has exposed the unfathomable, the unspeakable. It is pointless to avert my eyes, the image has penetrated deep, sunk its clutches into me. The fire burns fiercely before me. It won't let go, hits me in the face. My gut constricts, a knot reaches for my throat, my head is pounding.

Outside the house and its inferno, the cold bites. A scrum of people, half-dressed, heard the commotion, caught a whiff of the smoke, left the party, or crawled out of bed to see what was happening. They clutch and trip over each other, recoiling from the fire and its raucous cackling, its rage of colours—yellow, red, blue and green flames escaping windows with a squealing whistle, sucked into the wind's demonic frenzy leaping into the sky. Manic, hungry, gasping, guzzling, engulfing walls. Insatiable. The air is prickly and stinging, reeking of all manner of materials burning, melting.

Is anyone in the house? What happened? Asked over and over, and the answer is blunt and there are sobs and children calling *Nikaun* and help me, and they are calling out to be rescued, calling for mercy. Screaming. Their panic is under my skin. Their panic is inside me.

Oh mercy, that their small bodies shut down instantly—an inhalation, a quick surrender. Shock. A blast of pain, a lightning rush into a forever sleep, and then nothing. These children went ahead, went on their journey to meet death, the way was perilous. They went beyond. They discovered death. Did they see a long white light, the warmth of a benevolent God? Did they try to come back, the light extinguished?

I feel sick. I've seen too much. My heart is beating out of my chest, choking my breath. Dogs howl outside my tent.

There were dogs that night. They circled the crowd. They did not bark or growl or bite, but they were sniffing and must have smelled fear and panic, a feverish powerlessness, charred flesh. There was no entering the house, no pulling children out. There was nowhere to turn, nothing to be done. If there'd been water, there would have been a hydrant, there would have been a hose, water spraying. There can be vindication in a spray of water, in a purposeful, controlled jet of water.

The walls collapsed.

The cold in my tent feeds my dread. I should light the fire and I can't bear to light a fire.

Did someone go door-to-door to find out whose children were not home? Was it hours before people knew who and how many? Who told the parents? A mother remembered a head tearing through the birth canal, a first cry, face bright red and squinting in shock, the sweet lightness of chubby cheeks and a two-toothed grin, a first step, a first smelt caught through the ice.

Did anyone fall on their knees to pray—if they did, was it to God the Father or to *Mishtapeu*, a raw beseeching prayer? Surely God has miscalculated, he can make it right. Where is the *kamiteut* when you need him?

The children would have known fire: how to start one, keep it going, cool it down, put it out. They came in from the cold, convened around the wood stove, turned on the hotplate, fell asleep, and a curtain caught fire; or one of them lit a cigarette, gasoline on his breath. Was this a pact? No one knows. They held each other close, then changed their minds and called out?

The fire subsided. How did people pull themselves away? How long did the stench stick to their nostrils? They had to tell their children. Kids who witnessed the fire must have told brothers and sisters and friends, and the news spread, thrashing everyone in its wake. When and how hard did they land from this cyclone that picked them all up in a whirling human terror of ceasing to exist, set them down in a slow spin, futile and helpless?

Precious little children.

Crying is all there is. My chest heaves with a quiet sob.

The child has drawn his version of hell, like the picture Sister Paul showed our grade one class, a picture of the dark abyss of hell, enveloped in flames with human bodies wrenched into various states of agony plummeting into the bottomless chasm. Naked bodies. Shame mixed with horror.

All the things that might matter, small and big passions—love and pain, turmoil, beauty, hope—may arise, flare up, and subside in life, but how does anyone go on from this? The fire continues to smolder in every blood cell, every thought of the living. Parents are listening in the silence of their children's absence, and they must hear them stir in the morning, their footsteps coming in from the outdoors, their laughter, their cries for help.

My heart, split open, is still beating. The Milky Way, the moon, the mountains are all intact; branches still hang from the trees.

Nothing has prepared me for this, none of the sorrows of my own life, not the grief and betrayals that surfaced during the sweat. Nothing comes close, and there's no making sense of it. We are complicit, all of us fallen into the wreckage, fallen from grace.

In all my weeks here, I have not heard one bad word spoken about the parents, not one word of reprimand. There is no punishment to be meted out. There was a then and there is a now.

Chilled to the bone, it hurts to stand and it hurts to lie down, and it hurts to open my eyes to the light and it hurts to shut them, and all I can see are the drawings. Help me.

XXII.

The entrance to the gym is blocked, the space maxed out with people. The air fills with the sounds of crying babies, the consumptive coughs of Elders and smokers, of chairs being scraped across the floor, children running and screaming, outbursts of laughter. The basketball hoops are raised and out of the way; rows of chairs are lined up with an aisle between them and on each side. A boy on stage stacks a pile of wood teepee-style, like a campfire in front of a small Innu tent. Large banners serve as backdrop. Simple and stark, they feature silhouettes of a crow, a caribou, a leaping char, a goose in flight, a bear, and a sun, each outlined in a halo of white against a shadowy background.

The play *Boneman—Kaiatshits*, created by high school students with their teacher, is about to start. A couple of small kids have climbed on stage and are undoing the carefully stacked pile of wood. The boy stage manager quickly shoos them off. They bow and blow kisses to the audience as they exit.

The lights go down. Four youth dressed in caribou skins walk onto the stage and sit in a circle around the campfire. The noise in the room abates. I stand on my chair at the back to snap pictures. I'd prefer to just sit and watch, be swept away by the performance, but we need these pictures for the report. With no flash and an 800 ISO black-and-white film, the images will be high contrast with a soft focus.

One of the actors stirs, a boy transformed into a man, an old trembling man. He reaches for his walking stick and pries himself up, his movements slow and studied. He is hunched over, standing bow-legged. Mountains, rivers, lakes, trees, the sun and moon have shaped this body. It's Tshipesh, without his signature baseball cap worn backwards. Instead he sports a canvas Innu hunting hat, decorated with bric-a-brac, the earflaps tied up. Hard to imagine he's the same guy who was at the school workshop and at the gathering, sliding down the hill standing on his toboggan, a natural athlete, cheeky, joyful. Tonight his body and gait have absorbed the ancient sorrow and arthritic joints of an old man. He leans into his stick and takes a few small, deliberate steps. He bends to reach his hand down, teeters but regains his balance, grabs a large bone on the ground, a caribou femur, and continues on his way. Except for a few rustling noises, the audience sits in prayerful silence as he crosses the stage. Once he's disappeared, the others in the circle stand and scurry offstage.

A nurse walks onstage. She enters a home, snatches a baby from a mother's arms, and leaves. The mother is left doubled over, her hands cupped over her face, no one to console her. The lights fade and rise again. A store clerk stands a gun on its end and the Innu hunter slowly stacks a pile of skins to reach the height of the gun he wants to buy. He's a long way off his goal.

With a click of a finger, my camera captures each scene as it unfolds.

Words are sparse so far, sometimes in English and other times in Innu-aimun, always at cross purposes. The actors shout their lines in a desperate attempt to outwit the impossible acoustics of a gymnasium, but it matters not one bit. There is poetry and power in the simplicity of each scene.

Shuni walks onto the stage—the priest, with ghostly white makeup and hair pulled back uncompromisingly. Fearless and grotesque, she walks over to the front right side of the stage and begins to preach with a hoarse, spooky voice.

Sinners, awake! You must repent or you will burn in the fires of hell!

On the other end of the stage, the group in caribou skins circle around their Elder, as if dancing to an Innu drum. They circle closer and closer, with each step growing more aggressive and focused, stomp, stomp, and soon the old man is trapped.

I want to talk to you about pagan ceremonies, the priest cries out. I am talking about the *makushan* and the worship of false gods. I warn you. The power of the almighty Jesus Christ is the only power on earth! God has invested a power in me, your priest, that cannot and will not be challenged by such savage practices! They must come to an end!

Amen! Amen! Amen! the followers respond, as they push and shove their Elder across the stage, corral him before a cross that stands by the banner with the crow basking under a bright yellow sun.

What shall we do with the Boneman? the priest bellows.

Crucify him! Crucify him! Crucify him! the group shouts back.

They tie the arms of the old man to the cross, hammer a nail through the palm of each hand. He has surrendered. He is an island. His persecutors kneel around the cross to pray. The sun on the banner behind them forms a halo around the old man's head.

The viewfinder on my camera fogs up from my tears as I try to frame a picture. The room is still and silent, the audience in shock or dismay or heartbreak. An Innu shaman, *kamiteut*, crucified by his own. The play has ended, the actors walk to the front of the stage, take a bow. The applause begins as a low rumble, picks up momentum, and builds, propelling people to their feet.

A lump in my throat persists and my balance is off as I step down from the chair. A flood of spectators sweeps me up and towards the door. We are too devastated to talk. The night air ushers us out and across the road. A caribou carcass lies on the roof of a house, away from the ravenous stray dogs that roam the community, and stars choke the night sky.

XXIII.

We've had our last community meeting, mainly to talk about recommendations. What needs to change? Who needs to do what? We may not have reached everyone, but we've talked to many. The clock is ticking and the report needs to be written.

That's your job, Manish says. I trust you. That's why we hired you.

It's not my first report, but this one is different. Maybe you need a real writer.

I don't know, I say. How do we make sure it doesn't turn into a whitey-white-woman-speaks-for-the-Innu report?

Just write it.

You're a good writer.

But I'm chief, remember?

Okay, but you're in charge of finding people for the translation. Which you know means what people said will be changed one more time. There's what people said in Innu to start with, translated into English, filtered through my mind and back to Innu on paper. I hope people will recognize their words.

You think too much.

What about grammar? I ask. Should I standardize it? I kind of like the way people use English here, like it's your own dialect.

Just fix it, make us sound "correct," Manish says, with a sarcastic twist on the last word.

Just write what the people said, she adds, a hint of annoyance now in her voice.

Better wait to ask her about the acknowledgements, and I'm leaving the introduction for her to write. Her job as chief.

The transcripts are all typed up, and I've read every word over and over, so many times I can barely stand to look at them. My weekend solitude has me printing out the transcripts, cutting them up, sorting and glueing them onto sheets of flip chart paper according to themes. Words and quotes have been highlighted, tabulated, annotated. I've pulled my hair out, boiled the kettle for multiple cups of tea, staved off the urge to catch the next plane out of town. More cutting and pasting, like in kindergarten, but a whole day of it. Bits containing barely a whole line are stacked into piles by theme. Some don't fit into any particular pile and others belong in more than one.

The door opens and Tapit walks right into the midst of my sorting. He's followed by a gust of wind that sweeps up and scatters my careful little piles. Bits of paper fall like snowflakes, soundlessly, aimlessly.

Having fun? Tapit asks as we both stoop down to pick them all up.

Don't know about fun, but my nerves are shot, I say.

Nervous? Why nervous? he asks.

The writing. I keep thinking about what Mishta-Pinip said at the land claims meeting last year. About how the Innu have never written their stories in the past. This is not the Innu way, he said.

It's time we did, Tapit says, his left eye closed for some reason. Like he's not sure.

But you know how Mishta-Pinip says writing is lying. There are lies hidden in English words, he said. *Kakeshauts* use their words to trick the Innu.

But this report is the stories of the people. The true stories, their words. Nobody's making money from this, only to pay the workers. No one even asked to be paid for an interview. This is our report.

Tapit is circling the table, scanning the sheets now, squinting. He nods indiscriminately, his lips pursed.

You were there, I say, at that land claims meeting when Mishta-Pinip talked about how *kakeshauts* write things down, and Innu leaders too when they go out to meetings. Remember he was so mad? They write every word down, he said, but then where do they go? Their words and papers don't get shared with anybody.

We try to have meeting sometimes to let people know what's going on, Tapit says. But they don't always work out. You know that. It's very very hard to explain to Elders, we don't always know the words. He's right that there's secrets hiding in so many English words.

I really hope it's different this time, I say. But how can it be, with me writing, and in English?

We never do anything like this before. Innu people, anybody will see the report this time. Maybe they read it. See what happens, Tapit says with his usual optimism.

I thought he might have a suggestion or two, a comment, about the tangled mess he's just perused.

See you. Don't work too hard, he says with a grin.

That'll be the day, I say.

A blast of cold air enters as he closes the door behind him, and my bits of paper scatter again. I shiver and shudder. The true stories, he said.

Mishta-Pinip had ranted even longer about writing and truth. This land claims agreement, whatever it was, he said, is just another government "paper," not to be trusted. He talked about the knowledge of Elders, how the land was their library. Sepastien did his best to translate how Innu knowing was about doing, and Innu practices and ways were about beliefs and connections with the Spirits. Innu have to always be hunting and on the land, communicating with the animals, Mishta-Pinip said. They need to know the craft and care of canoes and toboggans; places, and their names and stories; how to make and break camp. He talked about protocol, showing respect, about ways the Innu must stalk game and set traps, the importance of never wasting anything, always watching for trouble, planning ahead and learning from the past. You couldn't know if you didn't do. It's wasn't about writing it down. You couldn't learn these things from a book. You couldn't sell knowledge, just as land was not anybody's to buy and sell.

Who will play the drum? he asked. Who will sing?

Was he pleading for dreaming, rather than writing? It was like he was saying writing was a kind of blasphemy. You could hear a pin drop in the room as he spoke. Sepastien had translated at great length. He seemed intent that the *kakeshauts* understand this. One of the government reps was looking down into his lap the whole time, and the other one was smiling awkwardly. I wish I'd taken notes.

If knowledge is always in the doing, it's always changing, never exactly the same. Mishta-Pinip had helped me understand why the Innu so often qualify their words. They'll say, This is what I saw or experienced myself, or This is what I've been told, I'm conveying secondhand information, I cannot be certain of the truth of my words. *Put* sprinkled throughout any conversation. Maybe. Theirs is a knowledge that is constantly interpreted and negotiated, singular, and deferential. Writing knowledge down makes it permanent, static, unchangeable, incarcerated.

Yet, Innu knowledge is key to survival. To what extent can it be improvised or compromised? Autonomy may be paramount, but there is little room for infidels, outliers making up their own rules, because if you believe and respect, life will reward you and won't let you die before your time.

Something like that, this was my understanding of Sepastien's translation: his attempt to reconstruct Mishta-Pinip's argument in English. Maybe I got it right?

My job now is to make meaning from these transcripts, write it all down, make these stories permanent, in English, a language sprung from a culture that has devastated this place. Sorry Mishta-Pinip. The words are typed, read, churned over in my mind. It's time to channel. Manish said stick to the transcripts, what people said. There'll be a chapter for each question. There is no one to show me the way. This can be a conversation between me and the words. I swallow my hesitance and forge ahead with the reckoning, consideration, calculation, estimation, summation of all these little piles of paper. This is the attack of a simple researcher, but my intuition also has ideas: inklings and hunches. Trust it. Don't stray, stay with the words, the very words. The best quotes are inserted to let them tell the story and dominate the page. Names are attached; forget confidentiality. Some remain anonymous, but most people said yes, you can use my name. They can stand proud by what they said. And the kids' drawings and photos, old and new, will show not tell, illustrate the words.

Before I know it, "we" has replaced "they." It's like I'm inviting the voices in to write with me, because what right do I have to write it on my own? My keyboard clickety-clicks as whole words and whole sentences are plucked from the transcripts to become the text. Some people said this and some people said that. Cut and paste, only this time on the computer. Is it plagiarism to try to write in their words, the way they use English? Why not use their very words, avoid another alteration? Let it be one less translation, but with minor grammar tweaks for clarity.

Clearly there's no need to interpret, change, or add to Utshimashkueu's words:

In the past, Innu live in innutshuap with open fire in the middle. He use caribou hides to cover the teepees. It was hard times, but we don't mind because it is our culture. We are safe in the teepees; we never have to worry about fires. Innu can also sleep outside, around a fire, for three nights. When the whites come to take and exploit our lands, they never ask permission from anyone. They never ask any Innu to sign a paper saying they take our land and destroy it so that he can make money whenever and whatever way he want off our land. The kakeshauts just come, give us houses with no water and toilets, schools, a clinic, a tiny amount of money each month for each family. He did this to keep us in one place so he can take and destroy our land. At the same time he kill our culture and our language, he steal our children from us, give them to white parents, put them in a white school, steal from them who they are. There never is a meeting to talk to us about these things, to ask us what we think about the changes. Never did a kakeshau say to us: We see that these beautiful and rich lands belong to the Innu, they are not ours. Never did the kakeshauts ask us if we agree that they come on our lands, that they exploit our resources and destroy it. Never did they ask if they could dam our rivers, fly their military jets, and pollute our lakes. Never did the kakeshauts warn us that we might regret them coming here. They just bring their bulldozers, their axes, build their mines and their dams, they never ask how we feel about drinking polluted water, eating poison fish. They never ask how we feel when we eat the animals poison with their pollution. The kakeshauts never ask us about the jobs they make off our lands only for kakeshauts. Maybe the Innu get a job for a few months but then the kakeshauts don't need the Innu anymore? The kakeshauts don't worry about what the Innu do now to feed his family.

I've never been one to write in a noisy coffee shop, yet this office, constantly full of people reading over my shoulder, doesn't rankle me. I'm on a roll and this is nothing like any writing I've done before. No sitting and self-flagellation, starting and deleting, cutting and bleeding on the page. Not the frightening solitude verging on madness, or staying up all night and sitting to the ominous point of searing pain in my hips, no longer able to carry on a conversation, hair like Medusa's, making it perfect, editing, and editing again.

There's no editing when you tell a story out loud.

Self-doubt can lead a person to try the untried.

My fingers on the keyboard are performing with eagles soaring over a cliff, riding thermals and updrafts, foraging, picking up and dropping bits. More cutting and pasting, moving paragraphs around, creating a logical flow and trajectory—all of this has me surrendering to an unconscious aerial current, steering me.

This is still a very painful time for us. This is not the first time tragedy struck our people. Since 1973 we lose 47 people to alcohol. Everyone here touched by tragedy. We decided to hold a People's Inquiry. It was time to stop and ask why these accidents and violent deaths happen. Too many people died. We thank the Minister of Indian Affairs for turning down our request for a public inquiry. He said they want to do an engineering study. This would be his government's inquiry. We thank Tshishe-utshimau for giving us the opportunity to do our own. We hope this gathering of voices break the silence of a forgotten people. We hope this report help us find a meshkaia for our children, so we know where we going.

Pause. I peer over the edge of the cliff, alert, aware. There is something outrageous about me writing this report. The joy in breaking rules. Throwing stones at the Voice of Western Science who is standing on guard. Is this honest? Should I be sharing my thought process, discussing the contradictions, revealing truths about how to bridge the worlds? What we did right and where we failed. Like I might really know? Do the Innu care about these preoccupations? What could I say about my intuition and performing with eagles?

Never mind. Everyone can see the unseen in proportion to the clarity of their heart. My heart is talking to me, to itself, and it is saying, Listen to me. Listen closely.

> *We didn't know moving to this village would bring so many problems. My son suicide himself. Twenty years stuck in village. I am angry all the time. My wife and my children scared of me. Alcohol control me. Then I quit and my family not scared any more. The things I neglect to tell my children, so many things, the voices of my grandparents, about the pakutshashkᵘ the snowshoes and the caribou, the spirits, respect the tshissenuat. I start to talk to my other children. Now one of my son dream. Maybe if he dream some more times, he can play the drum.*

If readers can listen carefully too, they'll hear a tone in the writing that says, you the uninvited have lied to us and this is the truth. There is no code to crack. Truth is woven within and between the words, crushing the lies, breaking the silence, an ocean of silence, the unspeakable, repressed, erased, unheard.

Deep breath, and my eyes look up to meet the ceiling, tiles stained from a leak, interrupted with a fluorescent light. My arms reach up and up to stretch. Outside the sky is a screaming red and orange and violet. This is a re-storying of the land, history remade. Bits and pieces of stories, opinions, rants, confessions, judgments, drawings, absolutions, nuanced and complex, are being arranged into a mosaic of their world. I could never muster such eloquence.

> *It is time to get up now. We been sleeping all along while the white people been doing everything for us. Something woke us up, and it's the noise of the jets. When we woke up, we see the jets are not our only problem. There is a pile of other problems in our community. The government think we will never wake up. It is time to clean up the mess while we were sleeping. We need to solve our own problems.*

A printout of each completed chapter is handed to the rest of the team and some leaders—Penute, Makuss, Shuash, Manish, Tanien, the office secretary, Pishum, and Katnen, and whoever else just happens to drop by. Chapters get swapped and taken home. People read slowly and quietly by themselves, for themselves. This is not a story shared in a circle; reading is a private act. Is this also the danger of the written word? Can it be communal if they are all reading the thing separately, but in the same space and time? Does the "we" throughout the report make it so?

Did I get it right? I ask. Should I change anything?

They hand the *mashinanikana* back.

Miam, Katnen says. It is good, repeated by the lot of them.

This is our bible now, Sepastien says.

Not a solitary edit suggested from any of them. I've been known to squabble, put my life on the line over a word, a point, a single comma. Is it possible that there is not one thing to dispute about this writing?

Once the report is printed, we won't be able to change anything, I say.

Aren't they wondering about this *kakeshau* woman reconstructing their story? Or it's more likely that you don't tell anyone how to tell their story in their world. And besides, no one's story is ever the last word; it's always evolving, depending on the storyteller.

Not one of them has asked about the "we," about what it might feel like to be a ventriloquist. I'd tell them it feels more like being a surrogate mother. I am the vessel, giving birth, but this is not my baby. "Surrogate mother" would make an interesting credit on the cover, but there is no way my name will appear on this cover. How could it? These are not my words. People will wonder about the writer. Let them.

There might be a ghost of me in this ghost writing, but I do not recognize myself. Can my writing really not be my own? Could this writing have its own intelligence, know more than me? The best thing to do is just get out of the way.

Thoughts vacillate this way and that, between certainty and doubt, so why don't I feel more unsettled?

Here, my gift to you, I want to say, but I don't. Knowing is in the act, Mishta-Pinip said.

XXIV.

I've been summoned? I say as I walk into Manish's office, a gentle tease in my voice.

Close the door, she says, her face deadpan. Her demeanour even more opaque than usual. She's still bundled up in her parka, the same one she wore when we went hunting.

What's up, *Utshimashkueu*? I ask.

She leans back in her chair behind the desk, the mountain of papers a dishevelled mess; a stack of trays in one corner bulges with more documents. Her filing system is the same as mine. She seems about to respond, but stops herself midway. It's not like Manish to be secretive. She ignores my question.

Tapit thinks we should have a meeting, she says. About the report.

You mean Tapit who keeps saying, We'll see what happens? I ask.

Tapit, who's president of the Innu Nation.

Yes, he is that guy too, I say.

As you know, he read your draft and he wants to talk about it. He's on his way.

She points her head to the window as she collects several sheets of paper, bounces them vertically to line them up, staples them together, and plops them into the top tray with a certain impatient aplomb.

So, is there a problem? I ask.

Wait. Tapit will talk to you.

On the wall hangs a blown-up photograph of Manish's late grandfather. I see the resemblance, the full lips, the same open and confident half-smile. He'd looked straight into the camera lens, like he enjoyed having his picture taken, dapper in his khaki green jacket, round glasses—like a professor might wear—and a wool fedora perhaps a size too small.

A pack of snowmobiles roar up to the building, and Tapit strolls in, followed by Makuss and Penute, both Innu Nation board members. Tapit closes the door behind him.

What's up? I ask.

I read the report, your draft, Tapit says.

You *really* read it?

This is *so* an oral culture, and I'm never sure things get read, or are actually readable. This report is different though. Manish's mouth stirs by a hair. Could that be a glint of a smile in her eyes?

This isn't a joke, Tapit says.

I wasn't making a joke, I say.

Is this really your report? he says. This is it, all of it? He waves his hand dismissively at the document on the desk.

It's not "my" report. These are the words of the people we talked to. What's the problem?

Outside the window behind Manish, a couple is arguing. Tuminik and Teinish. Their hollering penetrates the walls. His hand flails dangerously close to her face as she stands there looking anxious and cold, wearing only a Supergirl T-shirt and jeans. Where's her jacket? Oh good, she's turning and walking away, and surprisingly Tuminik lets her go.

Tapit had seen all the notes that day in the office, the flip charts, and people's words in piles, how I obsessed over them.

We can't give this to governments, he says. Or the media.

Why not?

Tuminik is still out there, shouting to what seems like the whole village now, shaking his fist, his long hair whirling wildly around his face.

It's like a child speaking...it's for children, Tapit says.

He spits the last word. It *is* for the children, but he doesn't mean it that way. Feedback finally, but this? Usually Tapit and I can agree to disagree. He often calls me, to talk things through, Innu Nation business, to bounce ideas off me and try to figure things out. We've been friends a long time, since our meeting at university in St. John's, when I'd sometimes lend him my car. I made a quilt for his firstborn son and his wife even trusts me. At least sometimes.

What do you mean? I ask, biting my tongue.

No one will take this seriously.

I disagree, I say.

I don't like it, Tapit says.

Tell me what you really think, I say, unable to stop myself. It's not academic enough? Should there be more jargon? Policy recommendations? Talk of jurisdictions? All of that is in there, just not in that language.

Being defensive is never a good defense. There are people in this room who read drafts of the work. Why aren't they speaking up? They look away from my x-ray glare.

I just tried to write it in a way that the reader could really hear people's voices, I say. These are the words people used. This is the way they talk, at least in English. And people here need to be able to read it, if they are able to read. They should be able to recognize themselves, understand it. I didn't make anything up.

I sound strangely sure of myself.

It's not professional, he says.

I'm not a professional. Remember? That's why you hired me.

Tapit is staring out the window, although the drama seems to have moved on. I glance back at Manish quickly, my mouth clenched back and downward. She smiles at my look of trepidation, but this report needs more than a smile of support.

Still no response from Tapit, and outside the window Teinish is face-to-face with Tuminik again. This time she's wearing her jacket. The hollering has begun again, the decibel level rising—something about *kamatshishit.* She steps back from him, tears off her gloves, and shoves them into her pockets. Geez, did she just haul off her wedding ring and throw it at him?

I really think this will be okay, I say. This report does not need me explaining what people said in my words.

More silence. Manish is my best bet, but I can tell she's not about to jump in. Thanks for the solidarity.

Tapit?

It's not like him to be without words.

Did Bob read it? he finally asks.

Yes, it's been vetted by the lawyers.

I want to get snarky, but I catch myself.

What did he say? Tapit asks.

He says it's good. He's mainly worried about the deadline. Will we be able to get it translated into Innu on time? It has to be in both languages and we have a little more than two weeks to get it to the printers, so it'll be ready for the press conference in Ottawa next month. Translation's a big job. The layout takes time, in both languages: Innu on one side and flip over to English on the other.

I don't like it, Tapit says again.

Bob's right, I say. The deadline is creeping up fast. It'll be okay. This doesn't need to be a *kakeshau* kind of report. Trust me.

He looks away to avoid catching my eye. Just let the people speak, I want to say. No one else will look at me either, not Makuss, Penote, or Manish. No one has defended the report, but they also haven't agreed with Tapit. The silence closes in on me and I can't just sit here.

Sorry, I really gotta go now, I say. There's something I have to do.

I march straight out of the office and out of the building, down the stairs, and right up to Tumunik and Teinish. He's got her by the sleeve now and I grab each of them by the their jackets and pull them apart.

You guys need a little time out, I say. You go home Teinish, and I point her in the right direction. Tuminik, to your parents, or your grandparents, anywhere but home.

The two of them head off in opposite directions, just as they're told.

Manish stands at the window looking out at me. Laughing and clapping and mouthing, You're crazy.

Sometimes it's no damn good just to stand there.

XXV.

Are you packed? Manish asks from the doorway of my tent. My humble abode of the last few months is swept and tidied, its buckets filled with water. The land of toilets and candlelit bubble baths beckons. Green vegetables, too.

Almost, I say, as I stash my journal into my bag. It's untouched, pages blank and white, not one word entered in it. No confessions of fear, love, hurt, or rage, no cloying feelings, humorous anecdotes, or brilliant epiphany. It's unfortunate. Oral tradition would die if it was left to my memory.

My moccasins are tucked again into the side of my bag, and the children's drawings lie carefully folded on top. They'll need to somehow be shrunk to fit in the report. The children's voices, the heart of it all. We might have to hire a proper photographer.

I'll drive you to the airport, Manish says.

She seems pretty cheerful. I'm trying to make a brave place in my heart as I head home, as home as any place can get for me on this planet. Water is dripping off the tree branches onto the tent. Spring has taken hold decisively, the days moved yet farther from the dark and sluggish hours. Still each day has continued to be a sad, sad day, and it's hard to leave this cocoon of sorrow.

What will you do now? Manish asks. Our eyes meet. The spring sun has tanned her face, coaxed more freckles across her cheeks. Freckles are a thing we have in common.

Well, I have a ton to do yet on the report. Pages of Innu still to type up. Letter by jeezly letter, I say, articulating each syllable with my nose turned up in disgust.

Manish laughs, like a big laugh. Haha.

My last days have been spent on this chore. Manish succeeded in finding a small army of helpers. Usually people run from translation work like flies avoiding a swat.

How will you find people? I'd asked her.

I'll bribe them, and if that don't work—threaten them, she said.

Those who'd read chapters signed up, and she must have hauled people off the road. But she actually pulled off a translation, all sixty-five pages of it.

Sheet after sheet of foolscap got typed up, by me. Mouthing each letter individually helps me to not lose my place. It's handy to be able to type eighty words a minute, without looking at the keyboard. Maybe forty in Innu. I ignored spellings—how the same word is spelled differently by different people, and sometimes even by the same person in the same paragraph. Best to avoid straying into the no-white-person-is-going-to-tell-me-how-to-write-my-own-language conversation, although I may live to regret it.

But I do have my limits.

Where are your commas and periods? I asked Sepastien. I can't figure out where I am in the English text.

Why you need to know? Sepastien asked. Just type it.

We need *some* commas and periods, I insisted as I handed him the sheet.

His punctuation hardly seemed to coincide with the original, but they'd have to do. I was not so naïve as to believe that the English version could just flow into the grammar and syntax and cosmos of Innu-aimun. The hazards of translation have truly sunk in again, the stakes that much higher. Every word is both compromise and compensation—almost right, kind of wrong in the search of the elusive equivocation. Creating new and different meanings, they betray their origins. How could I begrudge their choices?

Several bodies, a few committed souls, had worked well into the night with me, all of them moaning and groaning, joking and teasing me, as if they were doing me a favour.

Can you proofread this? I asked Katnen as I handed her the typed sheet of her translation.

She looked at me like I was cracked. There had to be typos, dozens of them. I'd have to check it myself, letter by letter, again. I had some word recognition, but not much.

But that's it.

The truth is this whole translation exercise brought relief to my last days.

You still need to write the acknowledgements and a foreword on why we did this, I remind Manish now. Soon. In both languages.

I'll fax it tomorrow, she says. What should I say?

You'll figure it out.

I grab my film from the shelf—three rolls to be developed—and throw them into my backpack. Ninety-six shots, the last captured a couple days ago. The band *Ashuapun* showed up at the office in the afternoon with the words to their song about the children lost. They wanted a group photo. All four members wore ball caps and fluorescent sunglasses, and carried their instruments—a guitar, a bass, keyboard, and drumsticks. We headed into the sunshine and they posed on the wharf with the white ice of the sea behind them and the sky a cobalt blue. Handsome Boy Samish looked sheepish until I called them to attention.

Look like you just killed a song, I said as I motioned for them to stand closer, and set the shutter speed to compensate for the bright light.

I'll send you a copy, for your first cassette cover, I called out as they hurried away, their shyness intact.

Done, I say to Manish as I zip my bag shut.

She grabs it, leaving me to carry my backpack and snowshoes, and we head out to her snowmobile. She decides to take the scenic route over the melting ice, squeezes the throttle tight, and we're skimming over huge pools of turquoise water. It's come to this. Death on the ice. Above our heads *nishkats* form an immense white V against the cloudless azure skies.

Look, Manish yells at me as she points to the geese.

Watch where you're going, I say.

We round the bend and soon we're at the airstrip. Sepastien, Akat, Shustin, and Kananin are all there, and it's hugs all around. Napaen said his goodbyes yesterday, even managed a half smile. Tapit is at the hangar too and walks over, gives me a discrete little pat on the arm as he sidles by. My bag reaches the plane just as the co-pilot is about to shut the luggage door. He swings it up into the compartment as I head back to prolong goodbyes.

By the way, your plane's leaving, Manish says, shooing me towards it.

She mouths a silent "thank you."

See you at the press conference, she says.

Ottawa won't know what hit it, I say. Are you sure you want me there?

Oh yeah.

Iame apishish, I say to the lot of them. It really is a little goodbye and I'll see them soon.

I'm running to the plane, climbing the steps, turning to wave one last farewell. I beeline it to the nearest window seat. I'm sitting and clutching my bag. I am not crying, and I'm unaware of who else is sitting around me; this aircraft is mine, mine alone, as it turns, taxis to the end of the gravel runway, turns again, and pauses to rev its engines.

A wolf stands at the edge of the runway: long bushy tail, thick grey fur with a swath of black across its back. His head and large broad muzzle point up, ears pulled back, eyes closed. I can see his breath, a glint of his teeth. Inaudible above the roar of the plane's engines, he is howling, howling for his friends, a wild defiant howl of sorrow for all that has been and will be lost.

The pilot twiddles the throttle and nudges the plane forward. It rambles down the middle of the bumpy runway, gradually accelerating. I'm still clutching my knapsack with my computer, notes, and film as the large metal bird frees itself from the pull of gravity and rises. Up and up we go and to the east a whole world is melting away. Far out to sea the turquoise ice seems tender, surrendering to the deep blue waters. There's no retrieving it.

Below, children stream out of the school for lunch. An-Pinamen is hobbling her way home from the store, a pack of dogs is circling with hackles raised, and snowmobiles criss-cross each other's paths.

This is another world, surely, but as real and defined as the one this plane is headed towards. Borders are diminishing midair.

The village gives way to the barrens and mountains and snow glowing in the sun. The plane bounces over this vast world of black and white, through a light that is pure, glareless, and transparent. The relentlessness of the landscape reminds me of the prairies, a weary monotony of a different, monumental kind with its unbroken flow of land, the way in which the sky is open from one side of the horizon to the other. Where a mountain could seem like some kind of impertinence. This vista, too, is indelibly lodged somewhere inside my skull.

The nerve to return home is white-knuckled. There's Mark, who'll be waiting for me, and our fight. It won't be a Hallmark card reunion. He'll be meeting a different person at the airport. Each time I come here I'm changed, but this time the place has sunk deep into me.

How was it? people will ask, and words will fail me as usual. It's like my story has only just begun; it's changed, and the implications are unclear. Where to start explaining? Again. The last few months have brought me to the precipice of unknowing, stumbling yet again on all that I don't know. There are anecdotes to be shared, but people will want to know why things are the way they are. They'll want me to pronounce and judge, but generalizations are dangerous, including this one: is it not my job to help people know what I don't know? There's no one to share the load and there's Mark who likes to point out that I have issues.

You need to get over your guilt complex, he's told me more than once. He's right.

It's so much easier to listen to a story than tell one. What are the words for sorrow in a world that denies death? And for bewilderment in a world that champions experts? Only a fool believes he understands the world. And how could anyone understand without experiencing the backdrop of this far north, its woodsmoke and candlelight, aurora borealis; the swelter of a sweat; an old woman sitting on boughs lifting a hot dipper of tea to her lips, a baby cooing in his *ueuepishun*; its uncut forest, unpenned animals, unmined land, all those rivers undammed. More than ten thousand years of bodies rest in the ground below, feeding the life that still lives there: the Innu and the caribou, furry and feathered and water creatures, the birch and the firs and the spruce, the lichen and fireweed. The encroaching thievery. What's a story without a setting? People only know of its misery and bleakness.

Dark clouds are growing out of the horizon to the south, casting blue shadows on the land ahead. Above us, white clouds are moving surely across the immense sky, their bottoms as even as if they had scraped themselves flat against the Mealy Mountains.

The world I am returning to has moved on without me for years, long before I came in March. I am an exile. And what have I missed this time? A season has passed in its journey around the circle and what changes might have occurred in fashions this spring, what new songs have been released, books launched? Which new war has been waged, and which of my friends have split with each other for what unforgivable transgression, and who is more right than the other? I am going back to the hypnotic drug of television and radio and newspaper, wildly erroneous news reports delivered in smooth professional voices, all cloned, the voices of gods beyond doubting.

We're getting rid of that television, I'm going to say to Mark. I'd said that very thing to Manish.

Maybe you should get rid of your TV, I told her.

Rid of my TV? She looked puzzled.

It's trouble.

Yeah, I know, but my kids will never let me.

I've dozed off and the jolt of our landing in Goose Bay wakes me. I switch planes in my grogginess and continue on my way.

We approach St. John's above the Narrows, the harbour engulfed in a thin fog. The sun shines above it and the town's bright colours permeate its haze. My throat hurts and my ears are paining. The pilot slides the plane onto the runway with startling ease.

Mark is waiting at the bottom of the stairs in arrivals, one hand in his pocket, the other waving as I step down towards him.

Anna, he calls out, even as he's looking at me.

It's a voice scared of being wrong, like, is it really me walking towards him?

He curves his arms into huge inviting brackets.

Hey, I say.

I lay my backpack down and let him hold me a while before I put my arms around him too, my hands against his broad back and my head resting on his chest. We stand like this, uncertain, for a long time. We don't know about tomorrow. People rush by unaware. An older couple by the luggage carousel is watching us, both smiling with their own longing.

How was it? Mark asks finally.

I pull away. He fingers the collar on my coat.

Another world, you know, I say, looking down at the ground. It'll take me a while to land.

Here we go. It's started. How long will it take before I'm able to respond? There's the story that's mine to share and the one that's not. It's a dangerous story, between seasons and between worlds, scary, uncomfortable.

I'm sorry about that call, I say.

Mark has reason to be annoyed. I've never been much of a talker, expect him to intuit what's happening with me. He'll go on and on, repeat the same thing over and over, while I expect him to know without me uttering a word.

In the car, I roll down the window to catch the breeze. We drive through suburbs and then streets of brightly coloured houses, attached and clashing more often than not. We peer out of our respective windows, skirting conversation.

In Labrador the bears will soon be leaving their dens.

Mark parks and as we get out of the car, my eyes rest on things that never caught my attention before. The cracks in the sidewalks, my shadow against the gate. Our house leans a little too much into the hill and the paint on the clapboard is peeling, and I arrive a little bit more.

It's good to be home. The air is briny, the sun has dissipated the fog and is shining above the Southside Hills. I missed the crocuses, but tulips and daffodils shine yellow and red and orange, the trees are contemplating leaves, and soon vast swaths of lupins will rise from the ground on those hills. Clouds are gathering from the northwest and snow and ice are a fading memory.

We're getting ready for supper; I light a candle and turn off the lights.

For my father, I say to Mark, and the children who died.

Oh yeah? he says, the tone in his voice nervous, like I've just shut him out.

Come in, come back, I want to say, but I don't. The candle burns as we eat; the wax spills down over the candlestick as the flame's shadows shiver across the walls. Like on the walls of the tent. Mark sits with his red hair down over his eyes, his cheeks glowing in the light, freckles against very white skin. He has shaved for the occasion. I stop eating and rest my fists on the table. There are crumbs caught in the crack that runs down the middle. The window beside us is prefab with smooth edges, sealed tight. My hand reaches for Mark's as my eyes wander the room trying to recognize myself in it. Mark shifts in his chair.

This time apart has been good for us, he says.

There's no point interrupting him as he explains our situation to me. His words are hard to grasp, and there's no taming my own thoughts long enough to nail down words to share. In a minute I'll arrive, really arrive. There's something I must do. I can't remember what, but I know it's important. It hurts more to not belong here. A minute is an awfully long time.

Mark has stopped talking and we continue to eat in silence. When we're done, we get up from the table, gather our plates, glasses, and utensils, and take them to the kitchen. I wash and he dries them, puts them all away. The tree from my dream never did talk to me. What was it Manteshkueu had kept to herself? And Akat and Sepastien? They were in cahoots. They were not going to talk to me on that tree's behalf, on the land's behalf. I had got close to hearing what the tree had to say to me, and now I was too far away again to hear it.

I lean into the kitchen counter, unsure what to do next. Mark walks over and gathers me in his arms. Rain beats down steady on the roof, a full gurgle of water flowing off the shingles, through the eavestrough into the ground, pelting against the window. The devil is in the wind, a creature puffed up with its own breath and outrage.

Thank God I'm not still in a tent, I murmur.

Mark holds me tighter, tucks a strand of my hair behind my ear, and the tangle in my heart lets go a little.

It's not like I even want my grief to go away. It's bound to keep returning. There's no leaping off the road back to how things were. Grief is more than a feeling. It's really an environment, a whole new landscape to my life that I have to get used to. You love someone so much and then one day you wake up and they aren't there. My father may continue to reach out and talk to me. It may take a while before all my memories of people and the land and the fire, recollected in sequence, come together to make sense. A whole community is trying to resurface, after having dove too deep, people's breath trapped in their chests, my chest. People huddled close, watching for one another's peril. Our throats may close and the pressure may seem unbearable, but our bodies will know how to navigate our breath, even if our minds don't. This isn't a puzzle I can think my way out of. There are the sorrows of my mother and grandmother, I need to make peace with them. And with the little girl who spoke up in that sweat, all that she lost. It's time I looked after her.

All that has accompanied me home, the whole weight of it in my body, is a lot, but it can no longer be too much, too sorrowful, too powerful, too scary to embrace it all. I'll have to work slowly, carefully, with every fibre in my body to navigate this new landscape. That's how survival happens—by gentle instinct—if I let it, if I can listen, keep listening, curious, to the soft and hurting part of me. To those things I didn't know I needed to mourn, the things that kept me hurt and small and angry, bred ways that clouded everything along the way: the inattention, distraction, indifference, the shutting down.

It would be very nice if I could tell where one thing ended and the next thing began, but there's always something ending and something beginning. I may not have the words, but my story now has a colour and shape and mood. The lens has been out of focus, but soon maybe the picture will become clearer. And it will change me again. Chances are I will be invited back, and I will return. These last few months will be filed away and I'll want to refer back to them, but they will be blurred and tenuous; the next time, the story will change again. The sins of my fathers belong to me. My hunger is mine. And there is forgiveness. I want to say, I forgive you, but I'm not sure to whom—myself, Mark, the parents whose children die recklessly, my own parents, those wreaking havoc on this planet. Can I ever get there? Forgiveness is a hard word.

Children who die are only remembered as good. Mishta-Pinip said Jesus went to the desert like the Innu went to *nutshimits*. That is what the land can do to a person.

All those tracks I left in the snow, they've melted away by now.

Let's go to bed, I say to Mark.

He lies down on his back, and then turns his back to me. I feel him shaking. I am crying, too, as I curl into him.

It'll be okay, I say.

Will it?

This is shitty and the stakes are high. I can't keep quiet and I can't be calling people out because I feel bad. This is going to be long and excruciating, finding a place for all my grief that is not in my body, and I can't do it alone. I need to start with Mark, and then we'll be two. There's no waiting until I know that I can; maybe I never will.

I move in closer to Mark, the warm bulk of him.

Let's go for a walk tomorrow, I say. I'll tell you about Labrador, and some other things you should know.

Acknowledgements

An earlier draft of this novel served as my thesis for a Masters in Education from Memorial University of Newfoundland. It was a privilege to work with Elizabeth Yeoman and Lisa Moore, the two best supervisors in the world. I am so grateful to Elizabeth for all the conversations, her generosity and belief in my work, astute guidance and helping me trust myself. Many thanks to Lisa for her uncanny and perspicacious eye, for so many lessons on how to flesh out and chisel a story both on and between the lines, for the tough questions and imaginative suggestions, including to look closer and deeper and freer in the first person.

I hardly know where to begin to acknowledge the Mushuau and Sheshatshiu Innu of the unceded territory of Nitassinan. Thanks hardly seem adequate. I am so indebted to all of them for what they have shared with me: their generosity, patience, friendship, forgiveness, skepticism and bullshit detecting, inherent leadership, steely grit and resilience as they endure, survive and thrive. For inviting me to visit and work with them over and over, for feeding me and providing me with a place to sleep both in the community and in *nutshimits*, for all the belly laughs and a lifetime of lessons—*tshinashkumitin.*

I am deeply grateful to Gregory and Akat Rich for their blessing to share this story, for their honesty and courage and resilience.

It was an honour to work closely with Nympha Byrne, George Gregoire, the late Marie Georgette Mistenapeo, Katie Rich, Prote Poker, David Nui, and George Rich on the Davis Inlet People's Inquiry. I am grateful to many other friends and colleagues for sharing their world with me over the last forty years: Manishan Edmonds, Christine and Prote Poker, Kathleen and Damien Benuen, Elizabeth Penashue, Mary Pia Benuen, Germaine Benuen, Jack and Rena Penashue, Natasha Hurley, Petapan and Madison, Kanani Davis, Edward Nuna, Basil Penashue, Peter and Mary Ann Penashue, Alex Andrew, Mary Martha Andrew, Jackie Ashini, Mary Adele Penashue and family, Ben Andrew, Alex Andrew, Elena Andrew, Jean Pierre Ashini, Janet Michel, Sebastien Piwas, Nora Pasteen, Theresa Penashue, Etienne Andrew, David Nuke, Greg and Jeannie Nuna, Victoria Nuna, Helen Aster, Raphael Gregoire, Guy Bellefleur, John and Martyne Nui, Emma Ashini, Joachim Nui, Mary Ann Nui, Amanda Rich, Ann Nuna, Shekau Piwas, Jolene and Jodie Ashini, Kenny Rich, Barbara Fiddler, Annie Pickard, and some who have passed away and are dearly missed: Rose Gregoire, Daniel Ashini, Ben Michel, Greg Penashue, John Poker, Tshenish Pasteen, Agathe and Edward Piwas, Charlotte Gregoire, Mary Jane Nui, Daniel Nuna, Mary Adele Andrew, Cecilia Rich, Matthew Rich, Frances Penashue, Kathleen and George Nuna, Angela Andrew, Mary-May Osmond, Mary Ann and Simon Michel, Anniet and Matthew Nuna, Apenam Pone, Louis Penashue, Caroline Andrew, Maurice Penashue, Yvonne Asta, Penash Pone, Charlie Andrew, George Ashini, Tony Penashue, and Mary Martha Rich.

A number of mentors and writers have helped me learn the craft over the years. Thanks to Sue Goyette, a wicked writing coach, and The Common—Wanda Nolan, Sue Carter, Jaime Forsythe, Ryan Turner, Sarah Mian, Stephanie Domet, and Carsten Knox, with whom I flexed a muscle and practiced spinning stories. Thanks as well to my colleagues in Lisa Moore's writing class, especially to Sharon Bala, Carmella Gray-Cosgrove, Olivia Robinson, Angela Antle, and Jacob Bachinger for their attention to detail and encouragement. Alissa York at the Banff Wired Writing Studio helped me find my feet, and Joan Clark inspired me to change direction and write the story I was really yearning to tell.

A number of people read early drafts of this novel and provided insightful feedback: Marjorie Beaucage, Ryan Turner, Andy Jones, Prote Poker, Kathleen Benuen, Peter Armitage, Sylvia Moore, Mary Pia Benuen, Manishan Edmonds, Kanani Davis, Kathleen Kearns, Debbie Sherrard, Mario Blaser, Bobbie Boland, Philip Lewis, Christiane Henningsen, Grace Bavington, Melody Morton Ninomiya, Linda Dale, Bernadette Power, Lynne-Marie Hickey, Nympha Byrne, Jacinthe Tremblay, Clara McCue, Wayne Boone, Karen Daley, Debbie McGee, Phyllis Artiss, Bruce Gilbert, Esmée Gilbert, Isabella St. John, Jane Robinson, Helen Murphy, Kathleen Knowling, Rosie Myers, Rita Kindl Myers, Aline Reid, Cathia Finkel, Christine Poker, and Anne Fouillard. I am indebted to these people.

During the course of writing this novel, I consulted many texts, and owe a debt to all their creators, but the following deserve particular mention for inspiring and influencing my thinking in the research and writing for this novel:

Mamunitau Staianimuanu: Ntuapatetu Tshetshi Uitshiiakuts Stuassiminut/Gathering Voices: Finding Strength to Help Our Children: the Davis Inlet People's Inquiry report, for source material and inspiration;

Georg Henriksen and John Poker (Kaniuekutat), for compiling a profound book, capturing and documenting Kaniuekutat's extensive knowledge, wisdom, and life experience before it was too late;

Peter Armitage, for his writings on history and Innu spirituality;

Paulette Jiles for spawning and Marguerite Mackenzie for informing my discussion on the challenges of learning Innu-aimun;

Linda Griffiths, whose courage inspired mine;

George Gregoire, for providing a view into the soul of an Innu man;

An Antane Kapesh, for not mincing her words in her account of the colonization of the Innu;

Franz Fanon, for his diagnosis of both psychic and socioeconomic imperialism;

Resmaa Menakem, Layla F. Saad, Alison Bailey, and Robin DiAngelo, for their insight into the weight of racism and white supremacy, and change from within;

Lou Byrne, for his stunning play *Boneman—Kaiatshits*;

Tomson Highway, for translating the most profound of sorrows into a story of breathtaking beauty and triumph of the human soul.

I am so grateful to Barbara Pulling for having faith in my story and connecting me to my agent, Stephanie Sinclair, as supportive and enthusiastic a champion any writer could hope for. She deserves a medal for her persistence. To Whitney Moran of Vagrant Press for giving my story a home, for her courage and belief in our need to unlearn. My warmest thanks to Carol Bruneau, a wise and generous editor, for her meticulous reading and acumen. And finally to those who worked on the design, marketing, distribution, and sale of this book, my warmest thanks.

A special thanks goes to Jane McGillivray, who aided and abetted, for her unfailing friendship, gorgeous food, soaring conversations and the Riversong where I was able to write ’neath the aurora borealis. Barb Neis, Natalie Beausoleil, Mario Blaser, Dorothy Vaandering, and Pam Hall helped steer me down my own academic adventure.

Thanks to Janice Meilach, for being my best friend forever, partner in crime, and for Lucas, a good man to have on any *meshkaia.*

My parents are with me always. Heartfelt thanks to them for their love and support—to Dad who taught me forgiveness and how to break the rules, to Mom for her strength and loyalty, for teaching me to love books and making sure I had all the opportunities she did not. To my sister Anne—my rock—and my brothers Jean, Henri and Pierre, who keep me honest.

So much love goes out to my Newfoundland family, the centre of my world: Bruce, partner, compañero, and father of my children; Esmée, for her shining smile, deep soul, exquisite music and grace; and Léo, my boy joy, for his kind heart, dry humour, smarts, and brawn.

The research for this novel was supported by the Social Sciences and Humanities Research Council of Canada. Thanks also to the Arts

Newfoundland and Labrador Council jury who many years ago gave me a grant, believing I was a writer before I did.

Glossary of Innu words and names

Akami-uapishk^{u}	Mealy Mountains
akuatshitakushu	s/he has a voice and is making him/herself heard
akua tuta	take care, be careful
apishish	little
ashini	rock
ashkui	open water on rivers, lakes and estuaries where waterfowl, fish and animals are abundant in the springtime
atanukun	legend or myth, plural *atanukuna*
atik^{u}	caribou, or plural *atikuats*
Atikuss	Little Caribou
atshen	flesh-eating being, monster
atim^{u}	dog
auassats	children
auei e	who is it?
auei tshin	who are you
ehe	yes
eshpishatshimeuan	fabric hung above sleeping area, like a tent within a tent
eukuan miam	I see, good, that's it
iame	goodbye, *iame apishish*, small goodbye, see you soon

Innu — human being, Montagnais/Naskapi, can also refer to the Innu language
Innu-aimun — Innu words or language
Innu kananatuapatshet — political organization uniting Innu from Labrador and Quebec set up in the 1980s
innutshuap — Innu tent
ishkueu — woman
ishkuteu — fire
ishpitenitamun — respect
Kaiatshits — Boneman
kakeshau — white, English-speaking, plural *kakeshauts*
kak^{u} — porcupine
kamakunuesht — police
kamatshishit — devil
Kameshkeshkatinau-nipi — Disappointment Lake
kamiteut — shaman, person with powers
kanatuiut — hunter
kapata — wait
kashiuasht — sugar
Katipenimitak — Caribou Master, Spirit or God
katshishkutamatsheutshuap — school
kukum — your grandmother
kushapatshikan — shaking tent
kushkunu — go straight
mak — and
makushan — Feast of the Caribou
mamu — all together
Mamunitau Tshitaianimuanu — Let's Gather Voices, People's Inquiry
Manitu-utshu — Evil Spirit Mountain
mashinaikanitshuap — building for paper, office
mashinanikan — paper

mashinanikana	plural of paper: document, book, booklet, newspaper, etc.
Mashinanikan Ishkueu	Paper Woman
Matshishkapeu	Fart Man/Spirit
mauats	no, also *mauat*
meshkaia	path
miam	good
Minushkuess	Pretty Girl
mishimenitakuan	it is sad
Mishtapeu	Great Spirit, Spirit-Helper of the shaman
Mishta-shipu	Churchill River
Missinak^{u}	Water Spirit, Master of the Water Creatures
Mishti-Shantesh	Daniel's Rattle
mitike	penis, standard Mushuau spelling *mitikan*
mitshikuai	scraper
mitshim	food
mitshim-utshimau	social worker, Food Boss
mitshuap	house
muk^{u} *tshin*	up to you
Mushuau	of the barrens, as in *Mushuau Innu*
Mushuau-shipu	George River
mushuma	his/her grandmother
nakatuapami	watch me
nakate	go away
namesh	fish
napeu	man
nikaun	Mother, my mother
nimish	my older sister
nimushum	Grandfather, my grandfather
nipi	water
nipishapun	tea

nishkats	geese
Nitassinan	Our Homeland
nitshik^{u}	otter
nukum	Grandmother, my grandmother
nussim	my grand-daughter
nutshimits	the bush or the country
nutshimiu	adjective, of nutshimits, of the bush or country
pakueshikai	bread
pakutshashk^{u}	mythical animal
passauaia	dried caribou meat
petapan	dawn
pets mini	give it to me
pimin	bone marrow (prepared for the *makushan*)
pineu	partridge, plural *pineuts*
pipun	winter
pipitsheu	robin
pishumu	sun
pushu	hello
put	maybe
shakutamuatsh	hawk
shaputuan	large gathering tent
shash	enough, done
shishi	pee
shuniau	money
shtapakuna	boughs
takau	cold
tan eshinikashuin	what is your name?
tan etin?	what's happening?
tanite	where
tapue	yes, that's it, I agree
tipatshimun	story, plural *tipatshimuna*
tshekuan	what, what is it?

Tshinetshishepateu	Early Bird, s/he leaves walking early in the morning
tshin	you
tshinashkumitin	thank you
tshishennuats	Elders
tshishe-utshimau	government
tshishtakanapun	alcohol, pronounced *shtakanapun*
tshishue matshen	it is bad
tshishushkateu	he pissed him/her off by walking too far ahead of him/her
tshissenitamun	knowledge
tshitimush	your boyfriend or girlfriend
tshitshinapun	milk or breastmilk
uapush	rabbit
Uashat	Sept Îles
Uashkaikan	Kuujjuag, Fort Chimo
Uhuapeu	Porcupine Spirit, also Owl Man, character in stories
uitsheuaniss	little friend
utauna	her or his father
uitshikassatikutshishu	it really tastes like caribou
ueuepishun	small hammock for a baby
uishkatshan	grey jay
ukuma	his grandmother
utinikan	scapula
uitsheuaniss	little friend
Utshimashkueu	Boss Woman
utshimau	boss, leader, president, prime minister, chief, etc.
Utshimassits	Place of the Boss, Davis Inlet
utshimashkueutshenimu	she thinks herself a grand lady
utshimashkueutshenitakushu	she seems to be a strong woman, or have a proud and honourable character

Germaine Benuen

Camille Fouillard was born in Manitoba on Treaty 2 lands. She has worked and collaborated with the Labrador Innu for forty years on storytelling and books, protests and activism, facilitation, land rights, social health and education. She served as editor for *Gathering Voices-Mamunitau Staianimuanu: The Davis Inlet People's Inquiry* (Douglas and McIntyre) and co-edited *It's Like the Legend: Innu Women's Voices* (Gynergy). She is a winner of the Larry Jackson Writers' Award, as well Newfoundland and Labrador Arts and Letters and Writers' Union of Canada competitions. She lives in St. John's, Newfoundland. This is her first novel.